Camilla is an engineer who l... the whimsical realm of roman...

She writes contemporary r... have big hearts, might be a little stubborn at times, and love to banter with each other. Every story she pens has a guaranteed HEA that will make your heart beat faster. Unless you're a vampire, of course.

Camilla is a cat lover, coffee addict, and shoe hoarder. Besides writing, she loves reading—duh!—cooking, watching bad TV, and going to the movies—popcorn, please. She's a bit of a foodie, nothing too serious. A keen traveler, Camilla knows mosquitoes play a vital role in the ecosystem, and she doesn't want to starve all those frog princes out there, but she could really live without them. Find out more at: **www.camillaisley.com**

By the Same Author

CAMILLA ISLEY

Sweet Love and Country Roads

A small town romantic comedy

Dedication

To all long-distance couples, may you find your happily ever after…

One

Bitter Pills May Have Blessed Effects

Dread fills me as I ask my boss to repeat himself because I can't possibly have heard him right.

See, certain things are annoying. Bad hair days. Not enough vanilla syrup in my latte. Pen clicking. Hiccups.

Then there's the truly hateful stuff. Cars that take up two parking spaces. People who read over my shoulders. Slow Wi-Fi. Humblebraggers.

And finally, there are the things with the potential to ruin my life forever, like the words about to exit Winthrop Cargill-MacMillan's mouth.

The head of Denouement Studios, the movie production company I work for, is presently holding my happiness in the palm of his hand and he's about to close his fist and squeeze.

Winthrop flares his nostrils. "I said I want you to move to Emerald Creek for the duration of filming, not fly over for a quick fix."

Yep, I'd heard him right the first time.

"But shooting will last at least three more months," I protest. "If I can settle things in a few days, I don't see why I should stay on location. I can always return should other issues—"

Winthrop bangs a fist on his desk so hard even the sturdy window panes of his Manhattan fiftieth floor office might've rattled. "We can't afford anything else to go wrong!" he shouts. Then, taking a steadying breath, he adds, "Three months is all it should've taken to wrap up the project.

Instead, we're already a month in and still deep in the weeds. For goodness' sake, they haven't shot a single scene in the past week." He points a finger at me. "Samantha, I'm tired of hearing excuses. You can either pack your bags and move to Indiana or pack your office."

I'm so shocked by the finger-pointing and by Winthrop's threat to fire me, I don't know what to say.

Thankfully, my boss seems to realize he went too far and backtracks right away. "Sorry, Sam, I didn't mean to threaten you. But we're hemorrhaging money on this movie and we can't afford to lose another penny. Not after the last couple of years," he says, referring to the global pandemic that stopped movie productions worldwide, kept movie theaters' doors shut for months, pushed new movie releases forward by one or two years, and left many film studios with serious cash flow issues. "Please," Winthrop continues, "I need you to make sure everything goes smoothly down there."

The carrot always works better than the stick with me... I swallow hard and regretfully agree to a three-month sentence in hell.

"Oh, come on," Winthrop says as I'm about to leave his office, "Emerald Creek isn't Siberia, and a few months of country life might even put a little natural color in those cheeks of yours."

Ah, easy for him to say when he'll still be living within walking distance of a Nobu. And what does he have against my Too Faced Papa Don't Peach blush, anyway?

***

Dazed, I stumble on my stilettos as I walk down the hall toward my office. The temporary relocation is making me dizzier than a third round of Cosmopolitans would.

As I reach my door, I beckon Celia, my assistant, to follow me inside. She eagerly scurries up from her desk and comes in behind me.

"Please close the door," I say as I collapse on my white leather swivel chair.

Celia eyes me with a worried expression—*as she should*—awkwardly standing a few feet from the desk.

"Please sit down." I gesture at the two empty chairs in front of her.

I sigh, ready to relate the awful news, when she anticipates me, "Oh my gosh, you're firing me." I close my mouth as she goes on, "I know the company isn't doing well. I have a friend in accounting," she explains. "But I never imagined layoffs were a possibility. Are the studios going under? Is everyone fired? What am I going to do now? I've still got a ton of student loans to pay—"

Before she can drive off a tangent, I raise a hand to stop her. "Celia, you're not fired."

She fans herself. "Oh, thank goodness." Still a little out of breath, she adds, "Okay, tell me what it is then, because this is the first closed-door meeting we've held since you hired me three years ago."

I don a reassuring smile. After a job-loss scare, a transfer to Indiana will sound marginally less horrific. Or at least so I keep telling myself.

"It's about *Sweet Love and Country Roads.*" Celia nods intently, hanging on my every word. "Winthrop has asked me to bring the filming back on track. And he feels the only way to achieve that goal is if I'm on-site for the entire duration of shooting."

Celia's hand goes to her chest. "You're moving to Indiana?"

I give her a steady look. "*We* are moving to Indiana."

The expression of horror on Celia's face deepens, and she couldn't have a more sympathetic audience than me. But the decision is made, and I don't allow her time to hope she might get out of coming with me. Instead, I carry on to the practical aspects of organizing the move.

"Do you have anything major planned in the next three months?"

Celia swallows. "My sister's baby shower is in two weeks."

"Then you'd better give her your present sooner." Before she can protest, I add, "You can take the day of the shower off and follow the event on Zoom. Everyone's used to digital events. Your sister won't even notice you aren't there in the flesh. Anything else?"

"No."

"Good. I need you to book the plane tickets and hotel rooms."

"When do you want to fly out?"

As expected, she has heroically accepted her destiny and turned businesslike.

"Sunday, the earliest flight you can find. We'll need half a day to settle in before we tackle the production team on Monday."

"You mean *this* Sunday, like in three days?"

"Yes, why? Did you have plans?"

"A Tinder date, but I can cancel."

"Great," I say. "Take tomorrow off to pack or sort anything else you might've planned outside of Tinder and say goodbye to the city. I sure will. The sooner we leave, the quicker we can return. And, Celia—" Here comes *her* carrot. "You want to be a producer one day?"

"Yes."

"Great, this will be a unique opportunity to gain in-the-field experience and build up your resume."

***

As I walk home from work, I search Emerald Creek, Indiana, on my phone. I usually take a cab, but today I'm skipping the ride in favor of a last stroll among the streets of my beloved New York City. I wait expectantly for the search results to load, but even the map app has trouble finding that speck of dirt in the world. To find a major nearby city, I have to zoom out six or seven times, and the closest result is Indianapolis.

What's in Indianapolis? Are they famous for anything other than the race track?

With a longing glance at Bloomingdale's bright summer clothing windows, I curse myself for the hundredth time for approving Indiana as the shooting location for *Sweet Love and Country Roads*. The movie will be my next romantic comedy blockbuster, assuming I can get the filming completed. And on paper, Emerald Creek looked perfect. The small town had all the features I needed: a lake, a quaint city center, endless fields, and it was cheap as hell compared to other sites. But now that I have to move there for three months, I'm wondering why the ranch we rented as the primary setting lowballed the rest by so much. Is the area so vile no one wants to live there?

I'm going to find out soon. I put the phone away and navigate the pedestrian-packed sidewalks, enjoying the view of tall skyscrapers, high-end hotels, and shops. My heart breaks a little more with each step forward as I say goodbye to my one true love: Manhattan.

At home, I kick off my shoes in the hall and move into the open kitchen to pull a bottle of white wine out of the fridge. As I work on removing the cork, I drop my phone on the countertop, shooting a group call to my two best friends.

Taylor picks up first. "Sam, what's up?"

"I just got home from work and I need moral support."

A short pause. "You left the office before eight? Are you ill?"

"Worse."

That's when Holly joins the call. "Hellooo—aaargh." A dreadful crashing noise comes through the speakers, then silence, scuffling, then Holly is back. "Sorry, I dropped my phone. What's up? Why are we having a three-way call in the middle of the afternoon on a random Thursday, is someone dead?"

"Sam is home from work," Taylor replies.

"Then someone is definitely dead," Holly concludes.

"Not just yet," I say. "Maybe soon." I pour myself a huge glass of wine.

At the telltale glug-glug-glug sound, Holly nails me immediately. "Are you at home drinking in the middle of the day?"

"Four o'clock is hardly the middle of the day," I retort.

"Come on," Taylor cries out. "The suspense is killing us. What happened?"

"I have to move to Indiana," I say, and take a long sip of wine.

Dead silence fills the line.

"Girls, are you still there?"

They recover from the shock at the same time and fire questions at me.

"For how long?" Taylor.

"Why?" Holly.

"Two to three months to supervise the production of my latest movie. Filming has fallen behind and Winthrop got tired of hearing excuses, so he sent his attack dog—aka me—to fix the mess. Apparently, the location manager and his two assistants can't manage on their own. This is punishment for being good at my job."

Taylor speaks first. "Well, three months isn't so bad. You'll be back just in time for Labor Day. And summer in New York sucks."

"No season sucks in New York," I protest. "Anyway, I'm calling because, as a dead woman walking, I have a right to my last meal. Cancel all your plans for Saturday. I want to spend the day soaking in everything Manhattan has to give."

***

And I do. I start my weekend by waking up at six to go to my Pilates studio for an early session. With my muscles toned and stretched, I take a sauna, a long shower, change, and meet the girls for breakfast at Tiffany's—or more precisely, brunch at The Blue Box Cafe at the Tiffany New York flagship store.

In the afternoon, we spend a few hours at our favorite salon, getting mani-pedis, facials, and I get my hair trimmed and refresh my highlights.

My shoulder-length bob requires constant maintenance. As I watch Jean-Luc, my hairstylist for years, expertly layer the tips so they'll fall beautifully without effort, I cringe. Who will cut my hair in Indiana?

I imagine an old lady with too much hair spray on and bright fuchsia and blue eyeshadow approaching me with a pair of jagged scissors. Panic strikes before I remember a SWAT team of professional stylists and makeup artists will be on set to take care of the actors. If I can't have Jean-Luc, they're the next best thing.

When we exit the salon, we have just enough spare time for a quick shopping spree at Saks Fifth Avenue before we cab to Momofuku Ko for our dinner reservations.

At the restaurant, the cocktails are delicious and incredibly pretty, and so is the food. After we open the second bottle of wine, I do my best to stay a happy drunk as opposed to spiraling down into a my-life-is-over rabbit hole. My friends cheer me and pull jokes on cowboys' stamina and rolls in the hay. Holly even hands me a printout of an article:

Ten reasons why moving to Indiana is the right choice for you.

That night in bed, I scroll a few.

- Great nature.

I'm not outdoorsy.

- Sports.

I don't follow any.

Item number three informs me that Indiana is the covered bridges haven of the Midwest. I didn't even know covered bridges were a thing. But when the article tries to pass off Indianapolis as a city with a beautiful skyline, they lose me. Guess whoever penned this deceitful list has never set foot in New York.

The only point I can agree with is the low state taxes, but since I won't be changing my residence, that won't apply to me.

And now I should sleep. I need to be up in less than four hours to catch my flight to the Hellish State—I mean, the Hoosier State.

Two

The First Hundred Yards Are the Hardest

Cocktails and two bottles of wine sounded like a great idea last night, but as my alarm goes off at four in the morning, I curse the day I was born.

Instead of coffee, I'm tempted to start the day with an espresso martini. Someone wise once said that to keep drinking is the best cure for a hangover. And, maybe, if I stay tipsy for the next three months, I could even like Indiana.

Pity I'll need a sharp mind to overhaul this production. So instead, I pop an Aleve and drag my two huge silver metal suitcases down the hall and into the elevator. The rest of my things—shoes, mostly—wouldn't fit, and Celia shipped those separately.

Downstairs, my assistant is already waiting for me in the lobby and helps me roll one of the suitcases to the black SUV that will drive us to the airport.

The driver takes the cases from us and struggles to fit them both in the trunk. Next to Celia's single, smaller bag, my luggage seems disproportionate.

Oh, well… One can take the girl out of Manhattan, but not the sense of fashion out of the girl.

Celia must disagree. She's wearing practical slacks and white sneakers, a sensible traveling outfit. But style will always win over practicality for me.

I stroll forward, proud in my intentionally distressed skinny jeans, high-heeled, leopard-print, calf-hair stilettos, and Armani power-suit black jacket.

In the end, the driver has to give up trying to fit both cases in the trunk and secures my second suitcase to the front seat with a seatbelt.

Time to go.

Goodbye New York, goodbye my love.

At the airport, I discover we're not even flying to Indianapolis but to Louisville, Kentucky. Emerald Creek is closer to the southern border of Indiana and the drive across Kentucky will only take an hour as opposed to the two and a half hours it would've taken from Indianapolis.

Whatever.

I navigate through the airport security checks like a malfunctioning human droid, and just before boarding, I indulge in the last decent cup of double-shot vanilla latte.

As I sit on the plane, I pull my sleeping mask over my eyes, ready to snatch a couple of hours' extra sleep during the journey.

Once we land, I rinse and repeat, pulling my sleeping mask on the moment Celia and I step into the black truck a member of the film crew drove to Louisville to pick us up.

I'm jostled awake a while later when the pickup comes to an abrupt stop. The arrest is so sudden, only a fastened seatbelt prevents me from bumping my head into the front seat.

I yank off the sleeping mask. "What's going on?"

Jerry Mallon, the driver and our on-set carpenter and handyman, turns back toward me. "A cow is blocking the street."

"A cow?"

I exit the truck to check the situation. We're on a dirt road in the middle of nowhere, surrounded by fields. No, not even fields—more like pastures. An endless expanse of grass on

11

both sides. And in front of us, blocking the way, a gigantic brown cow with white patches is grazing the grass growing at the side of the road.

I get closer and Jerry and Celia join me. "Can't we just side-step it? The ground seems pretty flat at the road's edges and we have a pickup."

Jerry inches his chin in that direction. "There are ditches on both sides, hardly noticeable in the tall grass, but I'm not sure how deep they go and I wouldn't want to risk getting tipped over or stuck."

I shield my eyes with my hand against the midday sun and squint at the winding road ahead. Nothing beyond the cow.

"Can we take a different route?"

Jerry removes his baseball cap and scratches the back of his head. "The thing is, the GPS gets iffy in these parts, and I'm not exactly sure where your farm is."

"My farm? What do you mean, *my* farm?"

"Sagebrush Ranch, isn't that where we're going?"

"No. We're going to a hotel in town." I turn to my assistant. "Aren't we?"

Celia wrings her fingers and looks at me apologetically. "That was the plan, but the two inns in town had most weekends booked and couldn't accommodate us for such a long stay. I had to find a more creative solution. A 'bed and breakfast' sort of thing." Celia puts her hands forward. "Which is much better because we'll have access to a fully equipped kitchen. We couldn't have survived three months on take-out."

I'm about to reply that I've survived most of my life on take-outs, but then I remember this is Indiana and not New

York. I'm not sure how many healthy delivery options they have in Emerald Creek.

Oh my gosh, what am I going to eat? Then, once again, I remember we have to accommodate a full cast of Hollywood-spoiled actors and their dietary quirks. Hence, we have an on-site chef and a community barn for meals and meetings at the ranch we're renting as the primary set.

"Don't be silly," I tell Celia, irritated. "We're going to eat with the rest of the crew."

"Oh, right. Sorry, I've never been on location. Anyway, the bed and breakfast was the only spot with rooms for the entire summer."

I wonder why. Oh my gosh, she probably booked us into a hovel.

"And what about the on-site cabins?" I snap.

"All occupied."

My head is already hurting. And not just for the lack of sleep or the excessive alcohol intake of last night.

It must be all the fresh air.

I need to sleep and, hovel or not, I don't care as long as they have a bed for me.

But before we can get there, we need to overcome our little cattle problem.

I stare at the other two and they stare back at me, expectantly. "So our only hope is to make that cow move?"

They nod sheepishly.

"Let's make it move, then. How hard can it be?"

Again, they both just stare at me.

"Oh, for goodness' sake."

I approach the cow and size up the animal. My opponent continues grazing, unperturbed. I give her a gentle pat on the hindquarters. Nothing happens. I slap her harder, saying, "Move."

The wretched animal lifts her head, still munching, and observes me, unimpressed. Once she's finished chewing, she moos at me.

"What does that mean? I don't speak cow. Can you please move out of the way?"

I try to push her forward, at which point she raises her tail and… I jump backward just before a pile of brown mush hits the ground, specks of the semi-solid substance landing dangerously close to my precious calf-hair stilettos. Then the smell hits my nostrils, making me want to gag.

Before I even have time to put a hand over my mouth, an uproarious laugh to my left makes me turn.

A man is sitting on horseback near the road. I take in his cowboy boots and hat, the faded jeans smudged with dirt and dust, and the checkered shirt.

Dude, you couldn't be more of a stereotype if you tried.

Under the shadow of that giant, ridiculous hat, and with the sun coming in from behind him, I can't properly see his face, but the smile is arrogant enough to irk me even more.

"Is this yours?" I ask, pointing at the cow.

The man tips his hat at me. "Sure is, miss."

"Would you mind moving her so we can be on our way?"

The cowboy whistles in response. "Come on, Betsy, yeeha, yeehaw, yeeee-haw, time to go."

The cow flattens one ear but otherwise ignores her owner.

I cross my arms at this poor display of cowboy showmanship.

In response, the man bends sideways over his saddle and grabs a rope that he swings over his head once, twice, and then throws it around the cow's neck.

Show-off.

Cow secured, he whistles sharply at her to move. Nudged by the rope around her neck, Betsy has no choice but to follow. She abandons her grass, hops across the ditch in a surprisingly graceful jump for such a large animal, and goes to stand next to the horse.

"Road's all clear," the cowboy says. "Where are you folks headed, anyway?"

"Sagebrush Ranch," Jerry replies. "Is it far?"

"Not at all." The cowboy points at a bend in the road. "Once you pass that turn, it's another two miles before the gate comes into view."

"Thanks," Jerry says.

"No problem." The cowboy tips his hat again. "Have a nice day."

He frees Betsy from the lasso, then turns his horse around and, emitting clicking sounds, he digs his heels into the stirrups and leaves at a trot.

I watch him go, then stare back at the pile of dung in the middle of the road that pretty much summarizes my impression of Indiana so far.

Three

Keep Your Problems to Yourself

The tires crunch over gravel as we stop before a massive wooden gate. Beyond the gate, a green hill rises in the distance, and on top of it rests a quaint, pale-yellow house with white trim. My home for the next three months.

"How do we get in?" I ask, not spotting any electronic interface. No cameras, no buzzers, no security-code pads. Only a white wooden gate strung between two stone columns and a fence sneaking around the hill on both sides.

Celia whips out her phone. "On the reservation, it said to call this number once we reached the gate." She taps the screen and waits on the line.

"Yes, hi, this is Celia Warren. We have a reservation—yes, that's us, we're at the gate." Celia hangs up and adds to me, "They'll be here in a moment."

Minutes later, a light-blue pickup winds down the hill toward us. As the vehicle gets closer, I can make out more details. It's an old battered Chevrolet that makes me feel suddenly transported into a Nicholas Sparks movie. Which isn't necessarily a bad thing. If nothing else, Emerald Creek will be perceived as authentic by moviegoers, evoking precisely the right sentiments for the *Sweet Love and Country Roads* target audience.

When the truck stops on the other side of the gate, an old woman at least in her seventies hops out and waves at us, smiling. Her hair is stark white but still thick, collected at the top of her head, and she's wearing a short-sleeved floral dress. She reminds me of Grandma Duck.

"Welcome to Sagebrush Ranch." The woman gestures at us to stay in the truck. "We'll make introductions once at the house." She opens the wooden gate.

As we drive past her, I look back. Grandma Duck has closed the gate and has gotten back in the truck, which she now reverses in a single, impressively swift maneuver to follow us up the hill. At the top, the farmhouse is perched on a large, flat surface with a view of the valley below. It's a two-story building with a large wrap-around porch lined with flower beds. The area surrounding the home is tidy, a contrast to the thickly wooded area made of tall, spiky trees we just coasted by up the hill.

Jerry parks in the open space before the house, next to a black pickup much newer than the one our hostess is driving. The Chevrolet pulls up right afterward.

A minty breeze blows in my face as I get out of the truck. The wind also carries a soft lavender smell in its wake with just a hint of honeysuckle. No livestock odors, thankfully. We must be downwind from the animal paddock off to the left of the house where cows and goats are grazing grass. Their large oval pen is delimited by a sturdy wooden fence with rose bushes growing alongside it. Ah, maybe that cowboy should come have a look at how to properly build an animal enclosure.

I look up.

The sky is mostly clear, but one cloud is hanging low, cloaking in its shadow a stable, what looks like a tool shack, and a giant red barn off farther to the left of the house. Behind all these buildings, green hills and pastures extend as far as the eye can see.

Grandma Duck dismounts with a friendly smile. "Hello, and welcome again. I'm Willette Hunt. I hope you had a pleasant journey."

We shake hands and Willette invites us into the house. Jerry carries one of my suitcases while I drag the other up the front steps. Celia breezily overtakes both of us with her single suitcase half the size of mine. How she managed to pack for three months in that tiny case remains a mystery.

Inside, the house is stylish in a country way. Plenty of whitewashed wooden furniture, vase flowers everywhere, and light pouring in from the wide windows.

"Your rooms are upstairs," Willette points to the stairs and eyes my attire—the shoes in particular—dubiously. "Do you want a hand carrying that?"

"No, thanks."

I grab the handle of my suitcase and stubbornly drag it up one step at a time. On the landing, Willette shows us our rooms and the shared bathroom.

Okay, the accommodation isn't ideal, especially the shared bathroom aspect, but I've slept in worse places. And my room is big and spacious with a small desk where I can power up my laptop if I need to work and, most importantly, a walk-in closet!

"Well, I'll let you settle down and once you're ready, I've made lunch," Willette announces.

"Oh," I say, surprised. "We wouldn't want to trouble you."

"No trouble at all, dear. I wouldn't feel right not giving you a proper welcome."

"If you're sure, thank you."

Willette nods. "I'm sure. Come down whenever you're ready."

I stare at Jerry, who, after dropping my case in my room, is waiting for instructions on the landing. "How far are we from the set?"

"I'd say fifteen to twenty minutes."

"And from the town center?"

"About the same."

"Okay, then it's better if Celia and I keep the truck so no one has to drive us back and forth. But we need to familiarize ourselves with the roads first. Can you pick us up tomorrow morning for our first trip?"

"Sure, what time?"

"Seven, I want to get the ball rolling right away."

***

Lunch is served under the shade of the porch. The large table is a rustic, wooden rectangle surrounded by benches in the same shabby-chic wood, which is a few shades darker than the whitewashed oak inside the house. The table is covered with an embroidered white cotton tablecloth and laid with wavy white plates with silver borders. The silverware has a Provençal feel, same as the centerpiece, which is made of an old wire basket containing six mason jars filled with lavender, wildflowers, and greeneries. All very stylish, very Pinterestable.

As I sit next to Celia, I count four plates. Mmm, who else is going to join us besides Willette? Her husband, perhaps?

The answer arrives pronto as I raise my gaze across the backyard and spot the same cowboy from before coming our way.

The cowboy hat and boots are the same, the dirt-smeared jeans unchanged, the checkered shirt, however, is gone. The man is walking toward us bare-chested with the shirt

19

casually draped over his shoulder. His skin shines with sweat in the midday sun. And if I had a thing for sculpted chests and washboard abs, the man could be making an impression… Thankfully, I prefer brains over brawn, so I'm not dazzled by this casual display of raw masculinity.

I avert my gaze and find Celia gaping at the incoming macho bomb.

"It's just muscles," I whisper to her.

Her eyes snap up to me, and she blushes profusely, closing her jaw.

Willette comes out bringing a tray of appetizers. Canapés and mini-sandwiches. Our host drops the tray on the table, and when she spots the man, her entire face brightens.

"Oh, Travis, were you able to mend the fence?"

"All done, Mom," he says, hopping up the steps of the porch.

He pulls his mother into a side-hug and kisses the top of her head.

Willette pushes him away. "You're all sweaty. You'll ruin my Sunday dress, dear."

Travis gives her another kiss all the same and then, looking at us, tips his hat again, "Ladies, please allow me to take a shower before I properly introduce myself."

And with that, he disappears inside the house.

Next to me, I hear Celia letting out a breath.

Oh, come on, he's not *that* good-looking.

"Does your son still live with you?" I ask casually.

"No, Travis helps me with the heavy stuff on the weekends. My back isn't what it used to be, and it's hard to manage the farm on my own."

That makes me wonder what happened to her husband. She's still wearing a wedding ring.

"Do you have many animals?" Celia asks.

"No. Just a few cows, chickens, three goats, two llamas, and the horses, of course."

And what if she had many? I comment in my head.

"Please, dears, help yourselves to the appetizers while we wait for Travis."

The canapés and mini sandwiches are delicious. Willette could charge a fortune for food like this in New York. I'm scarfing down my fifth mini sandwich when the man of the house makes another appearance.

The hat is gone, the jeans are clean, and a light-blue dress shirt covers his chest. He's also changed boots, wearing a pair less torn than the ones he had on before. His dark-blond hair is still wet from the shower and sticking out in all directions as if he simply ruffled it up with a towel and then let it be.

Mr. Cowboy gives his mother another kiss and then beams at us. "Hi, there, I'm Travis Hunt."

While he shakes Celia's hand, I have a few seconds to properly study his face: chiseled cheekbones, light-blond stubble, full lips, pearly white teeth, a slight chin-cleft, and intelligent hazel-green eyes. Admittedly, not completely unpleasant to look at.

Of all these charming features, the eyes worry me the most. As our gazes meet, they crinkle with some sort of untold mischief, as if he knew something I didn't.

To shake his hand, I stand up and find myself at an immediate disadvantage. Even off the horse, the man towers over me and he's doing nothing to lessen the gap. Travis Hunt seems to enjoy his physical superiority. The suspicion is confirmed when we shake hands, and he holds both my hand and gaze a few seconds longer than appropriate. Mr.

Cowboy has taken up the attitude of someone sizing up an adversary. Which makes no sense, unless he plans to have me battle another of his mother's cows.

"So, ladies," Travis says, sitting down on the bench opposite to us next to Willette. "What brings you into this neck of the woods?"

Celia jumps to answer. "We're with the movie production, we need to sort some—"

"We're here to supervise the shooting," I cut her off before she can utter the word *troubles.* A single tweet could start a rumor. And the last thing I want is for word to spread that my production is behind schedule. That would make investors and sponsors nervous, and I sure don't need that pile of crap on top of the dung—literal and figurative—I already have to deal with.

I shoot Celia a warning stare.

She nods back in an 'I'll keep my mouth shut' way, looking a bit mortified.

I smile now to let her know the crisis is averted, and we're cool.

"Of course," Willette says, serving the main dish: a quiche Lorraine that looks delicious. "The town has never been so busy, the population has doubled since you folks moved in. Which is great, right? Travis was telling me the other day how his office—"

"Mom, the ladies had a long journey," Mr. Cowboy interrupts. "I'm sure they don't want to talk shop at lunch."

"No, please," I say. "Tell us what you do, Travis."

"I'm a lawyer," he says, noncommittally.

At the announcement, Willette looks at him funny. But he gives her a subtle head shake, and she doesn't comment.

What was that about?

"Anyway," Travis continues. "The production will keep you pretty busy, I guess, but do you plan on seeing the sights as well?"

"I don't know," I say. "Is there anything to see around here?" Then I realize the comment could come off as offensive, so I hastily add, "I mean, what local attraction would you recommend?"

"The hike to the Potawatomi Waterfall, for sure, and the lake is always gorgeous in the summer..."

"And in a few weeks, we're having the Dubois County Fair," Willette chimes in. "It's a big event. A carnival comes to town, there's a baking competition and a horse-reining tournament. Cowboys come from all over the country to compete."

I've no idea what horse-reining is, and I'm dying a little inside that a minuscule county fair will be the most exciting thing for the next three months. I'm used to Broadway, to the Met Gala, to living in the pulsating, cultural and artistic heart of the country. Now all I have to look forward to is a baking competition.

FYI, I don't bake.

Travis seems to read my mind because he says, "Of course, it's small fish compared to the entertainment New York has to offer."

I raise my head quickly at the comment, lowering my fork. "How do you know we're from New York?"

Travis shrugs. "The accent."

"I don't have an accent."

"You think you don't, but New Yorkers have a pretty distinctive way of talking."

"And what makes you such an expert in New York?"

"Lived there a few years."

I compare him to all the lawyer types of Manhattan, trying to imagine him in their midst with his cowboy boots, but I can't reconcile the two images. What kind of law did he practice?

I finally take the first bite of quiche and shudder. "Oh my gosh, Willette, this is delicious."

No wonder she's excited about a baking competition. With food like this, she'll win.

"Thank you, dear. It's a secret family recipe."

"Really amazing, Willette," Celia agrees.

"Mom's the best cook in the world," Travis adds.

And while I might be ready to agree, I tease him a little. "Is that why you moved back home?"

"No." His face darkens. "I didn't want to live to work, and what else could compare to"—he looks behind his shoulders at the barn and green pastures—"this?"

I picture the Manhattan skyline, Fifth Avenue at Christmas, Central Park in the fall, the Hamptons in the summer… *Yeah, what, indeed.*

Travis and I exchange a silent 'agree to disagree' stare, and I let Celia take over the conversation for the rest of the meal. I'm too busy polishing off one slice of quiche after the other. Home-cooked food has risen to the top spot as the best cure for a hangover. I feel better with every bite.

When lunch is over, I get super drowsy, though. I'm stuffed, I haven't slept, and the king bed upstairs is calling to me with more passion than mermaids to sailors.

I thank Willette again for the wonderful meal and offer to help her with the dishes, but she refuses. I say goodbye to Travis and remind Celia of our early wake-up call tomorrow before I excuse myself.

Upstairs, I barely have the strength to brush my teeth and shimmy out of my clothes before I snuggle under the soft covers in my underwear, not bothering to put on pajamas. The room is cool despite the outside heat, and, as soon as my head touches the pillow, I fall asleep.

Four

The Early Bird Catches the ~~Worm~~ Goat

The silence wakes me up before the sun comes up. Considering that I've gone to bed at four in the afternoon, I'm not surprised to be stirring so early, but I find the complete lack of sound disconcerting, eerie almost. Where are the sirens, the traffic, the noisy neighbors? Those sounds are my white noise, I need them to sleep.

I should've recorded a night's worth of background sounds before leaving. But I'm sure someone invented an app for that. I grab my phone from the bedside table, 5:15 a.m. Gosh, I haven't slept for over twelve hours in I can't remember how long.

I download a few white-noise apps and scroll through the options: rain, crashing waves, logs burning... one even has a Tibetan singing bowl sound, but no blaring horns, wailing fire trucks, or construction work. When I finally find a city street option, it's a joke. I don't know what city they live in, but it clearly isn't New York.

One hundred percent out of sleep after the white-noise quest, I decide to use my time more productively and squeeze in a workout section before Jerry comes to pick us up at seven.

I change into leggings and a sports bra, grab my iPad, and move downstairs.

The wooden steps creak beneath my feet, and I try to be as stealthy as I can to not wake anyone.

The porch seems like the optimal place to take my virtual Pilates class. So I exit the house through the kitchen back door and roll out my yoga mat on the wooden planks. Outside, it's still chilly, but exercising should get me warm in no time.

Despite the shivers running down my arms, I pause a second to admire the sunrise. The morning light makes the pastures that expand beyond the fenced garden blossom with color, each grass blade tinged with the reflected orange of the sun on one side, and bright green on the other. And, okay, the setting is beautiful. But I'm still going to miss the sauna at my gym after I finish my training.

I place my iPad on the table, select my favorite on-demand routine—my gym has an app for remote conditioning, and press play.

Fifteen minutes later, I'm in plank when the app coach reminds me not to drop my chin. I raise my head and find myself nose to nose with a brown-and-white goat. She bleats at me and I scream back, falling on the ground in a heap of limbs.

We're still both screaming at each other when Willette comes out of the kitchen wearing a long-sleeved cotton nightgown with loose hair flying behind her in all directions.

"What's going on?"

"Sorry," I say, sitting back on my heels. "I was doing Pilates, and your goat attacked me."

"Oh, Hildi wouldn't hurt a fly. But she likes to take part in human activities. She probably wanted to join you."

Pilates with a goat. I still had to hear this one.

Getting to my feet, I apologize to Willette for waking her up.

"Not to worry," she replies. "I'm always up with the sun."

"Okay, then. I'll go take a shower and get ready for work."

"And I'll fix you breakfast in the meantime. What do you want to eat, dear?"

I don't suppose Willette makes kale smoothies. "Just coffee is okay, thanks."

"Nonsense, darling, you go take your shower and I'll feed you when you come down. You and your friend are both skin and bone."

She sounds like my grandma and seems just as stubborn, so I don't argue further. I simply thank her again and walk back into the house through the kitchen door.

The hot shower is a blessing after my chilly, unfinished workout. Under the high-pressure jet, I prepare for the day ahead, mentally scrolling the checklist of issues I need to tackle at today's plenary meeting with the movie crew.

By the time I finish drying my hair, the sun is already high in the sky. I grab my work bag with my notes, agenda, and laptop and move down to the kitchen. Before I can even enter, the smell of Willette's cooking reaches me. Eggs, but also a sugary scent of vanilla and cinnamon.

"Mmm." I turn the kitchen corner, crossing the room. "Are you making French toast?"

Willette is standing in front of the stove brandishing a spatula covered in egg yolk. "Oh, morning again," she says. "French toast is outside, I'm just finishing up my eggs. Unless you wanted some scrambled eggs as well?"

"No, thank you. You really didn't have to go through all this trouble. We'll have plenty of food on set."

She waves me off with the spatula. "Don't worry, dear, I enjoy cooking, and it's nice to have people around."

I guess the B&B isn't a preferred destination. In fact, I still feel a little weird about the setup. So far, staying at Sagebrush Ranch has felt more like being sent away to spend the summer at an old aunt's house rather than being on a business trip.

I step outside, welcoming the sunlight on my skin. Celia is already seated at the table, scarfing down French toast and scones.

I fill a mug with coffee and assess my options on how to sweeten the drink. I suppose soy milk, no-sugar vanilla syrup, and zero-calorie sweeteners won't be among my choices. I drop a sugar cube into the mug and then peer at the milk jug. As I pour some of the white liquid into my coffee, the fluid is so dense and creamy that for a moment I think I'm pouring actual cream, but when I taste the mixture, I have to concede that, no, it's milk. Ah, so this is what whole milk looks like. Who knew—my last taste must've been when I was still bottle feeding in the crib.

Despite my claims that coffee would be enough, I can't resist taking a slice of French toast. Then another, and a small scone, too. Thankfully, Jerry arrives at seven on the dot, preventing me from scarfing down more food.

Celia and I thank Willette again for the amazing breakfast and climb into the production pickup truck. Since we'll keep the vehicle and drive ourselves back tonight, I ride shotgun and pay particular attention to the road. Jerry's warning that map apps become confused in these parts is fresh in my mind.

The directions seem pretty easy to remember, though. Down the hill straight out of Sagebrush Ranch, left on the dirt road where the cow blocked our way yesterday. Then right on a bigger dirt road, right again on a smaller path, and we finally reach Lake View Acres' gates.

A guard waves at Jerry and asks us for our passes. Once we're past the security checks, we head straight for the pulsating heart of the set: the community barn. A tall, wooden structure painted in the quintessential barn-red color with white trim. The building is the social hub of the production, used for meals, meetings, and screenplay readings.

The dirt patch before the entrance is lined with an array of white golf carts. Lake View extends for over 260 acres, with cabins scattered all over the place for the live-in crew and actors, which is the reason why most people need to catch a ride to move between the communal buildings.

Jerry parks on a lot reserved for cars and, as we get out and head for the barn door, he tosses me the pickup keys. "All yours, boss."

I catch them in mid-air and stash them in my bag—brown leather to match my open-toe pumps. Since I wasn't sure how stiletto-friendly the terrain would be on this side of the fence, I opted for a larger, more practical heel that'd work better on gravel. And I was right.

Inside, the barn is already packed with people. Three rectangular tables are arranged in a U shape accommodating all the crew members Celia summoned for today's meeting. Actually, the production team is so vast, a few people are left standing.

Despite the large crowd, a free seat waits for me at the head of the U. I cross the room at a brisk pace, tossing a generic, "Good morning," around that has the desired effect of quieting the chit-chat.

I hate to play bad cop, but this production hasn't derailed on its own. Someone in this room is responsible. I need to find who and right their mistakes—fast. My stay in Emerald Creek is directly tied to the length of the shooting, so I'm going to make sure it won't be a day longer than necessary.

No more delays.

But first, I need to understand what went wrong and who to fire.

Over the years, I've noticed a little intimidation can go a long way to get straight answers out of people, so as I take my seat, I maintain a stern look and meet the eyes of a few unfortunate randoms who quickly lower their gazes.

Only the filming crew is present today, no actors or stunts. Still, that leaves me with a bunch of potential culprits: Set Decoration, Costume Design, Production Management, Location Manager, the Director and his Assistant Directors, Camera Crew, Property Master, Art Department, Sound Department, Constructions, Special and Visual Effects, and so on.

I adjust my chair under the table while Celia lingers behind me, leaning against the wall.

I clear my throat and the last background chatter dies away. "Good morning, everyone, I'm Samantha Baker," I introduce myself and note the usual reaction: people wondering if it's a coincidence I'm named after a teen idol of an eighties movie.

It isn't.

My mom loved *Sixteen Candles* so much that when she fell in love with a man named Baker and they had a daughter, she couldn't believe her luck that she got to name me as her favorite Molly Ringwald character. Hollywood has been in my destiny since the crib.

"I'm the Executive Producer for *Sweet Love and Country Roads,*" I continue. "And I've been rushed to Indiana because of the unacceptable delays this production has suffered. Now, the reason I wanted to see you all at once, is to determine what has caused such setbacks and how to fix the problem so that filming can resume at once."

Of course, I already know what's going on more or less from phone calls and Zoom meetings, but I've found that when people are held accountable in front of their colleagues, they seem much more eager to get off their rear ends and solve whatever the issue is, faster.

From what I gathered, most of the brunt is on the Location Manager. I want him to take responsibility publicly and explain exactly what is stalling him.

"Very well," I continue. "From my notes, I can see we got stuck at the beach scene at the lake. Why?" I turn to my left where Lionel Trumeau, the director, is sitting.

"We don't have the permits to shoot."

"What's the holdup?" I ask the Chief Location Manager.

The man, Bill—average height and build, mostly bald—scratches his brown beard. "The mayor's office hasn't signed the permits yet, ma'am."

"Did City Hall give you a reason for the delay?"

"I call them every day, but they keep stonewalling me."

"Stonewalling you, how?"

"First there was the Emerald Creek Barbecue Festival to organize, then the Founding Fathers Parade, and last week, the Memorial Day celebration—"

I raise a hand before he can tell me about the Stop Hedgehogs Deaths March or whatever other stupid event this town is organizing. "And what do all these celebrations have to do with our permits?"

"The mayor's secretary claims the mayor has been too busy coordinating the events to look at our permits."

"Is there a reason the mayor needs more time to review our applications? Did something change with respect to our initial agreement with the town?"

Bill shrugs. "Not that I know of, ma'am."

With all the supplemental collagen I apply to my face daily, if he calls me ma'am another time, he's going to regret the day he chose filmmaking as a career.

"You mean to tell me the only reason filming has stopped is that the mayor of an insignificant, small town in the middle of nowhere has been too busy to spare us the five seconds signing a piece of paper would require?"

"I'm only telling you what they told me."

"Who did we talk to in the mayor's office when we pre-negotiated the set locations?" I address this question at the tablet to my right where the location scouts and a few other crew members are following the meeting remotely.

"The mayor himself," one of the guys on the screen replies. "He assured us the permits were only a formality."

"Until they weren't." I sigh and go back to Bill. "Have you tried an in-person visit to City Hall to figure out what's going on?"

"Yes, but they've always turned me down, saying the mayor was busy."

"And did you try to schedule an appointment?"

Bill finally smiles. "Yes, ma'am, I've secured one."

I try really hard to keep my nostrils from flaring. "When?"

Bill checks the agenda on his phone. "On the seventeenth, at 10 a.m."

I stare at the date bubble on my watch. Today's the sixth of June. We're burning thousands of dollars every day and the idiot accepted an appointment almost two weeks from now on top of the week we already lost? Unacceptable.

I'm tempted to fire him on the spot, but I want to understand the situation before I make any hasty decisions.

I move onto the next scene on the shooting plan. "What about the bridge scene?"

I look at Lionel Trumeau, the director, who in turn looks at Bill.

The man has lost some of his initial buoyancy and now dries his sweating forehead with a handkerchief. "We haven't been able to secure the required permits from—"

"The mayor's office," I finish the phrase for him and lower my gaze to the production plan in my hands. The next ten scenes are all set in public spaces, which, I assume, would require a permit the mayor's office hasn't issued.

I've never seen the man, but I already dislike him with all my heart. That insignificant bureaucrat is single-handedly derailing my production.

But why?

All the stalling doesn't seem like a coincidence. If Bill was ready to eat out of the palm of their hands, I'm not. Willing or not, the mayor is going to receive me. *Tomorrow.* And I'll make him wish he'd dealt with Bill instead.

I return to the list of scenes until I find one that can be shot on the farm. "And in the meantime, why haven't we moved on with the barn scene?"

Lionel Trumeau takes on an offended air. "That would go against my vision for the movie. You know I need to do things my way, in a precise sequence, Sam."

Directors can be as much prima donnas as any member of the cast. So next, I speak in a conciliatory tone, "I know, Lionel, but we can't afford to be over-artistic here. Pragmatism has to prevail. Otherwise, the production will go belly up, and the movie will be canceled." I scan the room to make sure the concept sinks into everybody's head. Their jobs are at stake just as much as mine.

"Who's in charge of the Art Department and Construction?"

Two men raise their hands.

"Are the sets on the farm ready?"

"Yes," the older of the two says. "We've kept building everything this week while the ranch was relatively free. I'd say we're a month ahead of schedule." He looks at his colleague, who nods in return. "Much easier to build when we can bang a hammer all day without disrupting any sound take." He makes a mock military salute at the sound group. The guys wave back with a mixture of professional appreciation and friendly banter.

Finally, good news. And someone who's acting professionally.

"Great job." I nod at the construction crew, then turn to Lionel. "Can you readjust your plan to continue shooting on the compound while we secure the permits for the public spaces?"

The Academy Award Winner for Best Director isn't happy, but he gives me a resigned, "I guess so."

"Can you start today?"

Lionel Trumeau shrugs. "If you can make Chelsea Moreno come back, sure I can."

Chelsea Moreno is the lead actress in the movie. "Why, where is she?"

Lionel shrugs. "She left the set as soon as we stopped filming."

"Does anyone know where she went?"

A shy blond woman in a pink pullover, probably from the makeup department, comes forward. "Chelsea told me she might go see some friends in the Hamptons."

I turn to Celia. "Call her agent, make sure her skinny behind is back here by the end of the day. We're not paying her to go party in the Hamptons with her friends."

I keep a steely attitude while my heart goes out to Chelsea. What would I give now to be in the Hamptons partying with my friends!

But at least her paycheck has enough zeros to compensate for the hazards of country living, mine doesn't.

"Okay, everyone," I address the room at large. "Now that we have a plan, let's stay on track. It isn't too late to turn this movie around. You make sure everything goes smoothly here, and I'll take care of the mayor."

Five

There's More Than One Way to Skin a Cat

The room reacts with a round of applause and widespread sounds of agreement. The cheering, however, dies down the moment I stand up and say, "Bill, please come see me in my office."

Firing someone is never fun, but the Location Manager hasn't left me many options.

My "office" is a trailer about a quarter of a mile away from the communal barn. Jerry points me in the right direction and asks me if I need a ride. The trek is short enough that I don't need to take a golf cart. I walk down a low hill and up another until I reach my destination. Between the security gates and guards, locks are unnecessary, so the door is open. Inside, the space is equipped with the bare essentials: a table, a small couch, and a kitchenette with a coffee maker.

Bill knocks on the door a few minutes after I've entered. I usher him in, trying to block out his repentant, beaten-dog look. Sorry, Bill, too little, too late. We both know what's about to happen, and at least he doesn't make it more difficult than it needs to be.

Once Bill is gone, I sit at the table and connect my laptop to the satellite Wi-Fi link. I google "mayor emerald creek" and wait for the results to load with a beating heart. The City Hall website is the first hit. I click on it.

An official dot Gov page opens up titled: Mayor Theodor Abraham Hunt. No pictures. I stare at the surname, wondering if Emerald Creek is one of those small towns where everyone is related to each other. Probably. I shrug and read the rest.

> Mayor Hunt is the chief executive of the City of Emerald Creek.

Pompous. That's an introduction worthy of the president. The institutional rambling of the page continues to inform all interested citizens that the city's thirty-fourth mayor was sworn into office six months ago.

The recent appointment might be why they haven't put up a picture yet, seeing how swift and efficient they are at handling paperwork.

> As mayor, Hunt is responsible for the city workforce of over 30 employees and an annual budget exceeding $5 million. After attending St. Mary's High School and the University of Notre Dame, Mayor Hunt attained his law degree from Columbia University. Mayor Hunt is making government the best it can be for residents and businesses by demonstrating a commitment to engagement, innovation, and performance.

Uh-huh, Mr. Mayor, you're the boss man.

I skip the remainder of his boastful CV as it's just a sequence of one self-celebratory statement after the other.

Whatever. Whoever the elusive Theodore Abraham Hunt might be, he won't know what's hit him once I'm done dealing with him.

Between handling Bill and the unfruitful online stalking of the mayor, I need a palate cleanser. I make a cup of coffee, but as the first sip of the dark liquid comes in contact with my tongue, the blend tastes so awful that I spit it back out in the kitchenette sink.

I clean the mess and stalk out of the trailer, intent on finding a good cup of coffee.

One of Bill's deputies, Cameron, passes me on the way to the barn, driving a golf cart, and nods at me. "Boss."

"Cameron, stop."

The man hits the brakes and pulls up next to me. "Yes?"

"First off, you're promoted to Chief Location Manager. Bill is gone and I need you to pick up his slack."

"Of course, thank you." Cameron nods, with an expression not too dissimilar to the one his former boss had in my trailer a few minutes ago. The man looks like I'm firing him, too, instead of having just promoted him.

"Don't worry," I say. "You start with a clean slate. I won't hold you accountable for any past delays. I plan on sorting the situation with the mayor tomorrow, and once I secure the permits, it's on you to make sure everything proceeds smoothly from there on."

Finally, he smiles. "Thank you for the opportunity."

I wave him off. "You know what they say about Hollywood?"

He raises a skeptical eyebrow at me.

"There are only three ways to move up your number on the call sheet. If someone above you A, gets fired. B, quits. Or C, goes off to rehab."

"I thought that only applied to actors?"

"No, staff, too."

Cameron chuckles. "Duly noted. Anything else I can help you with?"

"Yes," I sigh. "Please tell me where to find good coffee on set."

He points behind his back with a thumb. "The one in the barn is pretty decent." Then, putting a hand to the side of his mouth as if he was telling a secret, he adds, "But I've heard rumors Christian Slade has a cappuccino maker at his cabin."

Christian is my lead superstar. I could catch two birds with one stone and drop by to say hi.

"Is the cabin far?"

"No, it's one of the closer ones." Cameron pats the empty seat next to him on the golf cart. "I can give you a ride."

I climb on the cart. "Thanks."

We ride down the hill and move on to flat ground until we reach Christian's cabin. Cameron parks next to two other carts and waits for me to get off before asking, "You want me to wait for you?"

"No, thanks, I can take one of these back. I should be able to find my way around. But let's meet at my trailer in about"—I check my watch—"two hours? I want to go over our applications and check that everything is in order. Could you also dig up city regulations, and county and state laws? Tomorrow, I want to walk into City Hall ready for any kind of ambush."

Cameron frowns. "Ambush? You expect foul play?"

"What I don't expect is for these delays to be casual. The mayor's stalling seems deliberate. We have to find out what his agenda is. And I want to be prepared. Make sure the paperwork is spotless and that City Hall doesn't have any legal ground to deny our applications."

"I'll dig up every town ruling on public space permits. See you in a couple of hours." Cameron waves and reverses the cart, heading toward the barn.

Christian's cabin is a brown log building with a porch. I walk up the front steps and ring the bell.

A thin, tall man with dark hair and dark eyes comes to answer the door. He's wearing black pants and a black shirt with a white cooking apron on top.

"Jeff, hi," I greet him, recognizing Christian's personal chef from previous appearances when Christian had to be on location for extended periods.

"Miss Baker, how nice to see you again."

"Is Christian in?" I ask.

"Yes, he and Miss Lana are having breakfast on the back patio."

"Is it okay if I join them?"

"Sure." He steps aside to let me in. "Would you like anything to drink?"

"If you could make me a vanilla latte, you'd become my new best friend."

"Something to eat as well?"

"No, thanks, my landlady is already stuffing me worse than a Thanksgiving turkey."

"Oh, please, you look as fabulous as always."

"Well, I've only been here a day."

Jeff escorts me across the small but cozy living room and opens the sliding French doors announcing me. "Mr. Slade, you have a visitor."

Christian, tall, blond, blue-green eyed, turns toward the doors and unleashes his million-dollar smile on me. "Sam!"

We hug.

Lana stands up as well and hugs me next. "What a surprise. We didn't expect you until wrap time." She and Christian got married last year, but we've been good friends since working together on the set of another one of my movies. A sci-fi flick that was instrumental in reuniting them after an emotional breakup.

"Well, yes," I say. "That was the plan. But filming will never end if things keep going at this snail's pace. So here I am, ready to wave my magic super-producer wand and fix everything."

"How long are you staying?" Lana asks.

I sigh. "Until the last cut."

Christian flashes me a teasing grin. "Gosh, you must be dying. Won't all the fresh air kill you?"

"Ha, ha," I say. Christian knows how much of a city girl, and New York fanatic, I am.

Jeff arrives with my latte in a steaming cup.

I take a sip and melt at how good it tastes. I raise the mug. "This coffee is a saving grace."

Jeff bows. "Much obliged." He collects a few dirty plates and bowls from the table and leaves.

I take another life-preserving sip of latte and ask, "Besides the production delays, how's everything else?"

"Oh, I love Emerald Creek," Lana jumps in to say. She caresses the table. "This is my office and you can't beat that view." I stare at the green hills and pastures with no sign of human intervention and silently disagree. "Plus, I can take the longest walks from the cabin. Just around that hill, there's a trail that goes straight to the Potawatomi Waterfall. It only takes two hours, and the view from on top is even better. We can do the hike together one day if you want to go."

That sounds like my idea of hell on Earth. Still, I say, "Thank you. Maybe, I don't know how much free time I'll get."

Christian chuckles. He knows I'd never voluntarily submit to hiking.

"What about the rest of the cast?" I ask. "Are you getting along with your co-star? I heard she's AWOL."

Christian winces. "Eh, I've had worse."

"But you've also had better," I say. "Sorry. Chelsea Moreno wasn't my first choice either, but she polls too well with the viewers."

"No, she's perfect," Lana says, surprising me.

"Oh?"

Lana grins. "I prefer Christian's co-stars a little nasty. Sorry, but I'll never get used to seeing my man kissing someone else, even if it's totally fake. At least if they're horrible people, I don't feel threatened."

"You wouldn't be threatened even if my co-star were an angel," Christian says, grabbing her hand from the table and kissing her knuckles.

These two are so sweet I want to gag.

"Okay, lovebirds," I say, getting up. "I've indulged in the scenic views enough. Time to get to work. Chris."

"Yeah?"

"Just a heads up, I've convinced Lionel to shoot the barn scene tomorrow, in case you need to do any prepping."

Christian wiggles his phone at me. "Yep, got the alert. We have an actor reading tonight. I guess the late timing is to give Chelsea enough time to get back."

"Yes, my minions are tracking her down as we speak. I'll see you peeps later, and let me know if you need anything."

Outside the cabin, I head for the parked golf carts. I'm about to jump on one when I stare back toward my trailer. The rectangular structure is visible in the distance. Considering the double slice of French toast I had for breakfast, I should probably walk. I still have an hour before I have to meet with Cameron and, as much as I technically despise walking for its own sake, it's also good exercise. Plus, my workout got cut short this morning, so...

I consider my pumps. Maybe not the best hiking gear, true. But no cows around, so it should be safe from the worst terrain hazards.

I'm halfway down the road when my phone chimes with a text from Taylor.

How's Indiana so far?

Before I reply, another message comes in from Holly.

Met any hot cowboys yet?

An image of a shirtless Travis Hunt pops into my head. But I refuse to acknowledge the guy, even if it's only in a text to my best friends.

So far, only an actual cow named Betsy and Hildi the goat

Taylor sends a perplexed emoji, followed by another text.

> Those are oddly specific names

> What can I say? People name their cattle around here

As I stumble down the hill, my left heel gets caught in a patch of wet mud. I curse under my breath and struggle to free my foot. The heel comes out with a cake of mud attached to it. I snap a pic and hop to the side of the road to clean my shoe in the grass. I send Taylor and Holly the photographic evidence of my wretchedness.

> Sorry gals, I have to go. Apparently, I can't walk and text at the same time or I might get caught in another quicksand

> Oh, come on, it can't be that bad. I googled Emerald Creek, and it seems like a lovely town

Holly sends her usual positive vibes.

Easy for you to say when your heels only meet blessed, solid concrete

I'm already fed up with all this nature

Haven't been downtown yet, though

I'm going tomorrow, will send an update

Six

Everything Comes to Her Who Waits

The mayor's office opens at nine, allowing me plenty of time to prepare. After an early workout, I convince Willette one scone is enough to meet all my dietary needs—if not more, then I shower and get dressed for war.

No occasion has ever called for a power suit more than today. At the cost of being banal, I opt for an all-black set. A clean-cut jacket with a silk satin sleeveless blouse underneath and skinny, straight pants. Very classy, very elegant, hyper-professional.

For footwear, however, I take a little more creative license. Nature might have not provided me with spikes, but thankfully, Christian Louboutin rectified that mistake. I wear my five-inch heel, studded pumps. The final touch is to apply matte-red lipstick to match the soles of my shoes.

Jerry comes to pick up Celia just as I'm ready to drive away. My assistant will be my eyes and ears at the compound while I'm gone. Before leaving, I double-check with Jerry that I understood the directions to get into town correctly. He repeats them to me one more time while also assuring me I only have to get a couple of turns right before I cross over a creek and into a land where satellite systems will resume functioning. I follow his instructions and as I pass over an old wooden bridge with flaking paint, the map app miraculously stops loading, and the reassuring "woman from the valley" voice instructs me to turn left.

As Jerry predicted, I reach the "city" center in fifteen minutes. The town square is for pedestrians only, and the street I'm on has no free parking spots. I make a few loops on the adjacent streets until a gray truck turns on the blinker. I pull up ahead, and once the car's gone, reverse into the spot.

In New York, I don't drive and I'm out of practice. So it takes me a few maneuvers to back into the space properly. When I get out of the truck to check the result, it's far from perfect. The pickup is skewed to the left and the front tire doesn't exactly fit into the parking limit line, but it's the best I can do. Plus, I'm already sweating more than with my earlier workout, and I'd prefer to get to the mayor's office in a presentable state.

The street is lined with parking meters. I take out my credit card to pay for a few hours parking—who knows how long the mayor will make me wait—but when I approach the column, there's no card slot or wireless sticker to signal where I should place the card for contactless payment. Confused, I study the meter. There's only a coin slot with a turning lever. Could... could this be one of those ancient mechanical-only meters?

I snap a picture and send it to my friends captioned: Have I suddenly stepped into the Eighties?

Holly gets back to me right away.

> Perfect, now all you need is a Jake Ryan

> Correction: all I need now is coins!

I don't have any on me. Already exasperated, I get back into the truck and search the glove compartment, cup holders, and under the seats for any spare change. I come up with a grand total of three quarters and ten cents. Mmm, probably not enough.

I check my wallet and find a five-dollar bill. In New York, I haven't used cash in I can't remember how long. Heck, I haven't used a credit card in months. I pay for everything with my phone.

Now I need to find a place where I can change the fiver. On this street, there's only a FedEx, a bike rental, and a closed restaurant. I lock the truck and walk along the curb to reach the main square. Here, fanned out around the wide circle of the plaza, the shops overlook a fountain in the middle. Flower beds full of anemones and multi-colored sweet peas are interspersed with wrought iron and wooden benches. And a large maple wood gazebo, probably used for public celebrations, sits at the edge of the square.

At the corner of the next crossroads, a blue-and-white striped awning catches my eye. I head in that direction, hoping for a coffee shop.

The establishment turns out to be more of a diner. As I walk in, the bell above the door chimes with the notes of an Elvis song. The fifties vibe is replicated by the interior. Not by design, I suspect, but simply as the result of the place not being renovated since it was built.

A portly woman in her early sixties is updating the day's specials on a blackboard behind the counter.

I approach her. "Hello, do you serve coffee?"

"Morning, dear, yeah, sure. Would you like a cup?"

"Oh perfect, I'll take a skinny vanilla latte with soy milk, easy on the foam, and with a double sugar-free vanilla syrup pump, please."

The woman blinks at me. She grabs a pot from the auto-drip coffee maker behind her and pours the dark liquid into a nondescript white mug. "Honey, we got coffee, black." Then she points at the counter. "Sugar is in the jar, creamer in the basket."

I search the pods for a vanilla flavored one and I'm thrilled when I find it. "Do you have any sweetener?"

The woman begrudgingly hands me a packet of Sweet'n Low. "That'll be a dollar fifty."

I hand her my bill and collect the coin change.

With the addition of the creamer and sweetener, the coffee is *drinkable*. I gulp it down in a few long sips and head out of the diner.

Back at the truck, I feed all the coins I've amassed to the meter. At a fare of two dollars an hour, the spoils of my scavenger hunt grant me a little over two hours of street parking. Busy or not, the mayor had better receive me.

I retrace my steps back to the square and cross it toward City Hall. The building is a three-story stone structure with decorative patterns on the windowsills and front pillars. Behind the double-entrance doors, a reception booth sits in the middle of the lobby, but I avoid stopping by, just in case they told me I needed an appointment to speak to the mayor and they'd be happy to provide me one in two or three weeks. Instead, I follow the directions pointing to the mayor's office as if I knew perfectly well where I was going.

When I reach the top floor, I chase one last sign to a spacious, blind corridor. The mayor's wooden and glass door looms at the end, Mayor Theodor Abraham Hunt spelled in golden lettering on the opaque glass panel.

And I wish I could just barge in, guns blazing. Unfortunately, the path is blocked by a young brunette manning an external desk. The secretary, nothing unexpected. To hope she'd be on a coffee break would've been too much.

With the self-assuredness of a woman who belongs where she is, I approach the desk and announce myself, "Samantha Baker, I'm here to see the mayor."

The secretary startles at my sudden appearance. "Uhm, hello, Ms. Baker, did you-mmm have an appointment with us today?" She checks an agenda. "I don't see you on the books."

"No, but I must speak with the mayor urgently. And since the only appointment given to my staff was two weeks from now, I tried a walk-in."

"Let me just check with the mayor." The woman picks up the landline and pushes a red button. "Yes, Mr. Mayor, I have a Samantha Baker for you... no... yes... very well, sir." The secretary hangs up and stares at me. "Sorry, the mayor is busy at the moment. He won't be able to see you. But I can check our calendar and book you an appointment."

"That won't be necessary, thank you," I say, struggling to keep a smile stamped on my lips. "I'll wait until he's free."

"I'm afraid that could take hours."

"Then I'll wait all day if necessary," I say with finality, sitting on one of the plastic chairs lining the hall.

The secretary doesn't pick up the phone again, but I see her typing a quick message on her keyboard. No doubt an email or a work chat message to her boss notifying him of the stakeout.

After sending the red alert, the woman keeps working at her computer but still throws me the occasional dirty look. After forty-five minutes of this silent battle of wills, the coffee I drank an hour ago demands out.

I get up. "Is there a restroom I can use?"

"Two doors down the hall," the secretary informs me.

I hate public restrooms, but thankfully City Hall has one of the cleanest I've ever seen. I enter a stall and exit again as quickly as I can. I wouldn't put it past the mayor to sneak out while I'm gone to avoid meeting with me. Before getting back, I pause in front of the mirror to reapply my lipstick. I'm going to need the war paint to handle the meeting.

At noon, I still haven't heard a peep coming from behind the mayor's door. And now I wish I'd brought a cereal bar or something to support me during my siege. But if I'm hungry, he must be, too. I mean, the man's gotta eat eventually, right?

After another half hour, the landline on the secretary's desk rings, making both of us jolt in our seats.

She picks up on the second ring. "Yes... yes, sir... right away." The woman hangs up and looks at me. "The mayor will see you now."

"Thank you." I stand up and iron the wrinkles from my suit with my palms. My heels click loudly on the marble floor as I close the distance to the door. I knock twice on the glass panel.

"Come in," a deep voice replies from within the office. Hand on the doorknob, I take a steadying breath and push my way into the mayor's office.

Seven

It Takes Two to Make a Bargain

My march to victory is very short-lived, though. The moment I step across the threshold, I freeze because opposite me, seated in a plush leather chair behind an enormous mahogany desk, Travis Hunt is regarding me with an amused expression. And, bless my heart, he's dressed in a suit! And not even a cheap getup from the mall, but a tailored outfit that must've set him back a few thousand dollars. The jacket is a dark navy blue that contrasts with the pristine white of the shirt he's wearing underneath. The shock is too much. I'm stuck in the doorway, eyes bulging and mouth dangling open rather unsophisticatedly.

"Samantha, good morning," he says, leaning his elbows on the desk. "How can I help?"

The clear mocking in his tone shakes me out of the spell. So much for the town's last cowboy.

I close the door behind me and narrow my eyes at him. "*You're* the mayor?"

Travis's grin widens, eyes crinkling. He's obviously enjoying my astonishment. Unfortunately, I'm distracted in my contempt by the way the tailored jacket shows off his broad shoulders as he shrugs, satisfied. "Last time I checked, it was my name on the door."

I turn back to the door and frown. On the glass, I can still read in reverse the words spelled in golden ink.

"Actually, it says Mayor Theodor Abraham Hunt."

"That's my given name, but no one's ever really used it."

"So you just give people false credentials for fun."

53

"Travis is what everyone calls me."

I study him, and he studies me back. Finally, at least, I can make sense of the intimidatory handshakes and hostile sizing up: we *are* enemies. But why? Why is this man stalling my movie? What's his angle?

He gestures at the chairs opposite his desk. "Please."

As I take a seat, he looks me over and says, "Nice shoes."

"Nice suit," I counter.

"A leftover from my lawyer days in New York."

"Ah, which reminds me how much I dislike lawyers."

His poker face is better than mine. Travis lets the comment slide without even flinching. "What can the city of Emerald Creek do for you?"

"Sign my filming permits."

"Ah, yes." Travis sits back in the chair. "I've been meaning to get around to them, but I've been swamped in paperwork lately." He points at a pile of documents on his desk.

"Yeah, yeah," I say. "I'm aware the Emerald Creek Barbecue Festival and the Founding Fathers Parade drained your office of precious resources. But if the city has no other impending events to supervise, may I ask you to sign the permits."

"Sure, I'll look at them and let you have a signed copy as soon as possible." He rummages through the pile of papers. "They must be in here somewhere..." He gives up searching after a while. "Well, I don't want to waste any more of your time. My office will contact you once the documents are ready."

Nice try, Mr. Mayor. My lips part in the most polite, fake smile. "Oh, don't worry, I've nothing but time. How about you sign them now?"

"Ah." He interlaces his fingers. "I'm afraid that won't be possible."

"Why? You have to supervise a protest to stop premature Christmas decorating?"

"No, but all the permits' parameters need to be in order."

"Such as?"

"Craft services, speed limits, structure altering activities, dock usage, cable guards, parking, vehicle access, and so on... then I have to check the dates and coordinate with the sheriff's department."

I lean forward and place my joined hands on his desk. "Mr. Mayor, how about we agree to cut the... *cow-manure* and get straight to the point?"

Travis's eyes flash with a shrewd glint. "Which would be?"

"You're stalling my movie on purpose, and I'm curious to know why."

Travis's mouth twitches with amusement and, dang, do his lips have to look so sexy? He soon schools his features in a mock-outraged expression while pressing a hand over his heart. "Samantha, such an accusation pains me deeply. Why would I ever delay your project on purpose?"

I lean back against my chair. "I have a couple of working theories..."

He raises an eyebrow. "Oh, I'm very curious to hear them."

"One, you're a sadist who enjoys derailing businesses. Two, you don't want the movie crew in your town for whatever reason—"

"And what's behind door number three?"

"You want something and the permits are your bargaining chip. So which one is it, Mr. Mayor?"

"No cow-manure you said?"

I nod. "No cow-manure."

The mayor sighs. "Having a live-in movie crew has been fantastic for the town. And since the news spread that Emerald Creek is the filming location of Christian Slade's newest rom-com, we've been invaded by tourists who lodge in our hotels, eat in our restaurants, and shop in our shops. The truth is, having you Hollywood people in town is a boost for the local economy. I just wanted to keep you around as long as possible."

"Well, that all sounds very nice, but you must understand that if you continue to delay the filming indefinitely, we'll eventually run out of money, and all you'll have accomplished would be to *not* make Emerald Creek the location of a major Hollywood blockbuster. You don't strike me as a completely idiotic man, so you must have something else in mind."

"I'll take that as a compliment." Travis opens a drawer and lays a set of manila folders out on the desk. He opens one. "Ah, yes, first, the lake scene... As you might've seen from the pictures, the location is gorgeous. Unfortunately, previous administrations have let it go to disrepair. The application states you plan to clean a small portion of the beach, enough for filming, and erect a few temporary structures."

"And what's wrong with that?"

"How about your crew cleans up the entire beach and you make the structures permanent, quality ones instead of props?"

"Why us? It seems more of a job for the town's government."

"I agree it would be, but my predecessor also left me with a gaping hole in the town's finances, and unfortunately, I don't have the budget to complete the task alone. But if we worked together…"

"Ah, I see what's going on. You heard Hollywood and you thought you'd found your golden goose. Let me give you a reality check, Mr. Mayor. Movie producers don't print money and our projects are carefully budgeted. And even if I could've met you in the middle if you'd made your extortionate requests transparent from the start, I surely can't now. You've jeopardized our cash flow with all the delays you've caused, while also, on a personal note, forcing me to move to the middle of nowhere to clear up your mess."

"Oh, come on, I'm sure you'll survive a few more weeks without your precious New York."

"You seriously expect me to believe the town is so strapped for money you have to resort to blackmail?"

"Blackmail is such a strong word. This is merely a negotiation."

Travis doesn't strike me as a mean man, and it's hard to reconcile this ruthless, bargain-driving weasel with the son who spends his weekends mending his mother's fences. Between the suit and the attitude, this Travis wouldn't fit half badly in a cutthroat New York law firm. So why do I like this suited version far less?

"But if you wanted our help, why be so antagonistic?" I ask. "Instead of making us waste so much time and money, couldn't you have just plain asked?"

"I apologize if I've put you in a tight spot, Sam—"

"I prefer Miss Baker."

"But your predecessor, Bill *Something*, didn't seem to have the executive power to negotiate with me. I wanted to get the attention of one of the top dogs."

"Careful, Mr. Mayor, 'cause this dog isn't all bark and no bite."

Eight

Beauty Is in the Eye of the Beholder

Two hours later, I walk out of City Hall stripped of every last penny my production had left. I might bite, but it's the mayor who just chewed me up and spat me back out a few hundred thousand dollars lighter.

Fuming, I stroll down the curb, not even caring that I've skipped lunch. I need to get back to the movie crew ASAP to loop in the others about the barbarous requests I just had to agree to.

At least now I'm the proud holder of signed permits for the first two public locations we need. The others, Travis will sign when I deliver my side of the deal.

Untrustful, conniving jerk.

The last drop in my already overflowing country-life bucket is getting back to my truck to the sight of a middle-aged police officer intent on writing me a ticket.

"Stop!" I yell. "I'm here, officer."

The man stares up from his notepad. "Ma'am, your time expired four hours ago."

"I know, I'm sorry, but I didn't have enough coins to pay for more. You should upgrade the meters to accept electronic payments."

"While I might agree with you, I still have to write you up. Rules are rules."

"It's okay, Peter," a voice calls from behind us. "You can let this one slide."

I turn around to find Mr. Smug walking toward us. I spin back toward the cop. "Officer, please write me the ticket, I insist."

"But—but just a second ago you were asking for a pass."

"And I was wrong. You said it yourself, rules are rules."

The police officer gapes at me and then at the mayor, who nods.

The officer nods back and puts his notepad away. "Good afternoon, Mayor Hunt."

"Afternoon, Pete. Please say hi to Dolly from me."

The officer tips his hat at me. "Good day to you, too, ma'am."

This day has been many things—enlightening, harassing, overtaxing, but *good* isn't one of them.

"I hadn't pinned you down as a rule-breaker," Mr. Teasing says.

"Provide a payment system that accepts something other than gold doubloons and people might actually be able to pay for parking."

The sexy crinkle of the mayor's eyes is insufferable. "Want to add that to the list of improvements you're bringing to the town?"

He's won, and he knows it. And I hate him all the more for it.

"Enjoy the feeling while it lasts," I spit. "'Cause in three months I'll be back to my life in New York and you'll still be mayor of this cesspit. A fresh coat of paint won't make this hellhole any less hideous."

"Oh, come on, don't be a sore loser. I'm only doing what's best for my people."

"Well, you don't need to look so damn pleased about it."

I don't wait for a retort. I round the pickup and get inside. Without saying goodbye, I slam the door shut and jerk the gear into drive. Rage dramatically improves my driving skills because in a single maneuver, I smash my foot on the accelerator and screech out of the parking spot.

As I speed away, I throw a glance at the rearview mirror and see the mayor waving at me with that infuriating, smug, and unfortunately, sexy grin still curling his lips.

***

That afternoon I call a general meeting, including both the staff and the cast, and ask Christian to bring Lana along.

"Okay, folks," I call once everyone has assembled in the community barn. "I have good news and bad news."

The room quietens down and I continue, "The good news is I've secured the permit for the town square scene and the other locations should follow suit. The bad news is, it's going to cost us." People exchange perplexed stares, so I explain the situation. "City Hall was stalling on purpose, guys. This is a shakedown, plain and simple. Now, I've negotiated with the mayor a few conditions to get the rest of the permits signed. The first is that we restore the Wilkins Mill Bridge." I address my next question to the construction crew chief. "Cliff, can your crew do the job? How long would such an operation take?"

"Is that the old wooden bridge that leads into town?"

"That's the one."

"If I put my entire crew on it, it might take two or three days to sandpaper and about the same to repaint. Is the color staying the same, ma'am?"

"Yes."

"Then it's the same shade we used for the barn reproduction. We've plenty of paint left and it's good for outdoor use."

"Perfect, thank you." The man nods at me and I nod back. "I won't lie, Cliff. Most of the extra work will fall on your shoulders. This brings me to the hardest part. The lake. The original plan was to clear a small portion of the beach and exploit different shooting angles to make it seem bigger. The mayor, however, would rather we cleared the entire perimeter and made our structures permanent. He wants picnic tables, a gazebo, a kiosk, the whole shebang. While the construction crew is at work on the bridge, I'd like the landscaping team to take care of the overgrown vegetation. You'll have the support of the town's urban forestry team for this job." The landscaping manager nods at me. "But the real issue is the amount of trash littering the area." I turn toward Christian's wife. "Which is why I asked you, Lana, to come along. The only way I can see to clear an area that vast is if we organize a volunteer event, and you're the only person I know who has experience in the field. Is it doable?"

"Everything is possible with a little hard work," Lana replies with a bright smile. And I swear I've never seen someone so excited about picking up trash. "How big of an area are we talking about?"

"The lake is roughly 330 acres."

Lana ponders for a moment. "I can contact my old organization to see if they can provide the basic equipment, trash bags, grabbers, and so on. But to clear such a large area, we'd require a massive turnout of volunteers. But nothing a few famous influencers can't pull off." She places a hand on Christian's arm. "Good thing we have a room full of them."

I shift my attention toward the rest of the cast. "This part is voluntary, of course, I can't force you to take part or promote the event to your followers, but all the help we can get is welcome. On my part, I can assure you your personal security will be my top priority."

Chelsea Moreno stands up. "Well, I'm not picking up trash, so count me out. Can I go now? I was supposed to have a facial half an hour ago."

The actress stalks out of the room, and Lana smirks at me. We exchange a silent yeah-a-man-would-be-crazy-to-touch-that stare, and we get back to work on the event.

The rest of the cast proves a lot more supportive, which is already half the battle. With their combined followers, I'm positive we're going to recruit a small army of volunteers. Next, I task the Graphics people with the design of a flyer to promote the event, put Celia in charge of the social media, and finally ask Lana, "When do you think we can realistically set a date?"

"Ten days should be more than sufficient to get the ball rolling. How about Sunday, next week?"

"Great. Okay, everyone." I clap my hands. "Thanks for grinding this out with me, let's get back to work."

The room slowly empties. As people file out, I massage my temples. My head is hurting from the lack of food and my ego hasn't felt so chafed in a long time.

And the worst part is I can't even go out for a drink with my friends to unwind. Two days into this nightmare of an assignment, and I'd already sell my soul to be back in New York.

***

The rest of the week is just as awful. All I do is work, work, work to satisfy Travis's requests. Friday and Saturday evening I don't even consider going out. I'm in bed before nine and up by six. But the stress must catch up to me because when I wake up on Sunday, the sun is already half up in the sky. I'm not even sure what woke me until a weight shifts on my feet. I open my eyes and meet the gaze of a large feline. I scream.

I've no idea how a lynx got into my bed, but the animal now lowers its large, pointed ears while its orange-yellow eyes meet mine in an annoyed scowl, as if my screaming was deeply inconveniencing him.

We stare at each other for a second longer, then the beast drops its gaze and begins licking its thick silver-tabby mantle.

"Gosh, how did you get in my room?!"

I check the window, but it's closed.

Anyway, it doesn't matter how the predator got in, only that I get out before it eats me for breakfast.

As I dash out of bed, my feet get caught in the blankets and I trip, landing in a heap on the floor.

The lynx pauses his cleaning routine and stares down at me with a pitiful air.

An unexpected knock on the door wrenches a second, small scream out of me.

Then someone calls my name. And I never would've imagined being grateful to hear Travis Hunt's voice, but I rush to the door and fling it open.

"I heard you scream. What's up?" Travis asks, looking worried.

"There's a monster in my room!" I say, hiding behind him.

"What monster?" Travis looks both puzzled and amused. "You've looked in the mirror and got scared?"

"Oh, you're such a gentleman, Mr. Mayor!" I snap, then point to the bed. "I'm talking about that feral beast, genius!" But really, can't Travis see the dangerous feline taking a spa break on my bed? "What kind of beast is it?"

"My mom's cat?" Travis asks back. The mayor looks so dazed it's comical.

I peek over his shoulder, inspecting the animal nestled between the blankets. It sort of looks like a cat. But a huge one that must've ingested a double dose of skele-gro as a kitten.

"That's not a cat. Cats are small, cute, and cuddly. That looks like a lynx!" I say, taking in its grim expression.

"Fluffy is a Maine Coon, a larger breed."

"Fluffy, uh? If he's your mother's cat, how come I've never seen him around the farm?"

"He's a bit of a vagabond," Travis says, approaching the bed to pick up the animal. "He comes and goes as he pleases. I thought it'd take more than a little furball to scare you…" Travis chuckles, looking me up and down.

That's when I realize how unpresentable I must look, wearing only a white T-shirt, crew socks, and with unbrushed hair. Instinctively, I smooth it down with my fingers, hoping it isn't too frizzy.

But what do you care? You hate this man! I mentally scold myself.

Precisely, and that's why it's even more important to appear presentable in front of the enemy.

Does the T-shirt even cover my bottom? I self-consciously pull down the hem. I need him out of my room.

"Well, thank you for retrieving the monster, I suppose," I say, hoping he'll take the hint to go.

"If you want to have breakfast, Mom is making her special Sunday brunch downstairs."

"I'll be down in a moment," I dismiss him.

After Travis clears the door, I search my bag for a pocket mirror to check my hair and yelp in horror once I flip it open.

The hair is the last of my problems.

This past week I've worked myself into the ground. And last night I was so tired I've fallen asleep with a purifying clay mask on my face. And now, I look like a green monster about ready to crackle!

I hear Travis chuckle down the hall. "I take it you've found a mirror!" he calls.

Insufferable, arrogant twit!

I grab a change of clothes, a set of fresh towels, and head to the bathroom for a hot shower. I lock myself in, drop the clothes and towels on the small white stool next to the sink, and get into the tub, yanking the shower curtain closed behind me.

As the water hits my face, I sneer at the prospect of another bright day in the country. Even the cats are freaks here.

I scrub the clay from my face, scraping at it with my fingernails. The mud is so dry, the process takes a while. I turn off the water and feel my face for any residual speck. I'd say I got it all, but I'd better check in the mirror. I pull the shower curtain open, but instead of my reflection, I meet Travis's stunned gaze as he enters the bathroom.

"What are you doing in here?" I screech.

Instinctively, I yank the shower curtain down to cover myself. But in my panic, I pull so hard that I dislodge the overhead pole that, in a whipping movement, hits Travis square on the forehead.

Travis stumbles backward, putting both hands to his forehead, and collapses on the floor with his back against the bathroom door.

Nine

Give Them an Inch and They'll Take a Mile

Blood.

Shoot, I broke his head!

As I watch the crimson liquid trickle down the side of his face, I turn white.

Okay, I hate him… but… I don't want him dead… it was an accident.

Travis barged into the bathroom while I was naked. And how did he even get in? Does he have a skeleton key? The door was locked.

I'm not saying he deserved a bash to the head for breaking and entering, but… is it normal to lose all that blood?

"Travis, are you okay…?" I ask him in a faint voice, while still covering my body with the shower curtain.

In response, he moves his hands and shows me his face smeared with a half mask of blood, and yet another scream escapes me.

"Gosh, Baker, I knew you were feisty… but this is a little over the top even for you," he says, running a hand over his eyes, wiping some of the blood that continues to smear his face.

"It was an accident," I stammer. "And you walked in on me."

But why am I justifying myself with a depraved maniac who is illegally occupying my bathroom?

"For goodness' sake, woman, if you don't want me to walk in on you showering, lock the door. Don't attack an innocent passerby."

"It was locked, and I didn't attack you. And, you might be many things, but innocent isn't one of them!"

"The lock is a little loose," Travis explains, ignoring my comment. "You have to really push for it to latch."

"And how was I supposed to know that? And since you're still arguing, the hit on the head couldn't have been that strong." I tighten my lips. "At worst, you won't be able to show off that arrogant face around for a few days."

His mouth curls up into that mocking grin of his.

"Show off, uh? So you find me attractive, eh, Baker…" he replies, smiling sarcastically.

I'm torn on whether I should help him or finish him off. In the end, pity wins over spite.

"Close your eyes," I say.

"Why?"

"Because I need to get out of the shower and you need that wound looked at."

Travis makes a theatrical gesture of squeezing his eyes shut.

"Not a peep," I order as I lower the shower curtain and get out of the tub.

I quickly wrap a towel around me and move my clean clothes from the stool to the closed toilet.

"You can open your eyes now."

He does so and winces slightly.

I temporarily push our differences aside and grab his wrists to help him up. I must catch him off guard because he looks gob-smacked at my gesture. Still, without a word, the mayor lets me pull him up and lower him down again on the stool.

Travis raises an eyebrow, his face questioning. And yes, I still notice how gorgeous, if slightly bloodied, that face is.

Travis Hunt, or whatever his name is, is obnoxiously handsome, too handsome for his own good.

"What are you thinking?" he asks, startling me.

I reassure myself the mayor may have many qualities, but reading minds isn't one of those, so he can't possibly know I was mentally acknowledging his good looks.

"Do you have a first aid kit somewhere?" I side-step the question.

He points a finger up. "Cabinet, above the sink."

I find bandages and disinfectant. With an exasperated sigh, I start to clean his wound.

We're enemies, but I don't want to come across as a heartless woman who'd leave her opponents wounded and bleeding on the battlefield. We can call a temporary truce in case of a medical emergency. And I might be acting nurse right now, but as soon as his wound is patched up, the hostilities will resume.

I unroll the long gauze, and he starts grinning.

"Hey, Baker, are you going to bandage me with that, or choke me? Because your gaze does not bode well…"

If he calls me Baker one more time…

"It's Miss Baker for you. And if you could please shut up and let me dress that wound…"

He gives me an amused look but has the good sense not to breathe another word as I get to work.

Turns out even his bleeding was overdramatic. The cut isn't that deep and I don't think it'll require stitches. I examine the small incision and proclaim, "You shall live.

But wash your face before your mom sees you and has a heart attack." Then I don't know why, I smile.

"Do my injuries tug at your heart, Baker? I'd call your smile almost sweet."

The smile, as it involuntarily appeared, drops from my face, and I purse my lips. "Yeah, the hit mustn't have been too strong. You've retained all your charming personality."

Okay, I've done my duty. Now it's time to put some distance between us.

"If you don't mind, now I'd like to finish my shower."

Travis stands up abruptly, and I'm once more reminded of how tall he is.

I'm waiting for him to leave, but as Travis takes a step toward the door, he puts a hand to his forehead and staggers. Without thinking, I close the distance between us and wrap his left arm over my shoulder before he ends up sprawled on the floor again.

Then he smiles.

My eyes narrow to two hostile slits and I quickly let go, pulling back.

He's making fun of me.

"You're incorrigible!" I say, and shove him out of the bathroom.

Unfortunately, the move lets me feel all the tight muscles under the soft fabric of his T-shirt.

"Nice to see you worry about me, Baker."

I give him a final push and slam the door in his face.

Cursing under my breath, I triple-check the lock, fix the shower rod as best as I can, turn on the water again, and get back into the maimed shower.

***

I manage to finish showering with no further incidents. And I pad back into my room with no more unpleasant encounters. But when I get out again ready for breakfast, there he is.

Travis is squatting in the hall, working a screwdriver into the bathroom lock, probably tightening it. He has washed his face and changed T-shirts. In this position, the white cotton hugs his shoulders and back, leaving nothing to be guessed about the level of muscle definition underneath. As he works the screw, his defined biceps bulge in the most hypnotizing way.

I bet his naked body could be used as a study manual in a myology class.

And I shouldn't be thinking about his body—naked or otherwise.

"You again," I say.

Travis stands up and gives me a once-over. And even if I'm fully dressed for the first time in our morning interactions, I'm still self-conscious. How much did he see in the shower?

I don't care if he got a full frontal. That man is… is… I get distracted by the tool belt hanging low on his hips.

Cowboy, suit, handyman. If I were into role-playing… *good thing I'm not!*

"I see you're taking to country living," Travis says, eying my stilettos sarcastically. "Two dead bodies were delivered for you."

"Two what?"

"Silver trunks, downstairs. From the weight of them, they could only contain dead bodies."

"My shoes!" I squeak in excitement, and head for the stairs.

"I'd offer to help," Travis calls after me. "But I suppose you'd just lecture me on how self-reliant and pro-equality you are."

I don't even care that he's mocking me. I fly down the stairs and hug my suitcases.

Two minutes later, as I have to stop halfway up the stairs to catch my breath after towing the heavy trunks along, I'm a little less cheerful. My mood further deteriorates as I look up and find Travis leaning against the wall and staring down at me with a teasing grin. That stupid tool belt still irritatingly unsettling on his hips.

"All you have to do is ask, Baker, and I could drag those up for you."

"I'm perfectly fine, thank you."

I abandon one suitcase on the larger, wider step and continue my journey upward one case at a time. As I reach the landing, I have to squeeze past Travis to pass. For whatever reason, he doesn't give way so that our faces end up a few inches apart. For a moment, I get lost studying the million colors in his irises, a perfect mix of green, golden flecks, and brown. My heart is pounding in my chest and I'm not even sure if it's for my recent effort up the stairs or for the way Travis is looking at me.

Then he ruins it.

"You're all sweaty, Baker," he says and takes a step back.

Still trying to get my breathing back to normal, I manage to spit an insult at him, "You're a jerk. I should've let you bleed to death."

"Now you break my heart," he says, theatrically bringing a hand to his chest.

I finally get past him and I don't even care that one of my suitcase wheels rolls over his stupid boots as I stalk toward my room and bang the door shut behind me.

Then I remember I have to go back for the other suitcase.

Ten

The Best Things in Life Are Free

That night, after my less-than-ideal morning and another full day spent on set, I need to unwind from the awful week behind me and get ready for a possibly worse one ahead. I might have no free days with the production being so delayed, but at least the nights are all mine. Blessed be Lionel's quirk for filming only with natural lighting.

Even if I'm super tired and every bone in my body is begging me to go to bed, I've gone too long without a proper drink and I'm also fed up with being alone. Willette is a gracious host, but I'm craving the company of someone closer to my age bracket—not her horrible son, who thankfully has left the farm this morning, never to return. I can't mingle with the people at work since I'm the big, mean boss. What would I do? Befriend them one night when I might have to reprimand them the next day?

The same doesn't apply to actors, and Christian is a friend. But hanging out with him and Lana would only make me feel like the third wheel. Plus, he's very private and the most I could hope for is dinner at his cabin. *Pass.*

Celia could be the exception. I'm still technically her boss, but she works directly for me and isn't involved in the production. We could go out for a drink without it being the end of the world.

Also, tonight is the first night she came back early to the B&B with me instead of staying behind to hang out with the crew and having someone drop her off later, so...

I cross the hall to knock on her door. "Celia, may I come in?"

"Sure, boss, just a second." She opens the door wearing a bathrobe and with her wet hair loose on her shoulders.

I bet her evening shower was less traumatic than mine this morning.

"Hey, Celia, I was thinking of going into town for a drink. Would you like to come along?"

Celia blushes. "Actually, Jerry is picking me up in an hour. We're going to the drive-in in Georgetown."

"Hollywood people going to the movies, cute. Is it just the two of you?"

"Mmm, yes. Is—is it okay if I... mmm... date him?"

I shrug. "Neither of you is in a subordinate position, completely different departments. I don't see the conflict."

"So it wouldn't be considered unprofessional or frowned upon?"

"Honey, if I had a dollar for every on-set romance I've witnessed, I'd be retired and living in the Bahamas."

Lie. I'd still be living in New York, but in a much grander apartment.

Celia finally smiles.

"Word of advice, if I may?" I add.

"Sure, boss."

"Be mindful of your geography before you get yourself in too deep, all right?"

"My geography? In what sense?"

"Last I checked, Jerry lives on the opposite coast from you."

"Yes, but Denouement Studios also has offices in LA."

I low whistle. "Looks like I should've given that advice a few atmospheres ago. Keep diving at this pace and you'll find the Marianas Trench in no time."

"You don't trust Jerry?"

"I don't *know* Jerry, and neither do you. I like him and he seems like a perfectly nice guy, but be sure you two are on the same page. Sometimes men are grand at making promises and become much smaller when it's time to follow through."

"Will do, boss," she says with a dreamy smile that tells me my advice has landed on deaf ears.

I go back to my room and let myself fall backward on the bed. I so miss my best friends and our outings in Manhattan.

"Nope, I'm all alone," I tell the ceiling.

"Meow," a ball of fur disagrees from the dresser chair.

I pull myself up on my elbows. "How did you get in?" The door was locked. "Is there a secret passage somewhere?"

The cat doesn't respond, only eyes me cryptically.

"No, you're right, I shouldn't sit here feeling sorry for myself."

If cats had eyebrows, he'd be raising one. With one last look of contempt my way, Fluffy starts licking himself.

Even if Emerald Creek doesn't offer much in the way of entertainment, I'm positive there's a pub in town. Time to check it out. And since tonight will be my only social outing of the week, I decide to pull out all the stops when I get ready. Same as if I was going out in Manhattan. I shave my legs, redo my nail polish, do my makeup with painstaking care, and dress to the nines. I pick a dark-green dress with white heart polka dots and oversized, see-through sleeves. The skirt starts at the waist and flares out—short and playful.

As for shoes, now that my full travel closet has arrived, I've plenty of choices.

The winners are nude suede sandals with a thin toe strap, even thinner ankle straps, and the cutest pert bow at the heel. I match the ensemble with a suede clutch big enough just for my keys, phone, and credit card.

But as I go to say goodbye to the cat with an ear scratch, my eyes fall on the pile of flyers on my desk. The design team did a stellar job with the graphics to attract volunteers for next week's beach cleanup. Should I combine business with pleasure and post a few in town?

Regretfully, I drop my clutch and opt for a larger bag. One last stop in Celia's room to ask for some Scotch tape—she keeps all the office supplies—and I'm ready to go.

When I get downstairs, Willette is coming out of the kitchen, and we almost collide.

Travis's mother takes me in and does a double-take. "Is someone getting married?"

"No, I've just decided to go out tonight, check out the local pub."

"I'm not sure that attire…" she starts, then stops. "I mean, the pub is more of a casual hangout."

"Don't worry, a little fashion won't kill anyone." I breathe a happy, "See you later," and leave the house.

Fifteen minutes later, I park the black pickup on Market Street. I get out of the truck and check the parking rules on an overhead sign—at least at night, there's free parking. I fish a flyer out of my bag and tape it to the sign pole. Next, I head for the town square and, as I pass City Hall, I stick my tongue out at the building, then tape a flyer on each side of the double front doors.

The mayor will be thrilled when he walks in tomorrow morning. I drop a few more flyers around the square and then head toward the pub. Being the only lit building in town, it's easy to find. Music is blasting out of its doors, as well as a few patrons holding beers. They definitely look like a casual bunch, all boots, jeans, and checkered shirts. No suits here, but I expected that. The wooden board above the entrance spells the words White Hart in white-flecked paint.

I walk past the outside drinkers, making heads turn, and push my way past the heavy wooden and colored-glass doors. As I step in, I feel catapulted into one of those movie moments. The dramatic scene of a villain who appears on-screen accompanied by a bolt of lightning and a clap of thunder, with the room going eerily quiet in response. Just as now, in the real world, all the chatter in the pub dies while all eyes turn on me.

Well, I always knew how to make an entrance. I ignore the startled stares and even a few slacked jaws and head straight for the bar to sit on one of the tall, wood-and-leather stools. Behind the counter, a young woman with strawberry-red hair held up in a ponytail is wearing a black T-shirt with the White Hart logo and taking orders. The barmaid finishes serving beers to two other customers and comes my way.

"Hi," she smiles. "Are you with the movie crowd?"

"What makes you say that?" I ask, wondering if I have a "Hollywood Producer" sign stuck to my forehead and never noticed.

"Oh, everybody knows everyone around here, and even if we get a lot of tourists lately, none look as stylish as you. Cute dress."

"Thanks," I say. "And, yes, I'm with the movie production."

"I knew it. You guys have brought this town back to life." Her smile brightens. "You know I even saw Christian Slade twice. He came here with his girlfriend for beers a few times, but then the word spread and the fans arrived, and I haven't seen him in a while."

"Yeah," I say. "Christian isn't a fan of the crowds."

"I'm Amber, by the way."

"Samantha."

The woman nods. "Nice to meet you. What are you having?"

"A Cosmopolitan, please."

The barmaid looks at me as if I've spurted a second head. "Sorry, we don't have triple sec—there are few fancy orders around here."

"No, it's okay. Can I have an espresso martini, then?"

Amber shakes her head. "No coffee machine either, sorry."

Disheartened, I ask, "Do you have a cocktail menu I can look at, or a wine list?"

"We don't serve wine," the barmaid says. "But I'll check in the back and tell you what I can manage for cocktails."

"Thank you, that'd be wonderful."

The moment Amber goes away, someone drops a half-empty beer mug on the wooden counter and sits on the stool next to mine. I turn and meet amused, hazel-green eyes.

"Did you just try to order an espresso martini?" Travis asks. He's in his cowboy costume: boots, worn-out jeans, unbuttoned checkered shirt. Underneath the shirt, he's wearing a black T-shirt with a scruffy old Metallica logo that's thankfully a little looser on the muscles than the white piece from this morning.

"Is it against the law to order a good cocktail in this town, Mr. Mayor?"

"I wouldn't call a mix of sugar, coffee, syrup, and alcohol *good*."

"Sorry," I say. "From your sophisticated order of a beer I hadn't deduced I was in the presence of a connoisseur."

Whatever answer he was about to give, gets cut off by a tall, dark-haired man taking the stool next to him, one over from me. "Vis-Vis, aren't you going to introduce me to your friend?" And before the mayor can say anything, the man offers me his hand, "Duncan West, the town sheriff."

The newcomer's style is still rustic, but a bit more refined than the off-duty mayor's. His jeans are less worn, he has a newer white T-shirt on that showcases his sculpted chest and he isn't wearing boots.

Also, when we shake hands, he doesn't crush mine. It's a firm but gentle grip.

"Samantha Baker," I say. "I believe we have a meeting scheduled for next Tuesday at ten."

Duncan does a double-take. "You're the gal from New York?" Then, turning toward Travis, he adds, "You didn't tell me she was so good-looking. You told me she was a—" He never finishes the phrase as Travis kicks him in the shin. "—a very nice lady," Duncan catches himself.

I'll never know what Travis actually told him about me. But I can make an educated guess: annoying, pedantic, haughty? I return whatever the sentiment with fervor.

The embarrassing moment is broken by Amber coming back with her findings. "So… err…" She falters in her speech as she throws Travis a quick side-glance and blushes, but then recovers quickly. "I can make you a regular martini—without olives, sorry—or a Moscow Mule."

I'm not a fan of plain martinis and I have never had a Moscow Mule. "Can you make the martini a Lemon Drop?"

"No, sorry," she says, embarrassed. I'm not sure if the sudden shyness is prompted by the lack of drinking options or by the clear crush she has on the mayor. "Again, we don't have triple sec or lemon juice."

Resigned, I go with the only remaining option. "I'll try the Moscow Mule, thank you."

With a big smile and one last furtive peek at Travis, Amber disappears again into the kitchen.

Duncan watches her go and pats Travis's back. "Man, that filly is eager to take you for a ride."

The mayor shakes his head as if he was dealing with a boisterous child instead of a grown man and the chief law enforcement officer in town, no less.

"Oh, come on, man," Duncan continues, squeezing Travis's bicep. "I don't waste three afternoons a week providing you free training for all these good muscles to go to waste."

I raise an eyebrow. "You're a sheriff *and* a personal trainer?"

Travis replies, "The sheriff kindly lets me join him and the other officers at the station's gym every once in a while."

"Yes," Duncan agrees. "And all my generosity is going to waste. If you don't jump on that horse somebody else will… and how long has it been since you went for a"— Duncan waggles his eyebrows and leans his head close to his friend's—"wild ride?"

My ears prickle at this last question. I suppose that in Emerald Creek even the number of Tinder users must be limited. Makes me wonder about the mayor's romantic life. Does he have one?

Travis pushes the sheriff away from his face. "None of your business."

"It's been too long," Duncan replies, nonplussed. "Man, you need a little female affection, trust me. And Amber would be perfect, she has such a crush on you." The sheriff closes his eyes and wraps his arms around himself, pretending to be two people kissing. In a fake shrill voice, he says, "Oh, Travis, yes," and makes smooching sounds.

Amber comes back in time for the second part of the show as Duncan, in a mock deep tone, replies to himself, "Yeah, Amber, just like that, baby." And back to the falsetto and smooches. "Oh, Travis. Ride me. Ride me."

Wordlessly, Amber drops my cocktail on the counter and fills up a huge beer jug at the water sprinkle faucet. She jerks her head at Travis to move aside and while Duncan is still busy making love to himself, she empties the jug square onto his head.

The sheriff ends up soaking wet and sputtering.

Eyes blazing, Amber calmly drops the jug on the counter and points at the door with her thumb. "You'd better take a *ride* outside, Sheriff West, and cool down."

Duncan pushes his wet hair away from his forehead. "Shoot, Amber."

"Yeah, shoot," the bartender echoes.

"I meant, I'm sorry," Duncan says. "It was a joke."

"In very poor taste, now go."

The sheriff pats Travis's shoulder. "Come on, Hunt, tell her it was meant as a compliment."

With a dashing smile, Travis turns to Amber. "I've never seen this man before in my life."

"Hunt, you coward," Duncan says. The sheriff is wringing his soaked T-shirt as he talks, but he's also smiling. "What's your favorite flower, sweetheart?" he asks Amber.

"I'm not telling you."

"Well, I'll find out and send you a bouquet."

Travis finishes his beer in one long gulp and retrieves his cowboy hat from a nearby stool, then he grabs Duncan's elbow, "Come on, man, I'd better give you a ride home. Even after the cold shower, I'm not sure you're entirely sober."

"It's my night off," Duncan protests at being steered away.

Travis ignores him and with his Duncan-free hand tips his hat at us. "Ladies."

As they head for the door, Duncan turns back, "Forgive me, Angel," he shouts at Amber. "I won't sleep tonight if I know you're angry at me." He blows her a kiss.

I can tell that, despite herself, Amber smiles at the sheriff, and he leaves the pub a happier man.

"What a man-child," Amber comments as she rounds the bar to mop the wet floor. "You must think we're all nuts in this town with our lack of sophisticated cocktails and me throwing water on unsuspecting customers."

"Actually," I say, taking my first sip of Moscow Mule— not bad. "I was thinking we could become best friends."

Eleven

Dreams Are Wishes the Heart Makes

A new friend and a few Moscow Mules aren't enough to shake off the jinx the Sunday morning shower started. Bad luck keeps close on my heels all of the following week.

No matter what I do, or where I go, I'm constantly running into the mayor. Monday it happens at the farm. Celia and I are on our way to work when we pass him on the road busy poking around the barbed wire fence that borders the ranch.

As soon as he sees us, he takes off his hat and approaches the truck.

Despite myself, I roll down the window. "You have no more out of towners to extort this morning, Mr. Mayor?"

He grins. "No, I set all my despoiling meetings for after ten." Travis jerks the pliers in his hands toward the property border. "And the fence needed fixing now, so…" He shrugs. "Ladies, let me get the gate for you."

He pats the roof of the truck and moves ahead to open the gate. As he walks past the truck, I try really hard not to notice how nice those jeans stretch on his bum.

***

Tuesday, I'm unsuspectingly sitting in the sheriff's office, discussing traffic stoppages and possible re-routings to accommodate the filming schedule when the mayor barges in, uninvited. Today he's in a suit again and the effect is breathtaking.

"Mayor Hunt," Duncan greets him. "To what do we owe the unexpected pleasure?"

"Just one of my regular rounds to check how our law enforcement department is doing."

"Cut the crap, Vis-Vis, you never show up in my office unless someone has died." The sheriff looks between me and the mayor and narrows his eyes. "Or perhaps, could you be checking on Miss Baker, protecting her from my undeniable charm?"

"More to protect you from her." Travis leans against the doorframe with a devil-may-care attitude, making my heart thump a thousand beats per minute—out of sheer irritation, I'm sure.

"Excuse me?" I say.

"I've been advised city girls bite."

"Forgive me, but when someone sticks his boots into my business, I get a little squirrelly…"

The sheriff cuts in, "Should I leave you the office? You two seem to have a lot to sort." I'm actually thinking Duncan is being serious when he adds, "The blinders come down for privacy, but you shouldn't get too loud in your *sorting*."

"No," I say. "We still have a ton of work to do, and I'm sure the mayor was about to leave." I turn to Travis. "Weren't you?"

"If my input isn't needed."

"It isn't."

Travis finally leaves, and with no more distractions, the sheriff and I can finalize our traffic plan.

By the time the meeting is over, I'm starving, so I opt for a minor detour to a bookstore doubling as a coffee shop Amber recommended. She assured me they make cappuccinos. On foot, I follow her directions to a small court nestled near the city park. The shop is impossible to miss, and I immediately fall in love with the quiet old building with its extensive selection of titles, comfy, mismatched furniture, and a small espresso bar. I decide to treat myself to a sandwich and a cappuccino and perhaps a good book to absorb over the weekend. I'm not sure I'll be returning to the White Hart anytime soon. As I sit at one of the vacant outdoor tables, the mayor comes up to me with a grin on his face.

"Is this seat taken?" he asks, pointing at the chair opposite me.

"Are you following me?"

"I could ask the same. This is my favorite lunch spot, and I arrived first."

I throw a pointed look at the empty table next to mine, but he's already sitting down, making himself comfortable.

"And do you always harass patrons of this establishment with your unrequested company?"

"Only the ones who wear ridiculous shoes." Travis grins again, glancing at my feet under the table.

Nu-uh, no one makes fun of my pink and aquamarine faux-fur slingbacks. I reach for my wrapped sandwich ready to take my lunch somewhere else, but Travis stops me with a raised hand. "Please don't go."

"Why not?"

"We might've started off on the wrong foot, but we don't need to be enemies."

"I didn't start this," I say.

"Fair enough," he says, baring a set of perfect pearly whites. "Let me apologize on my behalf and that of the entire city for…" he pauses.

"Threatening my livelihood, shaking down my business?" I offer.

"… for forcing your hand a little in collaborating with us."

"Ah, now I finally see the politician." I grab my sandwich, my paper cup, and stand up. "Thanks, but no thanks."

***

Wednesday at least I have a precise place and hour for when my path will cross with the mayor's: 10:30 a.m. at the Wilkins Mill Bridge.

Cliff made good on his promise, and today is the official inauguration of the restored bridge.

Two police cars are holding back traffic from both directions for the ceremony. In front of a small crowd, the mayor waits behind a golden ribbon tied to both ends of the bridge with a ridiculously large pair of scissors in his hands. As the official sponsor of the project, I have to stand next to Travis the whole time and smile as he hands me a golden engraved plaque that immortalizes Denouement Studios' generous donation to the city of Emerald Creek.

To add insult to injury, I have to wear one of those unfashionable yellow hard hats and screw the plaque to the center of the bridge's railing myself. What an honor, right?

"Need a hand with those tools?" a teasing voice asks in my ear as I struggle to half-squat in my tight pencil skirt. No one had informed me of the screw-in or I would've worn pants.

Now, I'm balancing precariously on my stilettos while simultaneously dealing with screws and bolts, hoping my skirt seams will hold. And to twist the knife in my wounded pride, a photographer from the local newspaper is presiding over the event, forcing me to keep a smile stamped on my face throughout this entire ordeal.

"No, thanks," I quip.

"Really? Because you look like you're about to drop your laurels lock, stock, and barrel into the river down below."

"If it makes you feel better, I might drop *you* into the river when I'm done."

I turn my head and find myself a few inches away from the mayor's face. Of course. His arms are casually folded over his knees, and I can't help but get lost staring into his stunning, sparkling, hazel-green eyes.

I accidentally let go of the screwdriver, but luckily Travis's reflexes are better than mine. He catches the tool and offers it back to me with an easy smirk.

Gosh, he's so infuriating my fingers are itching to push *him* over the railing and into the river below, but I settle with a death glare as I snatch the screwdriver from his grasp.

Instead of getting mad, he chuckles. "That's the spirit, Baker."

When I'm finally done with the infernal task, I stand up.

The final straw is when the photographer asks me and the mayor to pose for a few celebratory shots.

There's no escaping the request. Travis crowds my personal space by placing one hand on the small of my back while offering me the other to shake. I'm hyper-aware of all the spots where our bodies come into contact and the warmth radiating through his shirt and into my skin. And the worst part is that instead of wanting to escape, I want to lean into his touch.

My cheeks warm up, and I hope it's not noticeable.

"Miss, can you smile?" the photographer asks.

Travis squeezes my hand, and I feel like I'm going to die.

"Come on, Baker, don't be such a sourpuss."

The mayor's voice is husky and deep, and I think I might kill him.

The photographer snaps a few more pictures and then heads back to his truck.

Only when we're alone, I dare to ask, "What do you get out of constantly riling me up?"

Travis lets go of my hand and takes a step back, leaving me shivering even in the mid-morning heat.

"If you could see your face right now, you'd know."

Then, without adding another word, he walks away.

***

Thursday night, I'm all jitters as I enter Saint Mary's High auditorium for the town council meeting at 8 p.m. Tonight I'm supposed to invite the townsfolk to join the beach cleanup.

My strategy is to arrive at the last minute, hoping Travis will already be leading the meeting and won't have an opportunity to rattle me.

I enter the auditorium and tiptoe to a seat toward the back. My plan worked. Travis is already onstage talking, but when our eyes meet across the room, I don't feel victorious. There he is under the limelight, looking as dashing as ever. And here I am, cowering in a dark corner.

When it's my turn to speak, I have no choice but to join him at the podium. Travis introduces me to the crowd and ushers me forward with a gentle push on my lower back.

Is it just my imagination, or is he taking any excuse to touch me?

I deliver my piece, answer a few questions from the public, and get off the stage as quickly as I can, intending to leave as soon as possible. Unfortunately, a few of the people in the audience want to talk to me to ask more questions, thank me for organizing the cleanup, or simply gossip about the movie cast.

I politely answer all the questions, trying to be brief and efficient, especially since, out of the edge of my vision, I'm tracking Travis's struggle to make his way toward me through the crowd. Luckily, every time he edges closer, someone stops him. Mostly women of all ages, who all seem eager to talk to him. I wonder what that's about.

I finish my conversation and catch his gaze over the shoulders of the mother-daughter duo presently blocking him. Travis cranes his neck in my direction as if to signal he wanted to talk to me, but I flash him a delighted smile, wave, and I'm gone.

See? I'm completely indifferent to the mayor. I don't even care how beautiful the brunette talking to him is—I only want to throw her in the river after him.

***

Friday, I whoop in victory as I walk into my room and close the door behind me, ready to tuck in. Today I finally managed to avoid the mayor. Or at least that's what I think because this is the night he comes to see me in my bed.

I'm already sleeping when the weight of an arm around my waist makes me stir. Then Travis drops his head onto my shoulder and his soft hair rubs against the skin of my cheek, causing my entire body to shiver. Heart racing, I wonder if he's going to kiss me now. And the worst bit is that I want him to. My lips part as I reach out to him, still between sleep and wakefulness. Only, instead of coming in contact with flesh and muscles, my hands sink into a silky coat of fur.

I jerk awake and meet a set of glowing eyes.

"Oh, it's you," I say to the ubiquitous Fluffy, resigned and disappointed.

I push the cat off me and sit half upright to have a sip of water. My neck, my chest, my face are all sweaty, so I grab a tissue to wipe my sticky skin. That dreadful man is now also haunting my dreams.

Fluffy climbs back up on my chest, giving me a surreptitious head butt.

I scratch the cat between the ears and he seems to purr louder than normal.

Fluffy meows.

"I don't like cats. Actually, I hate all pets," I grumble. "And don't you think it's weird that you're here every night?"

He pushes his head under my hand with a low, sad yowl.

"Don't give me that," I snap, but I'm already mollified.

The cat keeps staring at me and I cave.

"Okay, you can stay, but keep to your side. It's too hot for cuddling."

The cat obligingly moves onto the pillow next to mine and, after a short kneading session, goes back to sleep. As for me, I spend the rest of the night staring at the ceiling, too worried about what I'd see if I closed my eyes again.

Twelve

No Good Action Goes Unpunished

The next morning I'm so terrorized about seeing Travis after my quasi sexy dream about him, that I leave the ranch before the sun is up and come back only when the moon is already shining high in the sky. The house is quiet, with no signs of Travis or his mother. Tiptoeing, I move up the stairs, dragging my feet to my room, and sink into bed. And, thankfully, I'm so utterly exhausted, I don't even have the energy to dream.

Unfortunately, the next day is the date of the cleanup. And the mayor will definitely preside over the event. My best bet to avoid him is to hide in the crowd. Let's hope enough people show up.

My prayers are answered because the turnout is bigger than anyone could've anticipated. The whole county must've come, heck, probably half the state—at least the female half.

I smirk at Lana. "The idea of pawning off your husband has been fruitful."

Christian's wife beams back. "Oh, you know my priorities, the planet"—she raises a hand level with her face, then lowers it to her navel—"my soul mate." We chuckle, then she adds, "We're about to open. Are you ready?"

"Sure," I take a seat at the greeting booth where she's stationed me and nod.

Lana grabs the megaphone. "All right everyone, thanks to all of you for showing up today. We're about to distribute the cleaning gear. Please come to the welcoming booth to collect your grabbers, trash bags, and of course to receive an auction ticket for a chance to be partnered up with none other than America's sweetheart, Christian Slade, and spend one hour helping him clean up this afternoon."

"Gosh," I say. "I'm now convinced you were a pimp in a past life."

Lana smiles wickedly. "Ready to start?"

I nod again.

Megaphone in hand, Lana yells, "Let's go!" and then sits down next to me.

The first volunteers are both women in their mid-forties.

"Hello," I greet mine, following the script Lana has given me. "Thank you for joining us today. Do you already have a partner or would you like to be assigned one?"

"Hi, I came with my best friend Delilah."

"Perfect. Here's your grabber and a trash bag. You and your friend should alternate using one or the other. You've been assigned to section A—"

"Don't we each get a grabber?" the woman interrupts me.

I smile. Lana already anticipated the question, so I read the answer straight out of her notes. "Studies have proven having one person pick up the trash and the other carry the bag is the most efficient solution."

"Oh, who knew?"

"Would you like tickets for a chance to join Christian Slade's team later today?"

"Yes, please, both for me and my friend."

"The winning number will be called at three this afternoon." I grab two numbers out of a red ticket dispenser and hand them to the woman along with two neon-yellow safety vests. "Your tickets and safety vests. Please wear the vests at all times while working."

Next, I hand her the last item in the volunteers' welcoming package: two dark-green steel bottles with the movie logo engraved on the front. "Before you start working, please fill these up at the water tanks over there." I point to where the medics have established the first aid tent. "It's important to keep hydrated, since it's a hot day. Should you or your partner feel lightheaded or fatigued at any moment, please stop working immediately and head to the medical tent to get checked out. Thanks again for joining us today and please remember to return your equipment before leaving." Before the woman can ask more questions, I yell, "NEXT!"

Lana stressed how important it is to get the volunteers sorted and working as quickly as possible.

Next in line is a young woman, I'd say college age. I give her the same speech, and then again to the next person in line. And the next.

After the fiftieth repeat, I become parched.

At the one-hour mark, I stare at the winding line of volunteers in front of me filled with despair. The sun is blazing in the blue sky, and even in the tent's shade, the temperature is sweltering. I'm wearing a white tank top and long-legged tawny jeans, as per Lana's suggestion. Apparently, I don't want to wander around the tall grass in shorts. Same reason my feet are taking a Turkish bath in my CK high-wedge suede sneakers instead of breathing in sandals. Still, I keep my eyes on the prize: getting the hell out of Emerald Creek. This cleanup is a huge contribution to my ticket out of Indiana, so I clear a bead of sweat from my forehead and soldier on.

By the second hour, I've turned into a machine. I don't even see the faces of the people I'm processing, or hear their voices. I just hand out tickets, grabbers, vests, and water bottles, trying to process as many good citizens as I can.

"Hello," I say, not looking up at the next volunteer in line as I check the sections map. "Thank you for joining us today. Do you already have a partner or would you like to be assigned one?"

"I already have a partner, thank you," a booming voice answers.

I look up and meet the amused eyes of the mayor.

"Morning, Mr. Mayor," I greet him stiffly.

"Baker."

Travis's smirk sends a zig of annoyance down my belly. I ignore it and proceed with the script at the speed of light, firing the words at him all in one breath until I'm able to yell, "NEXT!"

The mayor, instead of getting lost like any other good volunteer, circles the booth and comes over to my side.

"What are you doing?" I ask.

"You look like you need a water break yourself." He tosses me one of the steel bottles and I catch it on reflex. "Go have a drink. I can take over."

"No, you can't. You have to follow a precise script while welcoming the volunteers."

"Hello, do you already have a partner? Would you like a lottery ticket? Give them the grabber, trash bag, water bottles, yell next... I think I got it. And if I don't," he stares at the script on the table, "I can follow your notes."

When I still refuse to get up, Travis tilts my chair to dislodge me. "Shoo."

I stumble to my feet, seething. "You're a child."

"And you're welcome," he replies, taking my seat.

I storm off to the water tanks, fill my bottle to the brim, and basically down the whole thing in a few long gulps. As the fluids reach my system, I immediately feel ten thousand times better and loathe the mayor more than ever. I hate that he was right, and I hate that he thinks he can swoop in, sort the last few volunteers, and act as the hero of the day for having worked ten minutes. And, anyway, I wouldn't be dehydrated after sitting in the heat for the better part of my morning if it weren't for him.

I pity his partner. Whoever they are.

Has he come with a woman? From the jab the sheriff made at the bar last Sunday about Travis not getting enough female attention, it's safe to assume the mayor doesn't have a girlfriend.

But that doesn't mean he couldn't have a *date.*

What do you care either way? a voice asks in my head.

I don't.

Right.

I return to the welcoming booth just as the mayor dispatches the last of the volunteers.

"Great job, Mr. Mayor," I dismiss him. "Thank you for your invaluable contribution. Now you should join your partner and head to your section."

"My partner's already here."

"Where?"

"I'm looking right at her."

Her.

The word pierces my heart like a knife.

Oh, for the love of goats, no! No. No. No! I'm totally indifferent.

I'm not jealous of the mayor. I can't stand him. I actively dislike him. And I don't care who he spends his free time with.

Liar, liar, pants on fire!

I look behind my back, bracing myself to come face to face with a gorgeous woman—surely a brunette—and only find a family of geese plucking grass.

I turn back to Travis. "There's no one..." the words die on my lips as I see the safety vest he's offering me.

"No." I shake my head. "No way."

"Oh, come on, it'd be a humanitarian gesture."

I cross my arms over my chest. "Why? This is your town. You seriously expect me to believe you can't find anyone willing to spend half a day with you?"

Travis takes a step forward and pushes the vest in my hands. "If word got out I needed a partner, I'd be a dead man in the waters."

I raise my eyebrows questioningly.

"My mother's friends try to match me with their daughters of marriageable age every chance they get. Half the work I do at my practice is to rewrite wills for someone trying to marry me off to their daughters or granddaughters."

"And why aren't you married yet? The girls in town aren't good enough?"

"No, it's me, it's not them."

"Mayor, I should warn you I have a visceral dislike of humblebraggers."

"Okay," Travis concedes, pulling on his vest. "You want the real reason?"

I nod, trying to ignore how close we're standing.

"I left Emerald Creek at eighteen, and when I came back over a decade later, I had changed, but everything, *everyone* here, was still the same."

"Where did you go when you left?"

"South Bend first, then New York."

Ah yes, I remember the Notre Dame and Columbia references from his public page CV.

The mayor takes on a wistful air and my eyes widen. "Oh my gosh, you *miss* the city!" The realization hits me like lightning.

"Every day."

"So, why did you come back?"

A shadow passes over his face. "My dad died. Mom wouldn't have been able to run the ranch on her own, and losing the love of her life and the farm all at once would've killed her." The mayor makes big puppy eyes at me.

"Are you sad-dogging me into being your partner?"

The comment makes his mouth slide into a wicked grin before he asks, "Is it working?"

I catch a couple of old cronies pass us and stare daggers at me. Now the whole circus of women stalking him after the council meeting begins to make a lot more sense.

Travis gives me the sad pout again, and... I can't resist. "You and that awful cat are the worst."

"Is that a yes?"

"If you promise I don't risk any retaliation by the town's women for being seen in public with you."

Travis considers the same unfriendly-looking ladies I'm tracking and shrugs. "Nah, the Bethel sisters are sweeties."

They don't look so sweet to me. "Should I grab the megaphone and make a public announcement stating I have no designs on you?"

"None at all?" Travis teases, putting a hand over his chest. "I'm a little hurt by how categorical that statement sounded."

Is he flirting?

With an exasperated sigh, I put on my vest. "Let's go."

"Do you want the grabber or the bag?" Travis asks.

"The grabber."

I guide him to the least crowded part of the beach, noting how several heads turn to stare at us along the way. More glares bounce in my direction. "You know what? Next time I need to fundraise for one of your disproportionate requests, I'll auction you off alongside Christian. I bet Emerald Creek's bachelorettes would pay a small fortune to go on a date with the mayor."

Travis mock-shudders. "Please don't make jokes like that."

I give him an evil smile. "We'll see, Mr. Mayor. Make another demand from my production, and you know how I'm going to finance it."

As we work our way along the bank, I hate to admit I'm impressed by the view. The lake is a long pool of still, emerald-green water that stretches wide until it winds up on itself at the end. Contoured by reeds and tall grasses peeking out of the water, the surface sparkles in the midday sun. Tall trees grow around the shore, framing the beautiful picture.

A gush of wind rustles the leaves of the nearby trees, bringing in a respite from the unrelenting heat and carrying the smell of wet earth and water.

I track a family of ducks as they float among the weeds, passing a group of turtles sunning themselves on a white-washed, knobby log of driftwood at the water's edge. Then my eyes drift to the end of the log, where, tangled in together with an old fishing line, a plastic bag is swaying in the wind. Next to it, cigarette butts and bottle caps pepper the golden sand. And beer cans lie abandoned in the grass.

"Penny for your thoughts?" Travis's voice makes me jump.

I take another look at the trash littering the shore and sigh. "I don't approve of your methods, but I get why you wanted this place cleaned."

And with that, I brandish the grabber and pick up a discarded water bottle. Travis holds the trash bag open for me and I drop it in.

The work is repetitive and monotonous. After a while of having Travis follow me quietly around, I feel less guarded about him and more bored by our task, so I ask, "What do you miss most about New York?"

"The vibe, the energy, my old job, the bagel cart outside my office..." He shrugs. "Everything."

"I thought you said at your mother's that you didn't want to live to work."

Travis grimaces. "I can't tell her I came back just for her, she'd never have it. So corporate burnout is my official line and I'd like it to stay that way."

I nod. "Don't worry, I'm not telling." I drop a used condom in the bag and study him for a second. "You're the weirdest lawyer, cowboy, mayor I've ever met."

Travis flashes me a grin. "You know many?"

"Only you, admittedly. So what was your old job like?"

"Big firm, big cases. Gosh, I miss the thrill of walking into a courtroom, not knowing if I'll be able to win over the jury."

I've got a feeling he had no troubles in that department.

"And you can keep practicing while you're the mayor."

"Neither job is that demanding."

I flash him a stare. "Unless you have to review permit applications, of course."

The mayor can hardly contain his smirk, but I choose to give him a pass—only this once.

"Few big cases in Emerald Creek?" I ask.

"Nope, besides the wills, it's mostly estate planning, the occasional civil litigation, some neighbors' squabbles, and in the saddest cases, bankruptcy."

"You had many of those?"

"The pandemic didn't help the economy around here. But I guess that's true for about any physical business on the planet. Starving movie producers included."

I point the grabber at him. "Careful, Mr. Mayor, just because movie-making is a money-rich industry, it doesn't mean we didn't suffer like everybody else."

"I wouldn't dare to suggest otherwise."

Keeping quiet, I go back to clearing the trail of litter I've been absent-mindedly chasing to higher ground. When I can't find any more droppings to pick up, I check my surroundings and suddenly realize we're not standing next to the lake anymore but following a creek up a hill. The beach has given way to uneven terrain covered in undergrowth, and the reeds, to trees and bushes hemming the meandering flow of water.

Next, I realize that I have to pee—*badly*. All that water I drank earlier has reached my bladder and is threatening to have it explode. The sound of the water trickling over the rocks and twigs isn't helping.

We're completely isolated. No tents in sight or other volunteers. I squeeze my legs, trying to gauge how long it'd take to get back to the chemical restrooms.

"What's the matter, Baker? You're squirming."

"Nature's calling," I spat, embarrassed. "But I won't make it back to the main tent in time."

"Why would you voluntarily shut yourself in a chemical toilet when you have the whole woods to yourself?"

"I'm not exactly by myself."

"Oh, you mean me? I promise I'll keep my eyes shut." Travis puts a hand over his eyes and then peers between his fingers.

I walk up to him, ordering, "Give me the bag." I exchange it for the grabber and walk a few more yards uphill.

When I can no longer see the mayor through the vegetation, I squat down behind a bush, hoping a chipmunk won't mistake my exposed buns for its next meal.

I clean myself with a tissue, throw it in the trash bag, and re-zip my pants.

When I rejoin the mayor, I find him lying on a rock, sunbathing. He's resting on his elbows with his face tilted upward. His lids are closed, and he's the most handsome man I've ever laid eyes on.

And the most horrible.

I hate him, I remind myself.

Are you sure?

Ya-ah! Hate. Loathe. Despise.

I clear my throat.

Travis opens his eyes, tilts his head toward me, and smiles. Not his usual mocking smirk, but a smile with the power of a million suns. The air gets caught in my lungs, and for a moment I'm left breathless.

"Should we head back to our section?" I croak. Clearing my voice, I add, "There isn't much trash here. This area is clean."

"Actually, I wanted to show you something, if you don't mind walking a few more yards uphill in those."

Travis jerks his chin at my sneakers.

This man is treading a fine line, coming at my career first and now constantly attacking my shoes?

"Why are you always criticizing my footwear?"

"It's just amazing that even your sneakers have heels."

I wiggle my foot at him. "These are wedges for your information."

He hops off the rock. "Is there a difference?"

"An ocean."

"As long as you can keep up." The mayor precedes me up the meandering dirt path.

Without signposts or trailheads showing the right direction, I hurry after him before I get lost in one of the overgrown sections where the trail seems to disappear.

With every step, I risk stumbling on the uneven ground. Gosh, I'm not made for strolls in uncontaminated nature. What am I even doing following this man I barely know into the forest? Up here, it's only us and the squirrels scrabbling around the tree trunks.

"Are you taking me deep into the woods to make me vanish without a trace?" I yell.

"Sure, it's what I do with all the beautiful newcomers," he teases, throwing a smile over his shoulder. "That's why there aren't any left in town."

I'm alone with a man who's making serial killer jokes and all I can hear is that he called me beautiful.

"Don't you want a little thrill?" Travis calls, climbing forward. "Something you can't get in New York?"

"The most adventurous thing that can happen to me in the city is getting my heel stuck in a grate, and I'm fine with that."

"Don't worry," Travis adds, disappearing behind a bend in the road. "We're almost there."

I quicken my pace to keep up, and when I round the corner myself, I don't expect Travis to have stopped in the middle of the trail. I stumble back, then counterbalance by leaning forward. Only I go too far and land with my nose in the nook between his neck and shoulders. Before I can stop myself, I inhale. He smells like forest and sunlight.

"No need to fall at my feet, Baker." His voice is low and teasing. The tone threatens to melt me while the comment makes me sizzle with indignation.

I want to push him away, but before I can find proper footing again, Travis grabs me by the shoulders and spins me round to the most beautiful sight.

A frothy cascade of water is falling into a plunge pool surrounded by rocky outcroppings. Lush grasses grow out of the rocks, plants and flowers with shiny leaves and foliage. The water sprays as it hits the pond, misting the air with tiny droplets of water while a million rainbows shimmer at the edge of my vision.

"Welcome to Potawatomi Waterfall," Travis breathes down my neck.

A shiver runs down my spine even if I'm on fire. I'm not sure if the heat comes from the stroll uphill in the midday sun or from the searing touch of Travis's hands on my bare upper arms.

I need to break the body contact. I wiggle free with the excuse of going to check out the waterfall from a flat stone ledge that overlooks the pool.

I can't resist. I remove my shoes, socks, and dip my toes into the cold water.

"You know, Baker, there's a better way to cool off on a hot day," Travis says behind me. I hear shuffling of fabric, but don't turn back. Next, the air beside me shifts as the mayor runs past me and dive-bombs into the pond.

He reemerges, shaking water off his hair like a dog and then raking his fingers through his curls to free his forehead.

"Come on," he calls. "Jump in."

Nu-uh, not a chance.

I stand up and lock stares with the mayor. His hazel eyes taunt me. It's a challenge.

Still, I'm not jumping in the water with him. I'm not.

Of their own accord, my fingers begin to unbutton my pants and lower the zipper.

Never breaking eye contact with Travis, I shuffle out of my jeans and get rid of my tank-top in one fluid move.

Before I lose my cool, I take a step forward and swan-dive next to him.

Thirteen

You Have to Kiss a Lot of Toads before You Find a Handsome Prince

The cool water is a delicious shock against my heated skin.

I resurface, gasping for air, but can't get a full breath because of the mayor splashing me.

"Hey!" I scream, splashing him back.

The fight is on. We relentlessly trade water bombs, and I've never laughed harder in my entire life. For every splash I give, I get two back, though. I'm so busy repelling attacks that I don't notice Travis coming nearer. Before I can react, he dives below the surface, vanishing. Two seconds later, strong hands grab my ankles and pull me down so fast I barely have time for one last gulp of air before my head disappears underwater.

When I break the surface again, I receive one last splash, and Travis says, "I won."

"You didn't." My voice comes out in an indignant squeak.

"No?" He cocks his head to the side while water drips from the tips of his hair.

"No." I wipe the water from my eyes and grin.

Travis looks me over. "You want more?"

I do—I don't.

"I'm not sure what I want," I say, my voice hoarse.

I swim closer to him and trace the droplets of water on his left eyebrow with the tip of my finger. As soon as I touch his face, I can't break the contact. I'm spellbound.

"So," I whisper, our faces inches from each other. "If not to make me disappear, is this where you bring women to seduce them?"

"Oh, so now I'm seducing you?"

"I don't know, you tell me."

Travis's gaze burns into mine, and I can see the indecision in his eyes.

"You're so beautiful, Baker."

The words are a soft whisper. So much so that I'm not sure if he said them or if I only imagined them.

I bite my lower lip.

The mayor tracks the movement. Then, as if losing an internal battle his hand reaches for my waist underwater. His fingertips rest on the curve of my hip for a second before he pulls me flush against his chest. Travis threads the fingers of his other hand through my hair and tangles them behind my head. Then he tilts my face to his and kisses me.

Travis's kiss is soft, gentle, and promising. And he doesn't press for more until I kiss him back. And then he takes his time, teasing me with his lips, and sending sparks all over my skin.

I kiss him back until I'm breathless, until I can't think of anything but him. My hands reach his shoulders and trail upward until I can dig my fingers into his wet hair. I hold on for dear life. I press myself against his body, and the kiss changes from sweet to hot.

I moan, ready to bring things to the next level, but that's when Travis pulls back and puts some distance between us.

The mayor opens his eyes and looks down at me, his gaze dark and clouded. "You've no idea how much I want you." The words aren't a question.

The sentiment is reciprocated, I'm right there with him. I can't wait to tear off our underwear and go all the way. I kick my feet off the ground in an attempt to straddle the mayor. But instead of welcoming me into his arms, we engage in an awkward underwater battle where I try to get closer and he fights to stay apart.

When my feet hit the lake bottom, I start to move closer again, but he keeps me at a distance.

I frown, my thoughts still too hazy with lust to form words.

"We can't," Travis says.

"What?"

Travis lets go of my hips and takes another step back.

I suddenly become hyper-aware of how cold the water is.

"You know we can't."

I'm completely at a loss for words.

"I'm sorry," he whispers. "I shouldn't have kissed you."

The mayor is sorry for kissing me?

"We should get out of the water."

Travis turns away and heads toward the rocky beach.

I ignore the way the water slithers down his sculpted back and paddle-storm past him. With each step, tiny rocks stab at my bare feet, but I welcome the pain. It's sobering. And right now, I need to regain some composure and come down from the high of the kiss.

I arrive at the ledge first and start to grab my clothes.

"You can't get dressed," Travis says.

"Why not? You've made it abundantly clear you're not interested in naked activities."

His gaze darkens and his jaw tenses, as if he had to exercise all his self-control not to cross the three feet of rock that still separate us and show me exactly how keen he is on naked activities.

"If you put your clothes on now, they'll get wet," Travis explains, his tone unreadable. "And then everyone in town will know you took a dip with the mayor."

"Fine." I accept he has a point and throw my clothes on the ground.

I lie on the rock next to him, putting as much space between us as the ledge allows. I put my hands behind my head and close my eyes, quietly seething.

"Are you mad at me, Baker?"

"Are you mad at me, Baker?" I mimic his words. "Yes, I'm mad at you."

"What for?"

"You don't take a woman to a waterfall, trick her into taking a dip with you, kiss her, and then announce you've no intention of taking the liaison any further."

"I thought you hated me."

"Hate and sexual attraction are not mutually exclusive, apparently."

The air next to me shifts, and I sense the full force of Travis's gaze on me. But I stubbornly keep my eyes shut and my face tilted upward.

"I'm only trying to spare us both a heartache."

"I'm a big girl. I can keep sex and feelings separate."

"Maybe you can, but I'm not so sure I'd be able to," he says in a whisper that punches me in the guts harder than a kick. "Not with a woman like you."

"Like me how?"

"Smart, feisty... drop-dead gorgeous. Someone who hasn't spent her entire life in Emerald Creek and knows there's a world beyond this valley. Someone who'd laugh if

I made a joke about riding the 4-train at rush hour. Or if I said the NYC Marathon is really just a bunch of people running away from Staten Island..."

Despite myself, my lips curl up at the corners. But I press them hard together as not to smile.

"See?" Travis says. "You get it, no one else around here would."

"Okay, so I'd laugh at your jokes. What's so terrible about that?"

"That you're not here to stay."

I can't argue with that. The mere idea of moving to a place like this makes me shudder—gorgeous waterfall and semi-naked mayor notwithstanding.

"Got it, Mr. Mayor, our relationship will remain strictly professional from now on."

The second my underwear is dry, I stand up to get dressed.

The mayor does the same next to me.

I try to ignore his movements, to shield myself from his larger-than-life presence next to me. But then I make the mistake of looking up. Travis is leaning against a tree, still bare-chested, while he pulls on his socks. As our gazes meet, I'm undecided if I want to slap him or slam him against that tree and make him reconsider his views on casual sexual relationships with outlanders.

Fourteen

Hell Has No Fury like a Woman Scorned

The walk of shame downhill is humiliating. I've never thrown myself at a man like I did today with Travis, and I never got turned down so hard. Gosh, by the end I was practically begging for it.

To rub salt into the wound, as we make our way back among the volunteers, many heads bend closer—clearly to whisper speculations.

There's no hiding the strange vibe between me and the mayor. Not to mention the way I must look. My usually impeccable, sleek bob is all tousled and messy. Think Bryce Dallas Howard at the beginning and then the end of *Jurassic World.*

If I have to be gossiped about as Emerald Creek's newest scarlet woman, I wish I had at least earned my letters.

When we reach the main tent, I say, "I have to find Christian before the ticket draw." Travis is still holding the trash bag. I take it from him, and add, "I'll drop this off at the collection center."

The mayor seems to have a mind to state again how sorry he is. To spare me the indignity of a man having to apologize twice for not wanting to have sex with me, I take my leave with a dry, "See you around."

I turn on my wedges and, after dropping the trash bag into the giant dumpster truck at the edge of the beach, I search for Christian. My best bet is to locate his security detail. As celebrities go, Christian isn't overly fussy, but to mingle with a crowd as big as the one assembled today, I made bodyguards nonnegotiable.

America's number one heartthrob finds me first.

"What happened to you?" Christian asks from behind me, pulling a lock of my hair. "You look like you've been through the dumpster."

I spin on him. "Thanks, that sums up how I feel." *Dumped in the trash,* I add silently in my head. "It's this awful nature," I spit, swatting a mosquito on my arm. "I'm not made for it. It's time for the draw. Are you ready?"

"Tell me where I have to go sell myself for the good of the environment and I'll be there."

"Just follow me, Mr. Smarty Pants."

I drag him to the small platform that will become the beach's new gazebo, and we wait for Lana, who joins us shortly afterward.

"Do you have a hairband I can borrow?" I ask her.

"Sure."

Lana hands me one, and I wrestle my hair in a high bun to make my earlier indiscretions a little less obvious.

Christian's wife passes a hand over my upper arm. "Did you put sunscreen on? You're getting pretty red."

Oh, perfect. A sunburn would complement my bruised pride like dandelions with daydreams.

Oh shut up! Now I'm even talking like a doe-eyed, small-town girl with a giant crush on the mayor.

"I can lend you some of mine," Lana insists.

I thank her and have just enough time to apply the lotion before we have to announce the winner.

***

By the end of the day, the shore is unrecognizable. Without all the trash and rubble, and after the landscaping team has finished their job, the lake has turned from dump to wonderland—a paradise of wavy sand dunes and deep blue-green water sparkling in the glow of the setting sun.

Unfortunately, the smell doesn't match the view. Not yet, at least. Especially not from where I'm standing close to the dumpster truck. With the last garbage bags loaded, I urge the driver to leave for the landfill.

To end the event, Lana, I, and the other members of the support staff have to re-collect all the grabbers and safety vests that one of Lana's affiliate environmental organizations kindly provided for the day.

Then the temporary white tents have to come down, and, finally, we can leave the restored nature undisturbed for a night until the construction works resume tomorrow. I can already envision the pedestrian peer and the new boating docks on the water. And the kiosk, gazebo, picnic tables on land… this beach is going to become a major attraction in the area.

At least for as long as the mayor can keep it clean. But I have to commend Travis's vision. This looks like an entirely different place after today.

I walk up to Jerry and Celia now, as they help pull down the last temporary gazebo.

"Celia, I'm heading back to the B&B, are you coming or…"

She looks up at Jerry and they exchange an almost imperceptible nod.

"Don't worry, boss, Jerry will give me a ride later."

Mmm, I suspect not. In the past few days, I've woken up to texts from Celia saying she was already on set and I needn't wait for her. My assistant only comes back to sleep at the B&B when we have early appointments in town. And I'm not sure if it's the day spent in the sun or all the fresh air, but she has a bright glow about her.

Yeah, a sneaky voice says in my head, *'cause she's getting some—contrary to you. Or have you forgotten what it looks like to be all sexed up?*

"All right," I wave at them. "See you later."

I bump into Willette next and blush with a mix of heat and embarrassment at the memory of kissing her son.

"Hey," I say. "You need a ride back to the ranch?"

"No, honey, thanks, I came in my truck. I'll mingle a little more with my friends and meet you back at the house."

I say goodbye to Willette and, keeping my head low should another Hunt be in the proximity, I speed-walk to my truck. Thankfully, it's the first among a long line of vehicles lining the road to the lake. The sheriff's department lifted all the parking restrictions for the day, making it easier for volunteers to reach the location.

Letting out a sigh of relief at not bumping into anyone else, I climb into the truck. I start the engine and pull onto the street without even needing to turn on the navigator. Only a fortnight in town, and I already know my way around Emerald Creek like I've lived here my entire life.

Yeah, because there are only three streets to know.

Back at the ranch, I feel weird being here by myself. Well, alone if you don't count the cows, chickens, goats, llamas, and Fluffy, who has officially joined Hildi in my furry fan club.

I sit on the porch steps and watch the sun set over the paddock where Betsy is grazing grass. My gaze travels the length of the picket fence and the pretty wildflowers growing at its base in shades of lilac, yellow, and baby blue.

After a few minutes of contemplating, Fluffy joins me, sitting on the step beside me. Hildi is next. The goat hops up the steps and drops her muzzle in my lap.

I take my phone out of my bag and snap a selfie that I send to my friends in New York. I caption the picture: I had a weird day.

Holly's reply comes in first.

> Did you tame a lynx?

> Believe it or not, this is a cat

> Named Fluffy!

Two seconds later, my screen lights up with an incoming group video call from Taylor.

"Hey," I pick up.

Taylor winks at me. "I see you're embracing the bucolic lifestyle."

"Hi, gals." Holly picks up next.

Taylor is calling from her tiny patio with the tall Manhattan skyscrapers in the background, while Holly is sitting on a bench in Central Park, wearing workout clothes. She probably took a break from jogging to answer the call. Both views make me so homesick my eyes sting with tears. I blink in quick succession to fight back the salty water.

"Why is your hair up?" Holly asks. "It's never up."

"Never is a strong statement."

Holly's eyes narrow. "I smell smoke. Why is your hair up, again?"

"It got tousled, and this was the only practical solution."

"*How* did it get tousled?" Taylor asks.

I kept Travis out of our chats for as long as I could. I didn't want to give the man more importance than he deserved, but after today... I sigh. "The mayor of this awful town tricked me into going for a swim with him in the most beautiful pond at the foot of a waterfall... then he kissed me... and *then* he informed me we should never do it again because he's not into casual relationships."

Holly mock-fans herself. "That sounds heated. Is the mayor a good kisser?"

"Unfortunately, yes," I admit begrudgingly.

The best I ever had.

Taylor frowns. "Why is this the first we hear about this mayor? What's the story?"

To my chagrin, I bring them up to speed on my two-week acquaintance with Travis Hunt. From his first appearance riding a horse, to the ensuing bare-chest show, the City Hall trap, the head bashing in the shower, and all the other times I bumped into him. The only thing I don't confess are my quasi sexy dreams about him.

Holly's screen goes suddenly black.

"Did the line drop?" I ask.

"No, sorry," her voice crackles through the phone's speakers. "I'm googling Emerald Creek mayor."

"Yeah, don't waste your time," I say. "The town's website has no picture."

"The official page says the mayor is a Theodore Abraham Hunt," Holly continues, unperturbed.

"Yep, that's him, but everyone calls him Travis. Don't ask me why."

Next, Holly gasps.

"What?" Taylor and I ask at once.

"I found a picture of a Theodore Abraham Hunt, who used to work for Goldstein, Caldwell, and McDougal. I'm forwarding it to you gals. Is that him?"

My phone pings with an incoming message and I switch apps. I jerk my knees up and down, waiting for the photo to load, which causes Hildi to raise her muzzle and bleat in protest.

"Shhh," I pat her on the head and she goes back to sleep.

The picture finally loads and for a second, it takes my breath away. It's definitely a portrait of Travis, but younger and with a definite New Yorker feel about him. His blond-brown hair is swept back in a sleek haircut, he's wearing a suit probably even more expensive than the ones I saw him wear around town, and he's smiling at the camera, the image of an ambitious associate.

"Yep, that's him all right."

I go back to the video call and study my friends' expressions.

Holly is chewing on her lower lip while Taylor has both eyebrows raised.

"So you're basically dating Harvey Specter and forgot to mention it?"

"That's the thing, we're not dating. The man kissed me and then refused to put out."

They both laugh.

"Not funny," I say, dropping my elbow on my knee and my chin in my hand.

Fluffy chooses this moment to bump his head on my cheek and try to crawl into my lap, pushing Hildi out.

"Aw, look at you, Snow White," Taylor teases me. "Now you're only missing a couple of birds perching on your shoulders."

"With my luck, they'd take a dump on me."

"Jokes aside," Holly continues. "Do you like the guy?"

"No, I detest him. I'm just weirdly attracted to him physically. That's why I wished we'd done it already so I could get it—*him*—out of my system."

Before my friends can comment, a puff of dust from the road downhill warns me of Willette's imminent return.

"Shoot, girls," I say. "I have to go. Travis's mom is coming home."

"And you don't wish to discuss all the naughty things you want to do to her son in front of her," Taylor teases me.

"Shhhh," I hiss. "She's getting out of her truck. We'll talk later."

The last thing I hear as I lower my phone to end the call is Holly yelling, "Keep us posted on this mayor situation we—" then I press the red button and the line goes silent.

"Hello, there." Willette waves at me. "I see you've made friends. Hildi isn't bothering you anymore?"

"No." I pat the goat's head. "We've reached an agreement."

Hildi grunts.

"Good." Willette gives a nod towards the goat. "She's a fair judge of character."

"I don't know about that, but—" Hildi pushes her head against my hand. I rub the spot between her horns. "—she seems to have taken a liking to me."

Willette's lips twitch. "Perhaps she isn't the only one. Did you like the waterfall visit with my son today?"

I blush tomato red. How does she know about the waterfall? Does she know Travis and I kissed? Did he tell her?

Her lips curve up into a knowing grin.

I don't think Travis told.

I rub the back of my neck. "It was—interesting."

"Potawatomi is the most gorgeous spot in town," Willette says. "I'm glad Travis showed it to you."

"Yes." I shift my feet. "It was beautiful."

"Also refreshing, I imagine."

Heat spreads across my cheeks again. I seriously doubt Travis told his mother about our little swim or the kiss, but she seems to know, anyway. Is she a secret witch? She has the goats and the herb garden after all...

"The best view," I deflect.

Willette smiles and takes the first step up the porch. "Well, I'm glad you and Travis are finally getting along, and I hope you won't hold his fight for our town against him. You have no idea how much it meant to us folks to finally see our beach as clean and beautiful as it was today. We could've never done it on our own."

"Well, I still don't appreciate being strong-armed into things."

"Aw, well, Travis can get a little naughty sometimes." Willette winks at me, making me blush again. Then she pivots the subject altogether as if we hadn't been covertly discussing my involvement with her only child—both personal and professional. "I'm getting dinner started. Care to join me?"

The last thing I want is to spend more time under Willette's scrutiny. I clear my throat. "No thanks, I'll just make myself a salad and eat in my room. I'm exhausted."

Willette chuckles. "No wonder Hildi likes you so much. You follow the same diet."

I shake off the animals, ignoring their resented protests, and stand up, wishing Willette a good night. Then, forgetting the salad altogether, I rush up the stairs and go hide in my room.

I'm in such a hurry for privacy, I almost close the door on Fluffy's tail. The cat sends me a warning glare before paddling into my room with an offended pout.

"I didn't say you could come with me."

Fluffy ignores me and jumps onto the bed.

I collapse on the mattress next to him, ego bruised and cheeks still heating—I'm not sure if the warmth comes from sheer embarrassment or solar burns. To be on the safe side, I douse my face and arms in after-sun lotion, hoping I haven't damaged my skin too much today—or my heart, for that matter.

Fifteen

Every Gray Cloud Has a Silver Lining

The next few days are uneventful. I don't run into Travis, either at the ranch or in town—where I show my face only once to get groceries. I spend most of my time on set, behind the safety of security gates. By the time Friday comes around, I'm close to being back to my normal self. And not just me, the production is back on track as well. All smooth sailing, like Winthrop demanded.

In my room at the B&B, before going down to breakfast, I scroll my notes from last night to make sure I haven't forgotten anything for today's and tomorrow's shoots. As I turn the last page and read the schedule for Sunday, my heart sinks. The day after tomorrow is the date of the Dubois County Fair. I'll need to attend the event since part of my negotiation with the mayor was that he let my crew shoot enough external footage for all of the movie's carnival-like scenes. Cliff will build a stand at the fair for the wide shots, while all of the close-ups have already been shot back at Lake View Acres.

On the downside, there'll be no avoiding the mayor at the fair.

I close my eyes and sigh. Even if I haven't seen him all week, thoughts of Travis have been crowding my mind every day from dawn till dusk. Actually, whether I'm asleep and dreaming about him or awake and worrying about the next time we'll run into each other, he's been on my mind night and day nonstop. I've tried to keep busy and not think about him, but I can't help it. And now I'm getting anxious at the prospect of seeing him again.

Oh, for goodness' sake, be a grownup. I sound like a teenager who wants to skip school after her crush turned her down.

You're a tough woman, Samantha Baker. And you've held your own against bigger fish.

Right.

I stuff my notes in my bag and head down to breakfast, ready to tackle the new day. But as I enter the kitchen, something is off. Instead of bustling around with pots and pans, Willette is seated on a chair with her head in her hands.

"Willette," I rush to her side. "Are you okay?"

Travis's mother looks up at me with a glazed-over stare while beads of sweat dot her forehead.

I touch her temple. "Oh my gosh, you're burning up. Come…" I help her to her feet. "I'll bring you to your room."

Willette's bedroom is on the ground floor so that she doesn't have to take the stairs all the time. But even if her room is close, she's a dead weight to carry, and it takes us forever to reach her bed. When I finally drop her onto it, her head lolls to the side, her lids already half closed.

Celia didn't come home last night, so Willette and I are alone.

"Willette," I shake her gently. "Is there someone I can call, a doctor?"

She mumbles something unintelligible.

Should I give her a Tylenol to reduce the fever? Maybe, but I don't want to hand out medications to an elderly woman without knowing her medical history.

Fluffy comes into the room and looks at me interrogatively.

I pat the foot of the bed. "Come here, keep her company while I decide what to do."

There is only *one* thing to do.

With a heavy sigh, I exit the bedroom and go back to the kitchen to retrieve my phone from my bag. I don't have Travis's personal number. But I know where to find him.

I search online for the mayor's office number and dial with a mix of resentment and anticipation.

"Emerald Creek mayor's office, good morning. How can I assist you?"

"Hello, this is Samantha Baker, I need to speak with the mayor urgently, his—"

Before I can finish the sentence, the secretary cuts me off. "Hold on, please, I'll see if he's available." The line cuts to classical music.

She put me on hold! I groan in frustration and tap my foot impatiently, waiting for the secretary to come back on the line.

She keeps me waiting for a minute or so before the line clicks back. "Hello, Miss Baker, the mayor is in a meeting at the moment. Did you want to leave him a message?"

I grip the phone so hard I'm afraid it might crack. "If this is him playing hard to get again, you can tell him that his mother is burning up with a fever and I don't know what to do. Should I call an ambulance or a doctor to see her? Please tell the mayor I'll be waiting here until someone shows up. Have a nice day."

I hang up before she can reply.

I hate not knowing what to do and being powerless to make things better. So I google what to do in case of a high fever. All websites agree the most important and basic thing is to keep the patient hydrated. Fresh water seems like a pretty safe remedy to administer, so I fill a glass and bring it back to Willette's room.

Normally, she looks like she'd be light as a feather, but when her body is a dead weight, she's heavy to move. With great effort, I manage to shift her to a half-reclining position and make her drink half the glass.

Aware there's nothing else I can do, I sit on a chair next to the bed and keep vigil alongside Fluffy.

About ten minutes later, the screen door bangs open and Travis calls out, "Mom!"

Guess the mayor broke a few speed limits to arrive in such a record time.

"In here." I poke my head out of the room. "She's sleeping now."

Travis rushes out of the kitchen and I'm not ready for the ball of emotions exploding in my chest as I see him again for the first time after our kiss. Can a person become incrementally more gorgeous in just a few days? Then, as I take in his worried-sick expression, I get a grip on my inner lust.

Travis rushes into his mother's room and kneels beside the bed, taking her hands into his. I avert my gaze. Partly because this is a private moment between a son and his mother and partly because if I have to add "incredibly sweet" to Travis's qualities, I might lose it.

I'm about to leave the room when Travis calls me back, "Wait. What happened?"

Pausing on the threshold, I give him the facts. "When I came down this morning, she was slouched at the kitchen table and burning up. I helped her into bed, called you, and gave her water. Sorry I couldn't do more, but I didn't know what else—"

"Thank you," Travis cuts me off. "I mean it."

"No problem, I really did nothing."

"The doctor will arrive soon," Travis says. "When you go, please leave the gate open so Dr. Randall can drive straight up."

I nod and exit the room. And I know I should go to work. Willette is in safe hands, a doctor is on the way, and there's nothing more I can do. Still, I sit at one of the mismatched chairs in the kitchen and wait.

The doctor, a short, balding man in his mid-fifties, arrives five minutes later.

"Hello," he calls from the porch.

I usher him in, give him a brief account of the morning's events, and direct him to Willette's room. I don't feel like going back inside, so I sit on the porch swing. The screen door opens again five minutes later, and Travis walks out. He takes a few steps out before he spots me and freezes.

"You're still here."

"I wanted to make sure your mom is okay."

Travis nods. "Did you have any breakfast?"

"No, but I'm not hungry. Maybe just a cup of coffee?"

Travis retreats inside and comes back out shortly afterward with two steaming mugs of coffee. He hands me one and sits next to me on the swing.

I take a sip of coffee and am surprised to find it sweet and with a retro taste of vanilla.

"How do you know how I drink my coffee?"

Despite the worry-lines marking his forehead, Travis smirks out of the corner of his mouth. "City girls, so predictable..."

"Ah, bet you're drinking a very original black americano instead!"

"What if I was having a Cinnamon Dolce Latte!"

"You're so not!"

Both corners of his mouth curl up now, and I'm relieved he doesn't look as worried.

We sit in supportive silence, sipping coffee and waiting for news from the doctor.

The short man comes outside a few minutes later, and Travis immediately springs up from the swing.

"How is she?"

"Nothing life-threatening," the doctor says. "I suspect it's pneumonia, which, at Willette's age, can be dangerous."

Travis rakes a hand through his hair. "How did she get pneumonia in this heat?"

"I'm afraid it's viral, but I took a blood sample to make sure."

"Is viral worse?"

"Not necessarily, but I can't just prescribe antibiotics to make the infection go away. The disease will have to run its course."

"How long will it take?"

"Anywhere from a week to a month."

"Anything we can do in the meantime, Dr. Randall?"

"I gave her something to abate the fever and wrote out a prescription." The doctor hands a sheet of paper to Travis. "She'll have to take two more pills today. But I don't feel comfortable prescribing anything else until I've checked the blood sample. I'll get back to my practice and let you know right away. In the meantime, she shouldn't be left alone. At least for a couple of days and nights."

"I'll move in the spare bedroom downstairs, Doctor."

My heart does three or four somersaults in my chest at the announcement. Travis is moving in with me? Well, not with me... with his mother. But... po-tay-to, po-tah-to...

Travis and the doctor shake hands. Then the little man goes, and the mayor turns back to me, our eyes locking.

I swallow.

The silent staring becomes unbearable, so I give him back my half-empty mug of coffee saying, "I'd better go to work now."

Then I literally flee the premises.

Sixteen

Dinner for Two

As soon as I turn a bend in the road out of sight from Sagebrush Ranch, I stop the truck and hit the wheel repeatedly.

"Perfect. Just flippin' perfect."

I let out an exasperated scream.

The last thing I need is to live under the same roof as Travis.

I hate small towns and I hate not being able to safely hide among the eight-and-a-half-million people New York provides.

I slam my hand on the steering wheel another time.

Nice going, Samantha.

At this pace, I'll lose my mind before I make it back to the city.

I look at the time and start driving again. I'm already disastrously late, but I can still make it to Lake View Acres before the lunch break.

Good thing my presence is not indispensable. In fact, maybe I should test the waters with Winthrop to see if, now that everything is back on schedule and the mysterious delays have been solved, he'd let me go back to New York early.

I stop the truck again. The only good thing about being in a small town is that I can have as many mini-breakdowns on the way to work as I want. No chance of other cars honking at me from behind to speed traffic along. There is *no* traffic!

I grab my phone and dial Winthrop's direct line.

"Samantha," he picks up on the third ring, his voice echoing through the car's speaker system. "I hear things are finally looking up in Emerald Creek."

"Hi, Winthrop, yeah, everything down here is going great. It looks like we'll be able to finish in time after all." I stall for a second and then pluck up my courage. "That's why I was calling, actually. To see if now that the production is sorted there'd be any chance I could come back to New York. I mean, I'm not really needed on set anymore. And if you're afraid something else might go sideways, I could leave my assistant behind to supervise things," I add as an afterthought. I'd be doing Celia a favor, anyway. She'd be much happier in Emerald Creek with her new flame than in New York.

The line stays silent for a few beats, and I wait with trepidation for my boss's answer.

The first word out of his mouth is a dry, "No."

I sigh and steady myself for the tirade sure to come afterward. It arrives pronto.

"Samantha, I've already told you, you're overseeing this production until the last take. Look at how much you've already accomplished in three weeks."

"Yes, but Winthrop—"

"No buts, Samantha, I'm sorry. You're in for the long haul."

I sigh. "Yes, sir."

"Now that you've sorted the permits, I assume everything is going smoothly with the town's government?"

"Going smoothly?" I ask, my voice rising, but before I can start ranting with my boss about the mayor kissing me but not wanting to go any further and now moving in with me, I take a deep breath and say. "Yes, everything is fine. Super."

"That's music to my ears. Well, if there isn't anything else?"

"No, no."

We hang up and I stare at the long and twisting country road ahead, flopping back against the headrest, the phone still in my hand.

I can't believe the boss dismissed me so casually. Well, I tried. Nothing more I can do. I grab a bottle of water from the cup holder and gulp down a few mouthfuls.

Doomed or not, I can't spend the rest of the day in the truck. I put the pickup back into gear and drive on. With every turn of the road, I curse the picturesque scenery. Stupid fields of tall grass and wildflowers. Stupid river. Stupid lake. And most of all, stupid waterfall.

If the town hadn't been this quaint, the location scouts would've never picked it as the set of my movie. And the mayor of another city would've never delayed the shooting on purpose. I would've never had to move here. And I would've never met Travis.

But that's just wistful thinking.

When I turn on the road leading to Lake View Acres, the security guard lets me pass with a nod and a wave. Five minutes later, I finally pull up in front of the community barn and park next to the same old line of electric golf carts. I grab my leather satchel with all my notes and, as I drag myself out of the pickup, I let out a resigned sigh. This is my life now. I slam the truck door with a loud bang.

The day is warm, the sun bright. As far from my stormy mood as it gets. The idea of heading to the canteen for lunch makes my stomach churn. No matter that I already skipped breakfast, the thought of food right now is absolutely repulsive.

Still, I make my way to the barn and join Celia in the dining area.

"Oh, hey, boss, you're late," Celia says kindly.

"I know, I had a hell of a morning."

"Did something happen?"

"Nothing important." I wave her off as I search for my notes in my bag. After rummaging blindly without success, I stand up and dump the entire contents of the bag on the table: my phone, my moleskins, makeup, pens, and my agenda. I push stuff aside until I find the loose sheets of paper.

Celia fiddles with the chain at her neck. "Err... I already ate, boss, but would you like something brought up for you?"

I'm tempted to say just coffee again, but I can't survive on caffeine alone. "A sandwich, thank you."

Celia stands up and quickly comes back carrying a tray. She falters next to the table, undecided on where to settle the food with all the clutter from my bag scattered around.

I swipe the items back into my bag with an arm, except for the notes, and make room for the tray.

I manage to swallow down half the sandwich while Celia updates me on the morning happenings. Ah, finally I can bury my head into work and forget all about the sexy mayor who'll be waiting at home for me tonight.

***

I almost manage to. At least until I have to leave the set for the day. I all but beg Celia to come back with me, but of course, it's Friday night and she wants to hang with the crew. She's probably going to spend the night at Jerry's again.

No matter that I drive at an average speed under twenty miles per hour, I'm pulling up too soon next to Travis's black truck at Sagebrush Ranch. When I tiptoe into the house, Travis is coming out of his mother's room holding a bowl and a spoon.

He makes a finger-over-mouth shhh gesture and whispers, "She's sleeping."

I follow him into the kitchen. "How is she doing?"

"Better, her temperature is down and she ate a little soup. I made extra, you want some?"

"Isn't it a little hot for soup?"

I can't really tell the temperature because whenever I'm standing this close to Travis, my heat levels surge. We could be in the middle of Siberia and I'd still be sweltering.

Travis shrugs. "No, you're right. I can make something else. Join me for dinner on the porch?"

Say no. Say no. You'd better say no.

"Sure," I say instead. "Just give me a moment to change."

I rush up the stairs, hissing, "Idiot, idiot, idiot," under my breath.

In my room, I toss the day's clothes on the bed and ransack the closet for my sexiest, most-casual clothes. I want to look good but not like I tried too hard. Before changing, I dash into the bathroom to freshen up and retouch my makeup. Twenty minutes later, I walk out on the porch in jeans shorts, an off-the-shoulder white T-shirt, and low-wedge-heel flip-flops.

Travis has set the table for two with a white cotton runner on the short side. Between the plates, he's placed an old metal can filled with wildflowers. I wouldn't exactly call it romantic, but he made an effort.

The kitchen screen door creaks open and bangs shut. Travis turns the corner, holding two plates, and stops dead in his tracks when he spots me. The mayor is quick to recover, though, and says, "I almost didn't recognize you not wearing stilts." He drops the plates on the table and unleashes one of his lopsided smiles on me. "Dinner's ready."

I squash the butterflies in my belly and sit on the bench opposite him, taking in the three pretty tacos on my plate and the even prettier mayor across the table.

"Oh, I love tacos."

"You mean you thought you loved tacos, wait until you try mine. Everything you had before will pale in comparison."

I take a bite and almost have an orgasm. The chicken is soft and juicy, the seasoning on point with the right mix of flavor and acidity. Oh, gosh, if the mayor has sex like he cooks and kisses, maybe it's a good thing we're not doing it. Or he'd ruin all other men for me.

"So?" Travis asks.

"It's delicious," I say. Then I get distracted looking at his mouth and when I raise my eyes to meet his again, they crinkle knowingly. I blush. Next, I get mad because he caught me staring and my cheeks go even redder.

"What's up, Baker?" the mayor teases. "Too spicy for you?"

"I'm not the one who has a problem when things get *spicy*," I retort.

"Touché," Travis says, his eyes getting even crinklier with mischief before he breaks eye contact.

"What's the matter?" I say. "You can dish it out, but you can't take it?"

"What are you talking about?"

"You're smirking."

"I'm not smirking."

"Yes, you are."

"I'm smiling."

"It's a smirk."

"A smile," he chuckles.

I sigh. "Sure it is."

"I'm happy to stop if it bothers you."

You have no idea how much it bothers me, I reply in my head. But I won't let him know that. Best to change the subject.

"How was your day?"

"Long," Travis says, pushing aside his plate. "I thought the days of working from home were over. Plus, I've been a little preoccupied."

He's been preoccupied. With me? No, don't be pigheaded, probably with his mom.

"How's your mom feeling?"

"Better, thanks to you. I hate that she's out here alone, but she refuses help and I can't move back in with my mother at thirty-three—at least, not permanently. I don't know what would've happened if you weren't here this morning. I want to say again how grateful—"

"You're welcome," I interrupt. "But there's no need to thank me, I'm sorry I couldn't do more."

"You didn't have to do anything. Just being present made all the difference." Travis's eyes search mine, and then he says, his voice soft and deep, "You were more than enough."

I'm taken aback and I open my mouth to speak, but words fail me. Travis is looking at me with those hazel eyes again and I'm reminded of the first time he did it like that in the water. It's impossible to look away. The pull is irresistible, and it makes me uneasy, and a little angry.

I grab another taco, a hysterical laugh building inside me. If Willette doesn't get well soon, I'm going to go insane.

We keep quiet for the rest of the meal. The silence is loaded and a little more than frustrated on my part. I can see Travis would like for the tension between us to ease, but he should've thought about that before he fried all my brain cells with that searing kiss.

When we're both done eating, Travis reaches over the table. For a deluded instant, I think he's going to grab my hand. Instead, he goes for the plate. "Don't worry about the dishes. I'll take care of them."

"No," I stand up, throwing away my napkin. "Absolutely not! You can't do the dishes."

Travis's eyebrows rise in surprise. "Why not?"

Words tumble out of my mouth without filters. "Because you can't be a great cook, an even better kisser, and also be the kind of man who does the dishes."

"I swear I meant no harm with my offer—you look like you want to slap me."

"The problem is I don't want to slap you, I want to—"

"To?"

"You know."

His eyes darken for a second before the smuggest smirk of the night curls his lips. "Not gonna happen, Baker. Trust me, you don't want what's on the other side."

Travis takes my plate and disappears around the corner of the porch.

I'm left ogling his spectacular behind and thinking the real problem might be that I want what's on the other side too much.

Seventeen

Two Can Play

Saturday morning I wake up ready for vengeance, seething at the memory of Mr. Can't-Touch-This smirking on the porch. The mayor may act all cool and smug now, but I didn't start this. Travis is the one who kissed me first, which means he feels the attraction. The mayor wants to resist? Well, I'm going to make it a touch more difficult for him to do that.

I shuffle through my closet until I find a nude silk slip very much akin to the "naked dress" Carrie Bradshaw wore for her first date with Mr. Big. If I'm not going to have sex, at least I'm going to look like sex.

From the closet, I also select a calf-length, sleeveless button-down cream cardigan that will make the naked dress appropriate to wear at work. I roll the cardigan as not to wrinkle it and stuff it into my maxi bag.

I'd like to pair the dress with beaded stiletto sandals, but I have to be practical and not too obvious, so I opt for sensibly large-heeled suede mules.

Before exiting the room, I bend over the bed and kiss a still sleeping Fluffy on the forehead. "Wish me luck."

The cat looks up at me and rolls onto his back demandingly. I rub his belly and leave him purring on the bed to head downstairs.

The mayor is already up making coffee and cooking bacon. For a moment, I admire this homey version. Sweatpants and a plain white T-shirt have never looked sexier. Then, mustering my most casual tone, I say, "Morning."

"Morning." Travis turns, and the greeting gets choked in his mouth as his eyes widen. They roam over my body before they rise again to meet my gaze.

His lips curl up. "You look nice."

"Thanks." I force a smile. "And you look—distracted."

"Sorry," he says, but the subtle curl of his lips doesn't go away. "I was just... I mean, do you always dress so *casually* in the morning?"

I make a twirl. "You like the dress?"

"I, uh... interesting choice," the mayor says, his voice husky.

"I'll take that as a compliment," I say and continue to the porch, leaving him to gape at my backside.

Contrary to the treatment I've been used to expect from Willette, the table isn't laid with a million breakfast treats or, most importantly, coffee.

I drop my bag on the bench and poke my head back into the kitchen.

"No, breakfast, uh? Service is slacking at this establishment," I say, joking.

"I was working on that." The mayor points at the pans on the stove. "How do you take your eggs?"

"No eggs, thanks," I say, walking back into the kitchen. "Just coffee and I'll make oatmeal."

"I'm sorry," Travis says. "I know mom's breakfasts are one of the best things in the world, but I'm afraid I'm not such a skilled cook."

"Oh, don't worry, it's best this way. I was already getting fat on all Willette's food."

Travis's eyes roam the length of my body again. "I seriously doubt that."

His gaze on me makes me feel even more naked.

"How is your mom today?"

"Her temperature is not as high, but she still has a fever. The doctor is optimistic the pneumonia is going to resolve itself with nothing more than a scare."

"I'm glad," I say. Then, returning my attention to the practicalities of making breakfast, I reach for the empty pot resting on the stove. "I'll just put the water to boil."

"Let me," Travis says, also reaching for it.

Our forearms touch. It's the simplest, most innocent of touches, but it's like all the air has been sucked out of the room. I feel kind of... no, not kind of, I'm going to combust.

But I note with satisfaction that I'm not the only one who seems affected. Now that we're standing so close, Travis's gaze has dropped to my lips.

When he looks up at me again, the air between us crackles. For a moment, I think he's going to clear the kitchen island of all the clutter and give me a good "seeing to" on top of it. But then he must regain some self-control because he turns off the stove and takes a step back.

"I'll leave you the kitchen, then, I have to shower anyway."

Travis takes another step back, and another until he literally makes a run for it.

I smirk to myself. The naked dress always does the trick. I hope the mayor enjoys his shower. He looked like he needed a cold one.

***

139

The day at work is uneventful. If not for all the little things that remind me of Travis. The small pond on set brings to mind our kiss. The LBTA sandwich I eat for lunch makes me think of how sexy he looked in the kitchen cooking bacon this morning. I'm distracted all day. And even when I shut myself in my trailer to concentrate, I end up staring out the window, daydreaming.

The final straw is when I walk into the barn for one of the last takes of the day and see Christian in full cowboy costume from behind. For a moment, I mistake him for Travis and butterflies explode in my belly. And the worst part is that now I have to go home, and Travis will be there, unwilling to give me what I need.

Screw that. Maybe I shouldn't go home at all. I mean, I'm already dressed for fun and it's Saturday night. I should go to the pub, have a drink, and perhaps meet another hot cowboy. I bet not all men in Emerald Creek are so hell-bent on not sleeping with me.

***

"Samantha, you're back," Amber, the pub barmaid, greets me with a huge smile as I sit on a stool at the counter. "I thought we'd never see you again after the water incident."

"Sorry," I say, "I had a couple of busy weeks, but I'm ready to let my hair down."

Amber smiles conspiratorially. "And I have the perfect cocktail for you. I convinced Ernie to stock the pantry with triple sec and I got fresh lemons. A lemon drop martini?"

I beam at her. "You're literally my favorite person in town," I say.

"Mine, too." Muscular arms drop on the counter next to me. The sheriff unleashes a most dashing smile on Amber, who, in turn, scowls and disappears into the pantry, presumably to grab the ingredients to make my cocktail.

Duncan winks at me. "She's going to succumb to my charm one day."

"I've no doubts, Sheriff West," I greet the newcomer. "Off-duty again?"

"One night of rest before a fifteen-hour shift at the fair tomorrow."

"Ah, yes, for you and me both."

My phone pings in my bag with a text. When I open it, I'm astonished to find out it's from the mayor.

> You're not coming home for dinner?

I type back.

> I didn't give you my number

> Found it in the guest registry

> I just wanted to make sure you weren't stuck on the road somewhere with a cow blocking your way

> Only your cows block my way

> Don't worry, I'm at the pub having a drink

> Alone?

> Duncan is here

The three dots appear and disappear, then appear again until another text comes in.

> Are you wearing the same dress as this morning?

> Yes, why?

I wait a minute, two, five, but no more replies.

My cocktail arrives, and I want to weep for how good it tastes. I take another sip and check my phone again. But my inbox is clear. I shake my head and put the phone away.

"A suitor?" the sheriff asks.

"Actually, the opposite of a suitor."

Duncan chuckles. "What's the opposite of a suitor?"

"Someone actively trying to avoid a romantic entanglement with me."

The pub's doors bang open and Travis storms toward the counter. He looks disheveled in dark gray sweatpants and a black T-shirt. Not exactly the outfit of someone who had planned to go out, or a very mayorly attire at that.

"Speak of the devil," I say, pointing.

Duncan turns toward the entrance and leans backward with both elbows on the counter. He studies the mayor as he marches toward us. "Looks like a suitor all right to me."

Travis reaches us in a few quick strides.

"Did you fly here?" I ask.

"There was no traffic."

"And to what do we owe the pleasure?"

"Yeah, Vis-Vis," Duncan mocks him. "To what do we owe the pleasure?"

The mayor glares at his friend, sending a clear shut-up vibe, and then shrugs. "I suddenly felt like having a beer."

"What about your mom?"

"She was feeling much better. She could eat alone, and I left her reading a book in bed. Plus, I bought her one of those emergency chain pendants with the red button in case she didn't feel well."

Duncan pats Travis on the shoulders. "Glad to hear your mama is better. Willette is the heart and soul of this town." Then, looking at the barmaid he adds, "Amber, apple of my eye, gem of my heart"—the sheriff theatrically places a hand over his chest—"would you pour the good mayor a beer?"

Amber's glare would send children to cower into a corner and terrify even a grown man. "Keep that going, Sheriff, and the next jug of water I'll pour on your head will be boiling."

Duncan doesn't even flinch. If nothing else, he pumps up the charm. "Please say you'll go out with me and I'll stop."

Apparently, this particular police officer is a little harder to subdue than the average grown man.

"Not a chance in hell," Amber replies. But as she turns to fill a beer jug for Travis, I catch a little secret smile on her lips. Guess the attention isn't as unwelcome as she'd have us believe.

"What do you think?" Duncan asks me. "Do I stand a chance?"

"I'm sure every woman would capitulate under the force of your charm."

"Yourself included?" the sheriff asks, waggling his eyebrow at me.

"That's enough." Travis inserts himself between us, forcing Duncan to move down a stool.

If I didn't know better, I'd say the mayor is acting territorial.

"Can I talk to you?" Travis asks.

"You *are* talking to me."

He grabs my elbow and pulls me away from the counter and the sheriff, who is watching the exchange with an amused grin.

"In private."

I give the sheriff an apologetic smile, then reluctantly follow the mayor to a corner of the pub.

I stare at him. "What do you want?"

"What are you doing with Duncan?"

"Nothing, I was having a drink, and he joined me to chat."

"I've known Duncan all my life, and he's one of my best friends, but he's not famous for *talking* to women."

"No? What is he famous for, then?"

"Nothing that should interest you."

I don't take kindly to being told what to do—or what *not* to do. Even more by someone who, until recently, was a virtual stranger.

"So I can't sleep with you because it'd be too serious and I can't sleep with Duncan because it wouldn't be serious enough?"

The mayor positively growls his next question. "You want to sleep with him?"

"What if I did? It's none of your business how I spend my free time. Especially since you've clearly stated you're not interested in being a part of it. I'm a big girl, no need to go alpha mayor on me."

We both seethe in silence. When he doesn't speak again, I add, "And, anyway, in case you hadn't noticed, Duncan is really into Amber and he's flirting with me only to rile you up, which is working surprisingly well. Want to tell me why?"

"No, I'm tired of talking. I need a drink."

Travis abandons me in the corner and goes back to the bar, taking a long sip of his beer. The man is so frustrating I want to scream. I came here specifically to avoid spending time with him. Then he shows up, acts all jealous and possessive, and the moment I call him out on it, he chickens out again. My blood is boiling and I feel like kissing his stupid face until he faints—or kicking his gorgeous bottom. Either would be deeply satisfying.

Instead, I go back to the bar to grab my purse, ready to go home. The night is ruined anyway.

"Another one?" Amber asks me.

"No, thanks. I have to drive and tomorrow I have an early start. How much do I owe you?"

"Oh, the sheriff already covered your tab."

Both my and Travis's heads whip toward Duncan.

"Thank you," I tell the sheriff.

"It was nothing, Peach. See you tomorrow." He winks.

"Right, tomorrow, bye," I tell no one and everyone at the same time.

As I turn on my heels to leave, I catch Travis's last muttered words, "Where do you plan to see her tomorrow?"

"Relax, man, at the town fair. You seem a bit prissy tonight, Vis-Vis. Something the matter?"

I don't catch Travis's reply as I get out of the pub. But I haven't made it three steps toward my truck when I hear the door swing open and slam shut, immediately followed by the sound of footsteps behind me.

I spin around. "Are you following me?"

"Nope, just going home." Travis walks past me and hops into his pickup. I watch him put it into gear with an angry jerk of his arm and skid away into the night.

I'm half-tempted to go back into the pub, but I'm also tired and tomorrow is going to be a long day. Lionel wants to start shooting early and keep going until sunset—the most romantic natural lighting, so I might as well go to bed.

At the ranch, Travis has left the gate open for me. I drive in and get out of the truck to close it. By the time I reach the house, his truck is parked outside, and the mayor is nowhere to be seen. And just as well.

Eighteen

These Boots Are Made for Walkin'

I pick up Fluffy from the porch steps and go hide in my room ready to pass out. But once I get in bed, the frustration brings on a restless insomnia where no matter how tired I am my bloodshot eyes seem glued to the ceiling. At some point, I must doze off. But for most of the night, I toss and turn, thinking about the man sleeping one floor below me. By 5 a.m., I'm participating in another staring contest with the ceiling I can't win. At five-thirty, I give up and decide to make better use of my time. I pull on nude leggings and a nude tank top, grab my tablet and yoga mat, and go downstairs. The house is silent, but I still tiptoe across the living room until I make it to the porch.

Hildi joins my workout after a couple of sun salutations, trying to jump on me whenever I'm in upward-facing dog. After a few more awkward transitions, we reach an agreement where she takes the end of my mat and I make do with the lower half. Towards the end of the training session, I'm in downward dog when I hear boots on the porch. I look between my legs and see jeans-clad legs turn the corner to then stop dead. I don't see Travis's face, but from where he's standing, he must have a pretty spectacular view of my bottom sticking up in the air. The mayor mutters a curse under his breath, spins on his cowboy boots, and goes back to where he came from.

I shrug. He made his bed. Now he can lie in it—*alone!*

I follow the tutorial on my tablet through a few more sun salutations and finally, I'm free to collapse into corpse pose.

Hildi immediately takes advantage of my supine position to lie down next to my face and drop her muzzle on my chest.

Exhausted from the sleepless night and with the comforting warmth of Hildi by my side, I fall asleep. I wake up with a jolt—not sure how much later, but with the certainty that someone is watching me. Also, I'm covered with a soft blanket.

I blink and turn my head to the side. Travis is squatting on the porch one step down, smirking under his cowboy hat.

"For a moment I thought you were dead," he says.

"That's corpse pose for you," I reply.

He reaches across me to pet the goat, placing his toned biceps right under my nose.

I'm not sure if goats can purr, but the noises of contentment Hildi is making under the mayor's ministration definitely sounds like it. And now I'm jealous of a farm animal.

"I've made coffee," Travis says, his eyes crinkly in the hat's shade. "And left a pot of water boiling if you want to make oatmeal."

"You already had breakfast?"

"Yep, you were out for a while." He stops petting Hildi. "Sorry not to keep you company, but I have some farm work to do before I head into town for the official fair kick-off."

To Hildi's displeasure, I pull up on my elbows. "What work?"

"I forgot to harvest the spring cabbage. But the good news is Mom is well enough to remember it needed to be done and scold me for not doing it." Travis winks and stands up. "See you later, Baker."

I hate the way my stomach flips and how I never seem able to tear my eyes from his departing derriere.

Hildi tries to sit fully on my lap now, mercifully distracting me. I pick her up. "Come on, you can sit next to me while I have breakfast. Deal?"

The goat bleats in return.

***

When I get out of the shower thirty minutes later, grunting sounds coming from outside catch my attention. Against my better judgment, I creak the bathroom window open, careful not to make any noise, and spy through the crack.

Travis is working in the field off to the right of the house. He's wearing the same jeans and boots from earlier, but he's taken off his T-shirt and stuffed it in the waistband of his pants so that now the white fabric hangs over his bottom like a lopsided tail. The mayor is driving a pitchfork into the ground to pluck the cabbages out while his back glistens with sweat in the early morning sun. From my hidden spot, I study the movement of all his flattened muscles as he wrestles the pitchfork in and out of the ground. Travis is following a hypnotic rhythm and looks so darn sensual I want to cry. Feeling like a total creep, I grab my phone and shoot a picture. I send it to my friends captioned: Prince Farming.

I wait for a response but then realize it's probably too early on a Sunday for Taylor and Holly to be up. They still have social lives and must've gone out last night.

In front of the mirror, I take my time flattening my hair and doing my makeup. As for wardrobe, I opt for a pale-pink floral maxi dress with a spaghetti strap on one side, a short sleeve with ruffles on the other, and a high low asymmetrical skirt, also ruffled. Today, it's okay to wear beaded sandals as I'm headed into town and nowhere near a dirt road.

When I get downstairs, there's no sign of Travis. I peek out the window and confirm his truck is gone. Should I add showering at the speed of light to his superpowers?

I walk into the kitchen to make a cup of coffee to go and instead find Willette up and about tinkering with bowls and measuring cups.

"Willette, what are you doing out of bed?"

"Oh, hi, dear," she glances at me, frazzled, and then goes back to her utensils. "I forgot to make a cake for the fair. Sagebrush Ranch always presents one for the charity auction. I mean, I usually make two, one for the auction and one for the baking competition..." she trails off as if losing her train of thought. "I can skip the competition, but I have to make a donation for the auction. People count on me."

"Mmm, are you supposed to be up? Does Travis know you're baking a cake?"

"No, he'd already left when I realized the fair was today. And I don't care what the doctor says, I'm well enough to bake a simple vanilla cake."

On the contrary, she seems pale, and the effort seems to be wearing her down alarmingly fast. I reach her side and support her by the elbow. "Willette, you should go back to bed."

Travis's mom looks up at me, lost for a second. "But the cake..."

"I'll make the cake," I offer on impulse. "That way, the ranch's reputation will be saved and you won't risk a relapse."

Willette still has enough presence of mind to stare at me dubiously. "Are you sure you can bake?"

I smile at her. "I'm a master baker. I could bake in my sleep." I've never lit an oven in my life. "Do you have a recipe?"

"Yes, darling, my recipe card is on the counter."

"Then I won't have a problem at all."

I gently steer her back to her room and lower her into the bed. I've barely pulled the covers up to her chin before she's already sleeping.

With a sigh, I return to the kitchen and stare at the mayhem on the counter. Ingredients are scattered all over: flour, baking powder, baking soda—what's even the difference—butter, sugar, eggs, vanilla, and buttermilk. Plus a mix of spatulas, whips, bowls, and measuring cups.

I kick off my sandals and tie on an apron. I pick up the recipe card and skim over the instructions. How hard can it be?

Line one says to preheat the oven to 350°F.

I fiddle with the knobs and the light inside the oven turns on. See? Easy peasy.

Half an hour later, I'm covered in flour head to toe, the kitchen is splattered in a soggy mix of butter and sugar after a misjudgment incident with the mixer power, and I'm on my third attempt to separate an egg white from the yolk.

On the first try, I cracked the egg too hard and smashed the shell into a million tiny pieces. I didn't care to retrieve them one by one, so I set that aside. The second time, I dropped the yolk at the last minute and it opened into the white. And now, I've almost made it to the finish line when the yolk bursts in my hand for no apparent reason and starts oozing into the bowl of albumen below, irremediably contaminating it.

I slam my palms on the counter. "You gotta be yolking me."

On my phone, the YouTube tutorial on how to separate eggs gets interrupted by a notification.

Holly finally woke up and sent me a heart on fire emoji.

I use vocal control to send her a reply.

> **I can't talk now ladies**

> **Why?**

> **I'm baking**

The screen lights up at once with another three-way video call.

Taylor picks up still wearing a sleep mask over her forehead. "What's up? Why a call at dawn on a Sunday?"

I'm tempted to tell her nine-thirty hardly qualifies as dawn but abstain.

"Sammy is baking," Holly fills her in.

"What?" Taylor's eyes boggle. "Are you high on raw milk or something?"

"Yes," I say. "I'm super drunk on unpasteurized dairy."

"No, seriously," Taylor says. "What possessed you to take on baking?"

I explain the fair situation and Taylor low whistles. "Wow, you must have it bad for the mayor if you'd do this for his mother."

"Well," Holly chips in, "have you seen the picture she sent this morning?"

"No," Taylor says. Her screen goes momentarily black as she presumably checks her messages. I know when she's seen the photo because she exclaims, "Holy cow, girl, that's some serious country beefcake."

"Can we go back to present matters? Can any of you help me bake an *actual* cake?"

Holly has some baking experience and under her careful guidance, I manage to produce a half-decent, if-only-a-bit-lopsided vanilla cake—frosting and all. I search the cabinets for a cake carrier, find one, and successfully transfer the cake without breaking it or it falling apart.

I'm a mess, but I don't have time to take a second shower. I'm already terribly late as is. As a last resort, I wipe the flour from my face, arms, and hair, retouch my makeup and I'm finally ready to go.

When I arrive in town, the main road leading to the festival is packed with people in their Sunday clothes—polo shirts, crisply pressed jeans, and summer dresses, heading toward the town square. Being this late, I have to park miles away from the actual fair entrance, and by the time I reach it, I'm cursing the day I agreed to produce this stupid movie. I'm sweating in the mid-morning sun. The cake weighs like a ton of bricks in my arms, and these shoes weren't made for marching half marathons. The sandals are perfectly fine when all I have to do is step off a cab and cross the street to a cocktail bar. But trudging all the way across Emerald—son-of-a-goat—Creek, isn't their intended purpose.

When I finally reach the fair entrance, I have to begrudgingly concede how pretty the main square looks. The festival entry is marked by an arc decorated with a rainbow of flowers and bright banners. To the sides of the arc, red-velvet drapes with the words "Emerald Creek" emblazoned in gold leaf cover the metal fences delimiting the perimeter of the fair.

I step under the arc and take a deep breath. The air is filled with the scent of happiness, good cheer, and fresh-baked loaves of bread and cakes.

The crowd surrounding me is cheery. Children laugh and chase each other around, while birds chirp along with an eclectic array of festival music—boogaloo, bossa nova, rock—that is drifting on the summer breeze. The hot sun warms my skin. I tilt my head up and breathe in once again the sweet, earthy aroma of fresh baked goods.

White tents dot the inner and outer perimeter of the square and both sides of the roads leading to the center. I sigh in despair. Where am I supposed to drop off this thing? If I have to check every stand, I'm going to have more blisters than skin on my feet come evening.

I spot a free bench and sink onto it, dejected. I should probably call Celia. My assistant should've already arrived and maybe she knows where to find the charity cake stand.

I'm taking my phone out when someone drops on the bench next to me.

The mayor has changed into a black suit, his jacket casually strung over his shoulder in the heat. Travis looks at me, devastatingly handsome as always, and says, "I'd lost hope of seeing you today."

"I got deterred by an unexpected baking crash course."

Travis raises an eyebrow. "You can bake?"

I lift the cake carrier. "Evidence says I can."

The mayor seems even more taken aback. "Why did you suddenly decide to take on baking on a random Sunday?

You're aware the first prize for the competition is just a wooden spoon?"

"This is for the charity auction. After you left, I found your mom in the kitchen all frantic about how she'd forgotten to bake a cake for the charity event. The only way I could make her go back to bed was by promising to make the cake myself—by the way, you're going to have to do a lot of dishes when you come home tonight. No objections this time, I promise."

The mayor stares at me, dumbstruck, eyes wide with surprise and perhaps some other emotion I can't pinpoint. His mouth gapes open with no smart retort coming my way.

"My, my," I say. "If all it took to render you speechless was baking a cake, I would've done it a lot sooner."

Travis laughs despite himself. "I'm not sure whether to be flattered or offended."

I sigh. "You're weird."

"I'm not. I'm just... You're full of surprises, Baker, that's all."

Travis lays a hand on my shoulder, and I try not to let my body get all excited at his touch. "I'm in your debt again and the least I can do is relieve you of the cake and buy you a pair of shoes you can actually walk in."

"My shoes are perfectly fine."

"Baker, I saw you hobble all the way to the bench like a spancelled goat."

Can't argue with that.

"Do they even sell shoes at the fair?"

Travis's smile is killer as he says, "Shoes, perhaps not, but cowboy boots? Always!"

Travis asks me to wait for him while he drops off the cake—I wouldn't have a choice either way. I couldn't walk another yard in these beaded torture devices if my life depended on it. But when the mayor comes back, I still make a brave attempt at standing and walking. Travis takes one look at me and, shaking his head, scoops me up into his arms.

"Put me down. You can't parade me like this in front of the whole town. Can you imagine the gossip?"

"And you can't walk in those shoes, so it's either you go in my arms or you can piggyback."

That'd be even more infamous. Also, being in his arms isn't the worst thing. I lace my fingers at his nape and breathe him in.

He smells like summer and sin, a delicious mix of man sweat, clean cotton, and sage.

Travis carries me to a stand with racks and racks filled with leather boots, from the simplest brown leather ones to the most decorated, embroidered cowgirl boots.

The mayor drops me on a stool and, even in the day's heat, I shiver at being suddenly deprived of the warmth of his chest pressed against me.

"Mr. Mayor," the lady behind the stand greets us. "What can I do for you today? And how is poor Willette? I heard she's down with pneumonia."

"Mom is recuperating fast, you know her. And I told you a million times, Gladys, just call me Travis."

"Sorry, but you're still the mayor of this town last I checked." The lady scolds him, but her eyes are narrowed with mirth. "So, what brings you to my stand today?"

"I'd like to buy a pair of boots for a friend," Travis says.

"Oh." The lady pauses, her eyes sparkling with interest now. "Sure, looking for anything in particular?"

Travis turns to me. "See anything you like?"

I turn my gaze to the stand. Well, boots are still shoes, and I like everything. Wrapped in the scent of rich leather, I take in the rows and rows of orderly boots, musing this must be the only stand in the fair that doesn't smell like sugary powder.

All the boots are gorgeous, honestly, but my gaze keeps being drawn to the top right corner. Toward a soft brown suede snip-toe pair with a well-worn distressed finish and white flowers embroidered on the sides.

"Those," I point.

Gladys follows my finger to the top of the rack and grabs the correct pair. "Excellent choice. This is our softest leather and so pretty at that, too. What size do you wear, dear?"

"Eight," I say. "Eight and a half."

"Eight should be fine. These boots have some wiggle room." Gladys searches under the counter and hands the right size box to Travis.

He drops the box on the floor on top of the rug that covers the pavement and then stands up again. Travis goes to check out the rack sitting opposite the stools. "We need socks as well." His back shakes with a chuckle. "I think I've found an appropriate pair."

He turns to me and hands me a pair of brown-green socks with a goat peeking her muzzle out of a fence. "Hildi is convinced you're her new best friend. That goat is going to be crushed when you leave."

And dare I say that, for the first time since arriving in Emerald Creek, I don't sigh with relief at the idea of leaving. I might even feel a little wistful.

"I'm going to miss her, too."

I kick my sandals off with avenging satisfaction and pull the socks on. Thankfully, none of the blisters have busted yet and I can try the boots on pain-free.

I stand up and almost moan at how amazing they feel. Soft, supple leather wraps my feet in comfort like I'm walking on a cloud.

"You're right," I say to Gladys. "They're comfortable, a perfect fit."

I could walk a thousand miles in these boots and they wouldn't hurt.

The lady smiles at me. "Sturdy but soft at the same time and easy on the eyes, too." She glances at the mayor furtively, and I'm not sure if we're still talking about boots or men. "A solid choice."

"How much do I owe you, Gladys?" Travis asks.

"What?" I grab him by the elbow. "You can't pay for these."

"Sure I can," Travis insists. "It's my way of saying thank you for everything you did for my mom."

I lower my gaze, embarrassed. "Well, thank you."

"Mayor Hunt," a voice from behind us speaks.

Gladys looks past me and Travis and I turn around to find Duncan in full sheriff's uniform approaching us.

"Hello, Sheriff West," Travis says with a scowl, mock-copying Duncan's use of official titles even if these two are best friends.

The sheriff gives me a nod. "Samantha, looking as charming as always." He nods at my feet. "Nice boots."

"Ah," I mock-sigh. "You don't look too bad yourself. What do they say about men and uniforms?"

Travis's scowl deepens. "Are you here to flirt with fair patrons or on official business?"

The sheriff tips his hat at me. "As much as I'd like to banter with you all day, sunshine, I'm afraid I come on official business. Actually, I've been looking for you everywhere, Vis-Vis. I thought you, too, were attending the fair in an official capacity and not to flirt with the pretty city girl."

"We're not flirting. This was merely a foot rescue mission. Why do you need me? What's happened?"

"One of Templeton's ponies knocked down two crates of the Reinhard's jam, and now old Buck is threatening to sue Doug if he doesn't repay the damage. But Doug is claiming Reinhard is charging him double. And Buck is responding that the goods are his and he can price them however he wants. The gentlemen looked like they were about to exchange blows, so I left Officer Parker to keep them apart. But a higher authority might help solve the matter in a more civil fashion."

Travis gives him a considering look, then nods, resigned. "I'll be right there."

He turns back to me. "I'm sorry, Baker, but I've got to go."

"It's fine," I say, remembering I'm actually here to work. "I should go find my crew, anyway. See you around."

Travis gives me one last lingering look, then turns toward the sheriff and they walk away to solve the conflict.

I catch a few people staring at me and I squirm. Gossip about me and the mayor will definitely spread after the fair. Uncomfortable under the keen eye of the townsfolks—sorry, guys, I'm not about to become your first lady—I stuff my sandals in the boots box and leave the stand, waving goodbye to Gladys.

I find Celia and the crew intent on shooting background footage close to our mockup booth and ask her to bring me up to speed on the workings of the day. Her report is brief: no issues, everything is proceeding on schedule.

We spend the rest of Sunday supervising the crew and pitching in when needed.

After the sun has almost completely set, Lionel declares himself satisfied he's exploited the last shard of natural lighting and is ready to call it a day.

Celia, once again, opts to return to Lake View Acres with Jerry, so I walk back to the truck alone—never more glad for my new boots. Will Travis already be home? I should really thank him again for the gift.

Nineteen

A Man Chases a Woman until She Catches Him

As I turn the last bend on the road home, I find Travis's truck parked outside the property lines and the mayor opening the gate.

I honk in greeting.

Travis glances up at me and smiles. A broad grin that fills his face with joy, like a child who's just emerged from a water slide. Gosh, the man looks really happy to see me.

And just like that, my mind is invaded by a vision of what it'd be like to come home to Travis every night and be greeted by that smile. But reality cuts into the fantasy just as fast. Because in Emerald Creek, what would I be coming home from? The town isn't exactly renowned for its movie studios.

For the first time, I can see the point in Travis's stubborn refusal to give in to our attraction. Because if we crossed that line, then how hard would it become to leave?

I shake the idea away. Given Travis's mulish resolution, our involvement is a non-issue. No point obsessing over it.

With the gate open, he gets back in his truck and drives just past the fence, stopping at the foot of the hill.

I pull up behind him and watch him get back out of the pickup to close the gate.

The mayor comes my way and I roll down the window. Travis leans his elbows on the frame. "Hello, Baker."

"Hello, Mr. Mayor," I say in a teasing tone, and give a little wave.

"Stop calling me Mr. Mayor," he says.

With a zing of pleasure, I note he didn't speak in the same tone he'd used earlier with Gladys. He said not to call him Mr. Mayor as if the appellative was a big turn-on when coming from me. Another thing he had to resist.

Mmm... interesting discovery.

"Why?" I ask, intrigued. "Does it bother you?"

Travis just grins. "I'm going to close the gate now."

Definitely a turn-on. I track his movements in the rearview mirror and once the gate is closed, I follow his truck up the hill toward the ranch.

Travis parks first, and I pull up on his right.

When I get out of my truck, something disturbing catches my eyes in his passenger seat. The cake carrier I used this morning is riding shotgun in his truck. And while it'd make sense he'd get it back from the fair, it looks like the cake is also still inside it. I can't say for certain in the dark. To make sure, I yank his passenger door open and take the carrier out.

The container weighs a ton, and the cake is definitely still in here.

Over the roof of his truck, I meet his gaze. "Explain this."

"What?"

I round the truck and show him the carrier. "After all the hard work I put into baking this cake, you didn't even bring it to the charity auction?"

"No, I totally did. Sagebrush Ranch was represented, thank you again."

"Then what is the cake still doing in your truck?"

"I bought it back."

"Oh." The statement takes me off guard.

"Shall we go inside?"

I follow him up the porch steps, but stop before entering the house, as a sneaking suspicion slithers in my head.

I drop the carrier on the table and ask. "Why did you buy it back?"

The mayor shrugs. "It's charity. I like to do my part." He is the image of sanctitude.

I narrow my eyes. "Then why buy *this exact* cake?" I lift the lid of the carrier. "Why not another?"

Travis scratches the back of his head. "I was curious to try your baking?"

"Oh my gosh, you were worried it'd be inedible."

"Nu-uh, I have the uttermost confidence in your kitchen skills."

"Travis," I gasp and wince as if in pain, pleading, "Can you come here, please?"

Travis rushes by my side, and before he can guess my intentions, I scoop up a handful of cake and smear it across his mouth.

He sputters and wipes the frosting from his face with the back of his hand. "Baker, seriously, how old are you?"

"Did you like the cake, Mr. Mayor?"

"It's horrendously sweet. How much sugar did you add?

I gasp, outraged. "My cake isn't oversweet. I followed the recipe to the letter."

"Here." He scoops up some cake and returns the favor of smearing it across my face, only his hand lingers, cupping my chin.

I lick my lips and basically die of a sugar overdose. The frosting is disgustingly sweet.

"Delicious."

Travis brushes a thumb over my lower lip. "Really?"

In a low voice, I say, "So yummy, Mr. Mayor."

Travis's eyes darken. "Call me Mr. Mayor another time and I won't be able to control myself any longer."

I don't care if it's unwise, dangerous, potentially life-altering, I look him straight in the eyes and say, "Do your worst... Mr. Mayor."

Travis leans closer, his lips brushing my ear. "You look breathtaking in the moonlight."

And then he kisses me.

I lean into the kiss, desperate for more. I grab the collar of his shirt to pull him against me, but Travis breaks away.

He holds me at arm's length, his hands on my shoulders, his gaze searching mine. "I don't want to stop this time."

"Then don't," I say. And I don't just mean the kiss. I want him to go all the way with me tonight.

Travis's mouth descends on mine again, and I've been waiting for this for so long, I'm afraid my body will explode from the inside out from sheer anticipation.

The kiss is everything I remembered and more. It's not as tentative as our first kiss, it's fiery and passionate, even brutal. Travis doesn't hold back, making me melt into his arms.

I let out a strangled yowling sound and Travis seems to regain some control. His lips become more gentle and he takes his time discovering mine.

I reach up to wrap my hands in his hair, and when I touch him, he shivers. A telltale sign he wants me as badly as I want him.

Oh yes...

I press myself tighter against him, wanting more of his heat to sink into my skin, and breathe in his intoxicating scent. The vanilla still smeared on his face mixes with something else, something that is uniquely him, a scent that makes me think of a meadow in the early morning with dew on the grass.

And now I'm the one who shivers.

"I want you to be mine," I say into the kiss, as if he hasn't already figured it out.

Travis makes a sound, like a growl, and his hand travels down my back, pulling me even tighter against him.

Good.

The kiss goes on and on, and I'm lost in it, in him. I let myself free-fall. Travis is kissing and biting my neck, and it's the most glorious feeling in the world.

He lifts me onto the table, nailing me in place with his body. Instinctively, I wrap my legs around his waist without even realizing it and make the skirt of my dress ride up to my waist. I intertwine my ankles and press my thighs to hold him closer.

Travis presses his chest against mine and I lean back, ready to lie on the table. Pity the horrendous cake is still sitting forgotten behind me. Halfway on my descent to heaven, I land on top of it, squishing layer after layer of sponge and filling. I try to pull back up, but Travis's momentum is unstoppable, and he pushes me down on the table until the cake is completely splattered underneath me.

I let out a cry of protest.

Travis immediately pulls back and his eyes search mine.

"The cake," I say.

Travis stares at the table beneath me. "Is it just the cake? You want me to keep going?"

"Yes, but my dress is all dirty…"

Travis smirks. "Yeah, I'm afraid we'll have to get you out of it."

I stare into his hazel-green eyes, hypnotized, as his hands reach behind my back to pull down the zipper of my dress. Next, he gently brushes the straps off my shoulders until the bodice is pooling at my waist. The mayor lifts me from the table and I kick off the skirt until the whole dress lands in a messy heap on the floor.

Travis scoops me up into his arms, wedding-night style.

"Where are you taking me?" I ask.

He grabs a blanket off the porch swing as we go. "I want to make love to you under the stars."

Twenty

Maybe You Can Have Your Cake and Eat It Too

Afterward, we lie naked on the blanket, staring at the night sky.

I'm in Travis's arms, my head dropped on his shoulder, and I want to stay like this forever. We're both sweaty and a little sticky. Our skin glistens in the moonlight, and I feel my body still humming from the touch of his hands on me.

Travis kisses the top of my head. "You have a tattoo, Baker."

"Yeah, I was young and stupid." I push myself up on my elbow and lean sideways to show off the rose inked on my rib cage.

Travis trails a finger along the tattoo lines. "You regret it?"

"Sometimes…" I shiver under his gentle touch. "But not at the moment."

"It's beautiful." Travis kisses the rose petals.

"Thank you," I say, checking his body. "No tattoos for you?"

Travis frowns. "I don't think so. I'm afraid it wouldn't befit a mayor."

"But you haven't always wanted to be mayor of the small town where you were born and raised."

"No, but corporate lawyers aren't that keen on ink either, I suppose. And I've never been the rule-breaking kind."

"No, you're a good boy…" I smirk. "Except for tonight, maybe."

"What can I say, Baker? You make me want to break my own rules."

Those restrictions were in place for a reason, I understand it better than ever now, but I don't want to worry about the gloom and doom of me having to leave eventually, so I say, "You mean you don't usually ravish women in your mother's flower garden?"

Travis chuckles. "No, I don't."

I frown, unconvinced. "Never before?"

"I've done a lot of things in my life, Baker. But I've never taken a girl here for sex."

"Why?"

"Because I've never lost my mind as completely as I did tonight."

"I'm flattered, Mr. Mayor."

"Careful, Baker, you don't want to get in trouble again."

"Maybe that's exactly what I want."

"Ah, so you want your cake and to eat it, too?"

"Blessed be the cake. I would've never gotten you naked without it."

"I'm afraid it was more the cowboy boots. I had half a mind to leave them on you."

I stare at the heap of his discarded clothes next to my boots.

"Well, how about this? Next time I'll keep the boots on if you keep the tie."

He trails a finger along the stem of my rose and keeps traveling down. "Is there going to be a next time?"

I roll on top of him. "Sooner than you imagine, Mr. Mayor."

***

Eventually, we collect our things, the blanket, and move back into the house.

For a moment, I worry it's going to be awkward, me going to sleep in my room and Travis in his. But he eliminates the problem by scooping me up into his arms and carrying me up the stairs.

We scoot under the covers together and fall asleep in each other's arms.

The next morning I wake up alone. I stare at the pillow next to mine and find a short note.

I went down to make breakfast before my mom found out I slept in your room.

Ps. Morning, beautiful

And it's not like he wrote me a love poem or anything, but still, the fluttering in my belly spirals out of control. It could also be the teenage thrill of sneaking around without being discovered by parents.

I get up and dart into the shower, I'm pretty sure there's still cake in my hair. Once I'm properly scrubbed and dressed, the smell of bacon hanging in the air leads me to the kitchen.

The sight of Travis at the stove in an apron, making eggs, brings a smile to my face.

I sit down at the table, noting he's already cleaned all the cake-baking mess I'd left yesterday. Hopefully the porch, too. I don't know what Willette would have made of a smashed cake decorating her table.

"Hey," I say.

Travis turns to me, greeting me with a smile as warm as a summer day, prompting once again the question of what would it be like to wake up to this every morning for the rest of my life.

"Morning, sleepy head," he says, bringing me back to earth.

"Well, sorry I overslept, but someone kept me up past my bedtime last night…"

"Reading?" Travis asks with a fish-eating grin.

"Not exactly," I reply, blushing. "How long have you been up?"

"An hour. Had to cover our tracks."

Travis brings me a mug of coffee. "Are you sure you don't want any eggs? They're pretty restorative."

"No," I say, then pull him to me. "But I'll take a kiss."

I kiss him. And it's just a kiss, but my body reacts as it did last night, like he's a drug and I need another fix.

"I have to leave for work, soon," Travis says, breaking the kiss too soon. "I'm needed at the office today."

"What about your mom?"

"She's fine," Willette announces, entering the kitchen.

Travis's mom looks perfectly lucid and her coloring is back.

"And she's promised she'll take it slow," Travis chides. "Right, Mom? No work for you yet, promise?"

Willette pouts. "Since when did you start wearing lipstick in the mornings?" she asks her son. "It suits you."

Mortified, I stare at Travis's mouth and at the layer of my lip-gloss still smeared on his lips. I blush like a schoolgirl being caught making out in the locker room.

Nonplussed, Travis grabs a tissue and wipes his mouth. "Happy to see you alive and kicking, Mom! Dr. Randall will come to check on you later. Please promise you'll rest until he says it's okay to do more."

Willette grunts a reluctant agreement.

"I'll take that as a yes," he says. "Breakfast is ready. I've got to go shower now."

Before Travis can take off and leave me alone with his mother, I stand up. "I have to go as well. Willette, I'm so glad to see you're better."

She studies me for a second. "You look rosy yourself. Guess all this country air is doing you some good." Willette stares knowingly at her son.

"Well, thank you. I've really got to go now."

I grab my keys and positively flee the room.

Thirty minutes later, as I'm walking into the community barn to grab some breakfast, in my haste to escape from Willette's kitchen I completely forgot to eat, my phone chimes with a text.

> I bet you're not very good at poker

> And how did you reach that conclusion?

> Your bluffing skills aren't the best

You might've just told my mom we ravished her flower garden last night

Yeah, put that on me, Mr. Lipstick

It's not my fault if you can't keep your hands off me

Ah, because you're so great at keeping your hands to yourself

We both suck, agreed

But I think we should show some self-control while I'm staying at my mom's

Are you proposing we rendezvous in a shady motel instead?

No, I'm suggesting we behave tonight

I don't second that

Hear the whole proposal first

If the doctor clears her today, I'm going to move out tomorrow and I would like to invite you to my place for dinner

Okay for tomorrow

But definitely no sex tonight?

With you, Baker, I've learned not to make any promises

Another text arrives, not from Travis this time, but from Holly.

> You didn't tell us how the cake turned out

I smirk as I type.

> Couldn't have gone better

Taylor sends a skeptical emoji.

> So it tasted good?

> No, it tasted horrible

> But it still got me laid under the

I add a "cool" emoji.

My phone rings immediately with a group call.

"Don't you gals have to work?" I pick up.

"No," Holly says.

"Nope," Taylor agrees. "We want to hear all about your country-hot sexploits."

Shaking my head, while still not being able to stop smiling, I tell them everything.

***

When I arrive home that evening, Travis's pickup is already parked up front. The mayor, however, is nowhere to be seen. To avoid another run-in with Willette, I dash to my room. I close the door behind me and sigh in relief. No awkward encounters with the mother of the man who I'm not sure if I'm dating, but who I'm positive I want to see naked again soon.

I change into more comfortable clothes, a T-shirt and a pair of jeans shorts... and of course my new, get-lucky boots. But what do I do now? Dinnertime will be soon, and there'll be no avoiding Willette at that point, but at least I want to make sure Travis will be joining me eating crow the entire time.

Where is he? Is he doing some farm work?

I open the window of my room to scan the vast expanse of fields and pastures. Hildi is in her pen for once, grazing her last meal of the day before turning in for the night. A soft breeze blows in my face and I breathe in the scent of clean and fragrant sweet herbs—basil, tarragon, sage, cilantro...—drifting up from the vegetable garden underneath my window.

The wind also carries a distant tune. I track the sound to the barn. There, his legs dangling out of the hayloft, Travis is playing the harmonica.

Enchanted by the tune like the children in the Pied Piper of Hamelin, I sleepwalk out of the house and into the barn. Now that I'm close and can hear the notes clearly, the tune turns out to be haunting and sweet. The melody stirs up all the emotions of last night. If I'm not mistaken, it's an Irish song, but I'd better ask the player.

To get to the hayloft, I have to climb a rickety ladder. I pull myself up and join Travis in staring out the giant hinged window. The clouds are rolling like the sea, the sun setting behind the horizon in a blaze of orange.

"Hi," I say.

Travis turns to me, and gives me a smile, warm enough to melt my resolve to stay away from him, even if just for one night.

"Hey." He pulls me close to him and gives me a soft kiss.

"Don't stop playing," I beg.

Travis brings the harmonica back to his lips, filling the barn with music. I sit next to him, molding my side to his, and close my eyes while I listen.

Maybe it's the music. Maybe it's the romantic setting. Maybe it's the man himself. Whatever the reason, my determination to behave tonight crumbles. Of its own volition, my hand sneaks up his muscular arm to end up tangled in the soft hair at the back of his head, and I stroke his scalp in sync with the slow rhythm of the song.

Suddenly, Travis stops playing. In the quiet, he says, "We're going to be late for dinner."

"I know," I whisper.

***

By the time we lie next to each other, sated, dusk has fallen, and the barn is lit by a single beam of moonlight. Both of us half asleep, we lean into each other, our foreheads touching, our lips a short inch apart.

Travis opens his eyes and I open mine.

"We really should go now," Travis whispers.

"Your mom is so going to know."

I roll on my back and cover my face with my hands, then peek between my fingers. Travis is standing now, quickly getting re-dressed—hay randomly stuck all over his body.

I laugh at this point.

The mayor turns to me. "Something funny?"

"Well, yeah. Look where we are." I gesture at the hayloft.

"Something wrong with the barn?"

"No, I just never thought a roll-in-the-hay would be so literal."

"Ah, but barns and haylofts are notorious spots for horny teenagers to fool around. In fact, I lost my virginity in this very barn."

I try to suppress the surge of jealousy rising in my chest at the thought of him here with another woman—or girl, more likely. I don't care if it was years ago.

"Did your mom also catch you then?"

"Of course."

I stand up and get dressed, smirking as I pull on the boots. These sure have some magical, seductive powers.

When we get back to the house, the outside table is already laid with Willette sitting behind it.

"Oh, there you are," she welcomes us. "I was beginning to think the Gullywompus had taken you both."

Gully-what?

"Hi, Mom." Travis greets her with a kiss on the head. "Sorry we're late."

Willette studies us for a second. "You two must've worked up an appetite." Then, looking straight at me, she adds, "You still have hay in your hair, dear."

Twenty-one

Winner, Winner, Chicken Dinner

Travis moves out the next morning, and I'm glad to see him go. Tonight we will have dinner at his place, well, hopefully, not just dinner, and we finally won't have to worry about being discovered like a couple of teenagers.

He's texted me the address to his house, alongside a sketched map in case the navigator goes wonky.

To avoid having to explain where I'm going or why I'm dressed up, I bring my evening clothes to work and shower and change directly on set. I opt for a figure-hugging black dress with beige lace embroidery, simple spaghetti straps, and black fringes in strategic places. I consider wearing the boots but decide I need to break the spell and clear the road for more shoes to get lucky. So I go with killer high heel black stiletto sandals. The straps are super thin and crisscross over my insteps in a sexy net.

Between the map and the directions, I've no trouble finding Travis's house. He lives in a detached neighborhood, closer to the town's center and not as isolated as Sagebrush Ranch, but with enough space between houses to grant the inhabitants ample privacy. Each house has spacious front and back yards, most encircled by tall hedges.

Travis's house sits at the end of a no-exit road. A driveway flanks the house, leading to the back. I follow it into the garden and park. I honk in greeting and get out of the truck.

The property is fringed on three sides by tall hedges like the other houses of the neighborhood, but the bottom part is left free of trees and opens onto a magnificent view of rolling green hills.

I take in the house, a little surprised at how neat it looks for a bachelor pad. Travis's home is a two-story farmhouse, with white siding, large windows, and a dove-gray metal roof. The wide porch with its natural plank floorboards wraps around the side for privacy, and it's held up by white columns. A pair of ceiling fans are spinning lazily in the evening breeze while ferns spill out of baskets hanging from the rafters. A white swing covered in faded sage-green cushions sits at the edge of the porch, angled towards the sweeping expanse of lawn and pastures beyond.

So the mayor also has a good eye for design. Is there something he's not good at?

The man himself steps onto the porch now and gives me a skin-searing once over.

"You're not pulling punches, Baker."

"I like to show my best side," I say, taking in his jeans and button-down shirt—a middle road between suit and cowboy.

Travis leans against the porch column and crosses his arms, a faint smile playing on his lips.

"Are you going to just stand there, or can I get a kiss?"

I walk up the steps and stop once I'm level with him— the high heels help.

"I don't know. Is it wise to kiss you before dinner? I'm hungry."

His mouth is on mine in an instant, greedy and impatient while his hands find their way to my hips, and he pulls me into him. His fingers move up my back, stopping to massage my shoulders before they reach my neck. He gently pushes me away to stare into my eyes, and I run my hands through his hair.

Travis presses his forehead against mine, then traces his nose down my cheekbone, breathing against my ear. It tickles, adding to the flood of excitement, as my skin tingles in anticipation. His lips switch to my jaw, and then to my neck. His teeth graze my sensitive skin and the rush of pleasure is overwhelming. I'm shaking in his arms when he releases me and lifts an eyebrow.

"Maybe not so wise. Come on." He takes my hand and guides me into the house. "I'll give you the grand tour."

The front hall is as stylish as the exterior of the house. The foyer widens on an open-space living room to the right and the kitchen on the left. Hand-scraped oak flooring stretches across the entire house.

"Your house is beautiful," I say, taking in the staircase with its delicate whitewashed banister and timeworn treads.

Travis leads me down the hallway toward the luminous kitchen. I gape at how even at dusk the room is filled with natural light. Wide windows overlook the backyard and those magnificent green hills. Center-stage to the room, is a massive island with enough room to accommodate six distressed-leather bar stools. And something is cooking in the oven, filling the room with an enticing spicy fragrance.

We retrace our steps to the other side of the entrance, and the two-story living room that houses a leather couch, many tall bookcases, and a huge flat screen mounted above a spectacular fireplace. Imposing cathedral-like trusses force my gaze upward, while the last of the day's sunlight pours in through the windows and French doors that line both sides of the room.

"I love it," I say, walking back into the kitchen and lifting the lid of the pot on the stove.

An inviting smell of mushrooms, pancetta, and cream wafts up from the clear broth.

"What's for dinner?"

Travis comes behind me. "Does that mean you want to skip the tour of the upstairs?"

The prospect of seeing his room sends a thrill down my spine. "I thought we might reserve it for *after* dinner. I wouldn't want all this amazing food to go to waste. What are you making?"

"Chicken with a mushroom sauce."

"Mmm... smells delicious."

"Moan like that another time and you're never going to know."

"Noted, Mr. Mayor," I tease. "No more moaning."

He lets the Mr. Mayor slide and invites me to back away as he takes the chicken out of the oven.

"I laid the table outside," Travis announces. "If you want, you can wait for me on the porch while I put in the final touches."

I stroll out through the back door and study the table setting. A white cloth, white simple plates, but with candles burning inside small lanterns that surround a metal can filled with wildflowers. Simple but romantic. On this side of the house, fairy lights hang from the porch ceiling. As they turn on in the dusk, the atmosphere becomes even more fairytale-like.

A bottle of red wine is already open and breathing. I check the label, Cabernet-Sauvignon, and expensive from the look of it. And he accused me of not pulling punches. The mayor knows how to take the romance up a notch.

Just as I'm putting the bottle down, Travis comes out of the kitchen with two steaming pots in his hands and assembles the final dish on our plates with artful skill. Then he fills our wine glasses.

"What should we toast to?" he asks.

"To the end of hostilities," I propose.

"I thought that happened a while ago, but why not?"

We clink our glasses. The first sip of the cabernet is robust and thick on my tongue. The food is equally stunning.

I take another mouth-watering bite of chicken before I say, "Your roast is so good, even worth delaying sex for."

Travis chuckles. "Glad you enjoy my cooking."

I scarf down more chicken, drinking more wine as well, then pause to admire the view of the darkening hills.

"It's beautiful out here," I say.

"This is my favorite view from the house," Travis agrees. "I built a back extension to set up my home office to face the hills."

I raise an eyebrow. "The office where you deal with all the venerable old ladies trying to marry you off."

That smug grin again. "Exactly."

I compare the panorama with the one I have from my office. The two couldn't be more different, each with its merits. "I can see the appeal. No animals for you, though?" The backyard seems unfittingly empty.

"Not for now, but I wouldn't mind getting a dog one day."

"A dog?"

"Why, you're not a dog person?"

"I used to be a no-pets-at-all person, but lately I'm turning into a goat person, apparently. Don't tell Fluffy, he'd be crushed."

"Your secret is safe with me."

"Why a dog?" I ask, thinking about how it's the one animal Willette doesn't keep at her house. "Your mom's not a fan? Didn't have one while growing up?"

Travis stares out at the backyard. "Since I bought this house, I've always imagined I'd have a family to share it with one day. And, I don't know, I guess the image of kids running after a puppy is more common than goat-chasing."

I follow his gaze to the yard, the vision he's just depicted clear as day in my mind. A wave of want so strong it scares me crashes against my rib cage. Would I want that life? To be his wife? To be the mother of his children? To have our chubby toddlers run free in the backyard—*our* backyard— until they're so tired from the day they'd pass out in their father's arms as he brought them to bed.

The terrifying answer is that I could see myself being happy leading such a simple life. Before meeting Travis, the idea would've been repulsive. I would've never imagined myself living in any other place other than New York City, but now I'm wondering.

"Something the matter?" Travis asks.

"No," I say, and quickly tear my gaze away from the backyard. "I could see how kids would grow up happy in this house."

"What about you?" he asks. "It wouldn't be so bad, would it?"

I scold him. "Leading the witness, counselor."

"Too soon for that kind of question?"

"Perhaps," I say. "But the good part is we still have a few months to figure out the answer."

"But it's not a definite no," he says. "I thought you hated the country."

"I do, sort of. But, apparently, I don't hate all its folks, so…"

Travis's face becomes serious now. "When I told you about my time in New York, I left out an important part."

"Oh?" I drop my fork, giving him my undivided attention.

"When my father died, I wasn't single…"

"Did you break up due to the move?"

"Not right away. We tried to go long distance for a while until we both got too exhausted by conflicting schedules and missed connections."

"Your ex didn't want to move to Indiana?"

"She worked in fashion and Emerald Creek isn't exactly famous for its runway shows."

It all sounds a little too familiar. Now I understand better why he tried so hard not to start anything with another gal from New York.

"Bet you vowed never to date a city girl again."

Travis's smile is bittersweet. "I knew I'd break that vow the moment I saw you trying to reason with a cow." Travis's vulnerability is heartwarming. So genuine it tugs at my heart. We share a long, loaded stare until he breaks the tension with a joke, "What do you call a goat that swims really fast?"

"I don't know," I say.

"A motor goat."

"Oh my gosh, that joke is so bad I want to cry."

"I have an even worse one. Want to hear it?"

"Shoot."

"Why do goats hate waiting in line at the post office?"

I shake my head helplessly.

"Nobody's goat time for that!"

For how terrible, the jokes bring the atmosphere back on a more relaxed plain. The rest of the evening flows free of any more hard topics or existential questions.

"What's for dessert?" I ask when the last crumb of food is polished and the bottle of wine empty.

"Ah," Travis says, standing up. "Dessert will be served on the upper floor."

The toes curl in my sandals.

We stand up, and he takes my hand to guide me upstairs.

"This is my bedroom," he says, opening one of many white doors in the upstairs hall.

The space is cozy but masculine, accented in dove-gray tones. I gasp at the view of the valley on the other side of the hills and walk to the window to admire it.

The town lights dot the entire flatland and sparkle in the night like a million diamonds.

"How beautiful," I say.

"You're beautiful," Travis retorts, walking up to me from behind. His arms wrap around my waist, and he pulls me back against his chest. I turn, lacing my fingers in the short hair at his nape, and tug demandingly.

Travis doesn't need any more incentives to press our mouths together.

The kiss is slow and steady, with gentle brushes of the lips and deep feelings that translate into a fresh wave of excitement. The sensation is so consuming, I can't help but wonder if it's just the thrill of the novelty or if this man could make me feel like this for the rest of my life. Once again, I shake the thought away and concentrate on the present.

"That bed looks very cozy, Mr. Mayor."

"Let's get you tucked in, then."

We go to the bed, but Travis stops a foot shy. He takes my face in his hands and kisses me, with a more urgent feel to it. His hands are on my hips next, and I wrap my arms around his back, pulling him harder against me. With a sudden movement, he lifts me up and tosses me onto the bed. I lose one of my sandals in the process, which makes me laugh.

"That's the spirit, Cinderella," he says, sliding off the other shoe. The graze of his fingertips on my feet sends a tingle up my leg.

"You know Prince Charming is supposed to put the shoe *on* Cinderella."

"Oh, but we're doing the after-dark version of the fairytale, didn't I tell you?"

Travis begins to take off his shirt, but I sit up and I stop him.

"I want to do it," I whisper, and undo his buttons. First the shirt, then the belt, then the pants… The mayor's fingers are just as swift on my dress. When we're both naked, our bodies join, and as I look into his eyes, I realize we're not having sex, we're making love.

Twenty-two

Dance the Night Away

The next day, at work, I'm walking on a cloud. I can't stop smiling at everyone and being cheerful, which isn't exactly what I'm famous for. My bright greetings and bouncy attitude cause more than a few frowns and exchanged raised eyebrows.

Well, let them frown. I'm in love.

I'm not in love, I know that. In the cold light of day, I'm lucid enough to understand that I'm in *lust*. Badly infatuated, perhaps. Because, let's be honest, I've never been into anyone as I am into Travis. But since I'm not out of my mind, I'm aware this crush will end as soon as I board the plane to fly back to New York. The spark of attraction is strong now, but, as inevitably happens, it will die out and we'll move on.

I'll miss Travis when I leave, sure. If he lived in New York… I'm not sure what could happen. But given I'll be gone in a little over two months, I'm conscious this relationship has no future. And while I'm more than happy to take part in the remake of *9½ Weeks*, I'd better not worry too much about what will happen come September.

My calendar pings, reminding me I'm supposed to chair a budget review meeting in fifteen minutes. I sigh, numbers are so boring.

On the way from my trailer to the community barn, I pass Jerry and Celia kissing behind a tree.

"Morning, lovebirds," I greet them.

They pull apart and stare at me in horror. Yeah, any other day I would've probably berated them for making out while on the clock. I mean, at least wait until lunch break for smooches. But today, I appreciate that if Travis were around, I'd be doing much worse than making out behind a tree, so...

At my cheerful greeting, Jerry and Celia stare at me as if I've spurted a second head. They must think I'm drunk or something, but I'm way too happy to care.

Still, if I want to keep a shred of authority, I guess I'll have to tone the *joie de vivre* down.

I force my lips out of the smiling curve that has stretched them all morning and call out, "Celia, are you coming or what? We have a budget review in ten."

My assistant scurries toward me, readjusting her tousled blouse as she walks, and quickly falls into step with me. "I'm so sorry, Samantha. That will never happen again."

I put my hands on my hips. "If you're going to make out on the job, at least go somewhere no one will see you."

Celia nods, gaze downcast.

"As for you," I say, turning to Jerry, "Get to work, the meeting's in ten. You'd better have your numbers sorted."

"Yes, ma'am," he says and hurries away toward his cabin. To retrieve the latest reports on carpentry expenses, I hope.

I roll my eyes. Acting as love-police has sobered me up. I conduct the rest of the morning in business-as-usual mode. At least until the lunch hour, when I receive a text from Travis that puts my head right back in the clouds.

Can I take you out tonight?

I would love to

Great! I'll pick you up at seven

No, I'll come to you

I don't want your mom to see you picking me up

A bit late for that

She got the picture the other night

It's still embarrassing

Okay, be at my place by seven, then

Any dress code for our evening out?

Wear your cowboy boots and something not too frilly

Frilly like what?

Like the dress you wore at the fair

No long skirts

That seems like an oddly specific request for a date.

I shrug, thinking the mayor just gave me the perfect idea to torture him while we're out.

That night, at Willette's house, I act like a complete teenager. I hide in my room until I'm ready to go out and before leaving, I slip on a long, wrap-around maxi skirt over the jeans miniskirt I really intend to wear tonight.

I know I'm being irrational. I'm an adult and can dress however I want. Still, I'm now in the peculiar situation of living under the same roof as the mother of the man I'm dating… so…

Also, Willette seems pretty traditional with her wardrobe. I'm not sure she'd appreciate my style in a daughter-in-law. Not that we're becoming relatives soon… I really shouldn't worry about what Willette thinks of me. But I can't help wanting to impress her. And after the other night when I appeared at dinner with hay in my hair and just-had-sex-in-the-barn spelled across my forehead, parading my shortest skirt around the house doesn't seem like the right move.

Turns out my worries were totally unnecessary. When I get downstairs, Willette is nowhere to be seen. I cross the yard at a brisk pace and take off my camouflage skirt before I get behind the wheel.

When I step out of the truck at Travis's house fifteen minutes later, the mayor is waiting for me on the porch.

Travis takes one look at my mostly bare legs and swears. "Holy goats, Baker, are you trying to kill me with that skirt?"

"You said to go short!"

"I said not to go long, not to give me a coronary."

I climb up the porch steps and lace my fingers at this nape. "Agree to disagree." I kiss him.

The kiss soon turns heated, and Travis pulls back. "We'd better go before I try to take you on the porch again."

I give his lower lip a last nibble. "Where are we going?"

"It's a surprise."

We get into his pickup and another twenty minutes later, we pull up in a quaint little town that must be even smaller than Emerald Creek.

"Where are we?"

"Let me present you the oldest dance hall in Indiana, Coupland Dance Hall."

"And what are we doing at a dance hall?"

"We're going to enter a two-stepping competition."

"But I've no frigging idea how to dance the two steps."

"Don't worry, we have a little time to practice before the actual competition."

"How come?"

"I know the owner. Mary Sue has agreed to open early only for us."

Inside, the building is tall and airy, and I can tell at once the wooden floor has been danced on for years. A woman in her mid-forties is waiting for us on the dance floor.

"Hey, Travis, so nice to see you again." They hug. "And you must be Samantha? Very nice to meet you, I'm Mary Sue."

We shake hands.

As soon as the introductions are over, Mary Sue begins the dancing lesson. "Two-step is the most popular of all the country dances. Everywhere there's country music you'll find the two-step. Before we begin with the actual moves, I'd like to know what level we're starting at. Now, Travis, I know you're a pro…"

"Not really," the mayor self-deprecates in the sexiest way: gaze down-turned, a hand raking through his hair.

"Oh, please," Mary Sue counters. "I've seen you on the floor, *I know*. Now, Samantha, do you have any dancing experience?"

"I don't suppose clubbing in New York counts?"

Mary Sue chuckles. "Afraid not. We're going to start real slow, then. You'll have to rely on your partner and let him lead. Mutual trust is always key in couple dancing."

Our teacher claps her hands and guides us to the center of the dance floor.

"Now, partnership dancing is all about communication, always a great way to get couples together. I met my husband dancing twenty-two years ago and after twenty years of marriage, we're still dancing together, so… let's begin. Please stand in front of each other and hold hands."

Travis gently grabs my hands and pulls me toward him.

"Now, now, leave some space in there." Mary Sue fans herself. "I don't want you to step on each other's feet."

Travis and I pull a foot apart, and Mary Sue continues with the next instruction, "To begin, I just want you to walk in a straight line. Lead, you're going to start with your left foot, and lady, with your right. Can you guess why?"

I shake my head dumbly.

"Because ladies are always right!" Mary Sue jokes.

As we keep walking in a wide circle around the floor, she adds complications. "The basic rhythm is two quick steps and two slow steps, so now instead of going at a steady pace, try quick, quick, slooow, slooow. And go! Quick, quick, slooow, slooow."

Travis and I make a trial lap and so far, so good.

"Now the trick is, even if your feet are following a rhythm, overall, your bodies should glide steadily at the same pace. So quick, quick, slooow, slooow, on the lower body and nice and fluid on the upper body."

"Fantastic," she praises us after another lap. "Let's try the correct hand position now. Travis is going to hold your right hand with his left. While Travis's other hand should go on your back, and Samantha, place your left hand to the shoulder seam of his shirt."

We get in position and we're not doing anything special or particularly compromising, but still, the intimacy of being dancing partners is simmering. As if reading my thoughts, Travis smirks, and ever more heat goes to my cheeks.

"At least we don't have to bathe in a lake to learn how to do this," I whisper.

Travis frowns.

"*Dirty Dancing* reference," I explain.

His smirk goes feral and, disregarding Mary Sue's instructions, he pulls me in to breathe down my neck, "I thought you enjoyed bathing in lakes with me."

"Not when you shun me afterward."

Teeth graze my earlobe. "That wouldn't be a problem anymore."

Thank goodness I'm wearing next to nothing because the air is getting scorching hot. I push him back, scolding him. If he wanted to get right to the fun activities, he shouldn't have brought me dancing.

"Let's dance," I order.

We do a few more practice laps, then try a few turns and more complicated moves until Mary Sue announces our rehearsal time is over and that she has to open her doors to the general public. People are already waiting in line outside and the dance hall quickly fills up.

The more crowded the place gets, the more nervous I become.

"Hello," Mary Sue says into the microphone on stage a while later. "Thanks for coming to the Coupland Dance Hall's Wednesday competition in Indiana's oldest dance hall."

As we step on the dance floor, the jitters worsen. "Travis," I pull him back. "We're not ready." I stare around. The room is full of the most authentic, honky-tonk folks. The various couples practice their moves and darn, they know what they're doing.

Travis smiles at me reassuringly. "Sure we are."

I shake my head, pulling back. "No, we're going to trip and fall, I'm sure."

Travis pulls me close and whispers in my ear, "Don't worry, I got you."

My insides melt at the honey-like sound of his voice, and a shiver spider-walks down my spine. All the objections I had dissipate in a cloud of lust and, surprisingly, complete trust. If Travis says we got this, we do.

We do a warmup lap of quick, quick, slow, slow while Mary Sue continues presenting the night. "I'd like to take just a minute to introduce our judges tonight. With the United Country Western Dance Council, Betty Jo, Mary Jane, and our only male judge of the evening, Mr. Billy Bob."

Billy Bob is an ancient, thin man with a mane of white hair. The judge stands up and demonstrates a few steps, moving incredibly springily for a man that old.

The crowd cheers, and Mary Sue continues, "He's been dancing for longer than some of you have been alive. Let's hear it for Billy Bob." The cheers intensify until Mary Sue talks into the microphone again. "Tonight we've got dancers from all over the state competing, so... without further ado, may the best couple win!"

***

Of course, we don't win. But as we walk outside and Travis twirls me on an impromptu turn to then pull me to his chest and kiss me, I still feel like a champion.

We break the kiss, which leaves me high. High on dancing, high on life, high on him.

"Oh my gosh, I'm starving," I say. "Please tell me there's a place nearby where we can eat?"

"Are beers and burgers too unsophisticated for you?"

"Are you kidding? I'd kill for a burger right now."

"Great, c'mon then, I'll show you my favorite place in town."

We lock hands and walk around the corner to Billy Bob's famous BBQ joint. Apparently, the man is a local legend, not only for his dancing skills.

Sure enough, they have the best burgers and the most beautiful view. The bar grill is by the water, and the lights of a nearby bridge are twinkling like stars against the dark sky.

We eat on the patio, taking in the gorgeous weather and the quiet river, not hurrying anything. The music from the bar indoors is just loud enough to be a perfect background noise to the peace of the evening.

I dip my fries into the best homemade mayo and, after a few bites, I ask, "What's the best thing about being mayor?"

The corner of Travis's lips curls up. "I always meet interesting people."

"Uh-huh. And you blackmail all of them?"

"Only the beautiful ones." He laughs. "But that's not what I meant. As mayor of a small town, I get to know pretty much everything going on in my city, and all its people."

"You really care about Emerald Creek, don't you?"

"Yeah, I do. And I try my best to advance our town. To preserve its history and traditions, but also giving it a chance for the new."

"And what's the worst thing about being mayor?"

Travis looks away for a second, then brings his gaze back to mine. "Sometimes, I have to make some tough calls."

"What kind of decisions?"

"The kind that makes some people's lives better and others' lives worse."

I stare into his eyes, trying to figure out what he's talking about, but his face is so expressionless that I can't. And I'd hate to put a sad note into an otherwise perfect night.

"What about you?" Travis asks. "What's the best part about being a movie producer?"

I smile. "Seeing a project come to life. I follow every step of the production from start to finish. Do you like to read? Fiction, I mean?"

"Yeah, sci-fi and space opera mainly, but I don't have as much time as I'd like."

"Uhh, I didn't take you for the lightsaber kind of guy. Anyway, can you believe *Star Wars* started like words on a page? A screenplay that would change people's lives for generations. I love seeing the characters get out of the written page and brought to life on the big screen. And I know most readers will always say the book was better than the movie, but my goal is to make the movie as good, if not better than the book. And when I succeed…" I sigh. "It's just the best."

"And the worst part?"

"Uh, definitely rogue mayors who blackmail me."

Travis takes my hand from across the table and brushes a thumb on the back of it. "I thought you liked me being a little *rogue.*"

I take my hand back and stand up. "The view is fantastic and the food delicious, but it's time you take me home for dessert, Mr. Mayor."

Travis chuckles and stands up. "As the lady commands."

***

Later that night, we lie in his bed, my head resting on his shoulder.

"So Tuesday was dinner at home, Wednesday dancing. What about tomorrow? What do you have in store for me?"

Travis grimaces. I don't see it, but I can sense the movement. I roll over on my belly to face him.

"Thursday nights I have town council meetings."

"Like every single week?"

"Yep, our community is very hands-on."

"Oh, okay, how about I take you for ice cream afterward?"

"Baker, are you aware a date to Scoops Of Delight after a town meeting would be worse than posting an engagement announcement in the Emerald Creek Gazette?"

"Should I wear chain-mail then, under my clothes?"

Travis frowns, confused.

"To avoid being backstabbed by all the disappointed ladies in town, and their mothers, and grandmothers, and aunts…"

"Are you sure you want to make this official?"

"We're just going on a date, I don't see what the big deal is…"

"Don't say I didn't warn you."

Twenty-three

Kiss the Rain

The meaning of Travis's admonition becomes clear the following night as I'm sitting at the back of St. Mary's High School auditorium. I'm the only person present who is not a council member or a town resident.

Before the meeting starts, the elderly lady sitting next to me asks, "You have another charity event to present tonight, dear? I loved what you accomplished at the lake. That beach has never been prettier. Now I'm so happy to take my grandkids."

"Thanks. Yeah, the lake cleanup was a great collective effort. I could've never done it without the town's help."

"So, what's the new endeavor?"

"No, nothing new. I'm here to see Travis, we're going for ice cream after the meeting."

The woman's lips turn into such a thin line they all but disappear. And I'm not easily scared, but at the sheer look of contempt the lady gives me, I'm tempted to move to a different bleacher.

Thankfully that's when Travis officially opens the meeting. After greeting everyone, he jumps right into the main item on the council agenda. "Thanks for coming. Tonight we're assembled to discuss the sale of the Petersons' property on Ironwood Road."

"What's to discuss, they're selling." The comment comes from Mr. Harley, a nice but very old man whose family has lived in Emerald Creek since before the town was even a village—or at least so Travis told me when I got in and interrupted them speaking to greet the mayor. Not with a kiss like I would've wanted, but with a too-formal handshake.

"Well, yes, but I'm not sure the Petersons understand the full extent of the new zoning laws we're about to approve," Travis says.

"They understand it all right, I bet that's why they were in such a hurry to sell," another man shouts. He's a big man, with an even bigger belly.

"That's not true," the lady next to me comes to the Petersons' defense. "You know Tom needs the money."

"A sale is a sale, and should be carried out in good faith," another woman with a round face argues, and half the people in the room nod their heads in agreement. "The Petersons should know better than to try to sell under false pretenses,"

Mr. Harley speaks up again, "Are you sure about that? The Petersons have lived in Eastern Indiana for generations, they know the land and the regulations better than anyone. The property is theirs to sell. It's the buyer who should investigate any pending changes to the conditions."

"And an honest seller should disclose them."

Travis clears his throat to put an end to a discussion that's spiraling out of control. "Each of you is right. The problem is I don't want to block the sale because as Mary Jane said, Tom needs the money, and we all know why. But I also don't want a buyer coming in from out of town and getting blindsided with a new zoning area on his building. That'd be a poor signal to outside investors."

"What do you propose, Mr. Mayor?"

"An adjustment to the new zoning areas."

At this announcement, the towners all begin to protest, shouting over each other with various arguments: the zoning took ages to decide, why should someone else be penalized, and on and on…

I watch Travis navigate all the objections while trying to come out with a constructive solution that'll make everyone happy. Of course, it's an impossible task.

Now I see what he meant last night.

By the end of the meeting, the assembly hasn't reached a decision. The council members agreed Tom Peterson and all other citizens who have properties in the area should be notified of a possible change to the new zoning areas and be present for the next meeting to discuss the issue further.

When all the attendants stand up to leave, I go to Travis— not failing to notice how Thin Lips scurries over to her friends and then begins to furiously whisper. In no time, half the room is staring daggers at me.

Guess I'm being accused of stealing one of the few decent men of marriageable age from the community. Heck, probably the best bachelor in town.

I reach Travis and whisper in his ear, "Please, let's go before the neighborhood watch decides to have at me."

Travis's lips break into a smile. He loops his arm through mine, and we make a hasty retreat out of the room to a flurry of whispers and stares.

When we reach the school's front court, I lean against a column and sigh. "Phew, I made it out alive. You weren't kidding last night."

"When will you learn I'm always right?"

"Not always."

Travis laughs and kisses my forehead. "Want to go grab that ice cream now?"

"On one condition."

"Name it."

"I get double whipped cream."

"Ha! You're so demanding. But you can ask for anything. I live to please you."

I bite my lip and smile. "Uh, wait until after the ice cream to learn just how high maintenance I am."

Travis's eyes glint. "I've already got a good idea of that."

I blush and scoot my head under his arm, dropping it on my shoulder. "No, you don't. I was just warming you up these past few nights, but wait until we have to burn off all that sugar."

At the ice cream shop, I order a double-scoop, double-whipped cream sundae that comes with a bright red cherry on top. If my friends saw all the dairy I'm consuming, they'd faint. Travis goes for a slightly less disgusting single-scoop, single-cream sundae, but has his topped with cookie dough chunks.

We sit at an outside table, sharing a bench under the fairy lights that dangle from the shop's roof to the nearest tree.

I lean my head on Travis's shoulder, sighing contentedly as I savor my first spoonful of ice cream. As I watch the town people walk by, some smile at me, others glare as if I were some kind of parasite from space.

"Why does Tom Peterson need to sell his property?" I ask.

"Tom's a farmer. A hard job with slight margins. The Petersons lost most of their crops two years in a row. First due to bad weather and then with a bug infestation. Bank loans are hard to come by, and selling the property on Ironwood is the best solution to keep their farm afloat."

"Did many properties suffer the same fate?"

"The weather, yeah. The infestation, not so much. But another long-standing resident who went under is the owner of Lake View Acres. It's why they had to give up the land and rent it out to your crew."

I didn't know that, and I feel a little stupid for never wondering what such a big ranch was doing empty of cattle and with no cultivated fields.

"Why don't you start a town fund to support struggling farms?"

"With what money?"

I smirk and look up at him. "You could always auction yourself out, I'd pay a pretty penny for that."

"Thank you. But I don't think that would be enough."

"I hope the movie will help," I say, straightening up. "I'll make sure to promote Emerald Creek as much as I can."

"Even after the poor welcoming the mayor gave you?"

"Oh, he's making up for it in other ways…"

Travis laughs. "That's true. I'm getting little sleep these days."

"If you need to recover your beauty sleep, I can go back to my place tonight—I came with my truck."

He scoops me closer on the bench. "Not a chance, Baker."

I laugh and kiss his cheek.

After we finish our sundaes, Travis and I wander to the nearby park. Travis acts like a tour guide as we pass the few sculptures the town council has paid for and named after the most important historical figures in Emerald Creek. After the park, we walk along the river and then head back to the school parking lot.

The night is cool, but not cold. A light breeze fills the air with the scent of rain, distant enough for us not to get worried about a storm but close enough to make the air feel fresh.

"We should go before it starts pouring," Travis says.

"I agree."

The first drops of water begin to fall just as we arrive at Travis's house. We get out of our vehicles and rush under the porch, where Travis, without a word of warning, presses me against a column and kisses me. But we don't need words. Not right now. My desire for Travis is a living thing, growing inside me, a fire, burning hotter, brighter, and more demanding every minute.

I need him.

I push him back only to grab his hand and pull him inside the house.

Behind closed doors, his hands and lips hurry to remove my clothes. My hands mirror his actions, pulling at his clothes and then mine.

We never make it upstairs.

Half an hour later, we're naked on the living room rug, a blanket casually tossed over us while the rain outside is making the world disappear.

I turn to Travis and trail kisses down his jaw, the barely-there stubble of the day scratching my lips in the most delicious way. I take my time... I want to explore this man's body until I know it better than my own. We have all night. We have all the time in the world.

Panic stabs me in the chest as I realize that no, we don't have much time at all. If the production will be done at the beginning of September, we only have what sixty, seventy more nights together. When I got sentenced to Indiana for the summer, it seemed like my time here would never end. But now... my stay has suddenly become too short.

Twenty-four

Time Flies When You're Having Fun

Travis doesn't text me all the next day. He mentioned lack of sleep last night. At the moment I thought he was joking, but maybe he wasn't. I sure kept him up until the wee hours of the morning this past week. And I wouldn't want to waste a single one of the few nights we've left together, but if he needs a break... Plus, I seriously need to do laundry.

Once the set gets wrapped for the day, and still no texts have landed in my inbox, I have no other choice but to go home and face Willette. I'm sure news of Travis and me getting spotted in town has reached her, and that she has no doubts about where I spent the last three nights.

But as I get out of the truck at Sagebrush Ranch it's not Willette who I have to confront, but another displeased lady. Hildi stalks towards me from across the yard and bleats frantically. I guess it's a mix of "I've missed you and I'm happy to see you" and "where the heck have you been!"

"Hello, gorgeous," I greet the goat, squatting down and patting her on the head. "I've missed you, too."

She bleats, then stands on her hind legs and drops her front hooves on my thighs.

I scratch her chin and then, acting slightly out of character, I sit on the lawn, not caring if I get grass stains on my designer jeans. I have to wash them, anyway. After a few minutes of playing, I'm back on my feet, dusting my jeans and forearms. Hildi is reluctant to let me go, so I promise more cuddles for later.

The house seems empty. I take advantage of Willette's absence to rush to my room and change. Inside, I find Fluffy curled up in the middle of my bed.

Upon seeing me enter the room, he lifts his head in an unhurried gesture.

"Did you miss me too?" I ask. "Or were you happy to have the bed all to yourself?"

In response, the cat rolls onto his back, offering me his belly. I sit on the mattress and promptly oblige him with a rub. "Of course, you've missed me, you giant, soppy furball."

Fluffy purrs and stretches and even goes as far as getting up to bump his head on my chin. The cat tries to go back to sleep in my lap.

"Sorry, Mr. Fluff, but I really have to do laundry today." I give him a few extra rubs and chin scratches to show him how much I care about him, then I get changed into sweats and throw my day clothes in the dirty laundry bag.

I grab the bag and my phone, and move down to the basement where the washer and dryer are.

I'm in the middle of sorting my laundry when I hear Willette's voice drifting down from the kitchen. "Yes, her truck is here, so she must be, too..."

Is she talking about me? She must be. My truck is the only other vehicle parked outside.

"No, I don't know where she is or why she isn't picking up. But I haven't heard any screaming, so I'm pretty sure she's all right..."

I take my phone out of my pocket and check the bars. No service in the basement. I quickly load the washer and tiptoe upstairs.

Halfway up the stairs, I realize how ridiculous I'm being and take the rest of the steps in confident strides.

When I reach the kitchen, Willette has already hung up.

"Hi," I say.

Willette's shoulders jolt as if I'd scared her and she turns toward me. "Oh, there you are. Travis was trying to reach you."

"I was in the basement doing laundry. I hope that's okay."

"No trouble at all. You and your friend are the easiest guests I've ever had. You're never here."

"Oh, well, I…" I don't know how to segue… *I've been too busy knocking boots with your son* doesn't sound right.

Willette takes in my agonizing face and must be moved to pity because next, she says, "Relax, dear, my son is an adult. He can date whoever he likes."

"So you don't have a problem with us seeing each other?"

"A problem, no. But I'm still his mother, I worry."

"Worry about me?"

"About if you're here to stay or not…" Ah, the million-dollar question. "It's been a while since I saw Travis so taken with someone." My heart jolts at her words. "Travis brought you dancing the other night, right?"

Small towns. I guess there's no hiding anything around here.

"Yes?"

"Well, relationships are a lot like dancing. If you're a good dancer it means you must have good communication. You have to trust each other and learn each other's moves. And you have to put up with each other's mistakes…"

"I hope I haven't made any mistakes so far."

"Not yet, but please don't break his heart."

My phone rings and I'm saved by the bell!

I nod, letting Willette know I understand her. "I'd better take this," I say, and move outside to the patio.

"Hello?"

"You're late," Travis says.

"Late for what? Did we have a date tonight?"

"You mean you didn't plan to come over?"

"You didn't text. I just assumed you wanted a night by yourself."

"Baker, this isn't New York. You don't have to follow some stupid dating rules like waiting three days to text back or not have sex on the first date."

"Well, I had sex with you *before* our first date, so I shouldn't be accused of being that strict with 'the rules'..."

"Okay, but for the record, I don't want to spend tonight, or any other night by myself."

"Are you sure?"

"Positive."

"So I should just drop by your place unannounced whenever I feel like it?"

"My door is always open."

The mayor is being literal, as I think neither he nor Willette nor the majority of Emerald Creek's residents ever lock their doors.

I shake my head. Both his approach to dating and house safety is as far from the New York scene as it gets. Do I mind? No, I like it.

"So what's the plan for tonight?" I ask.

"I'm actually kind of tired. I thought we'd have a quiet night in..."

"Sounds perfect. I just have to finish doing laundry before I come over. It shouldn't take long."

I go back to the basement to unload the washer, throw whatever is dryer safe into the dryer, hang the rest on the backyard clothes line, and go shower.

Draped in a towel, I study my closet.

"Quiet night in, uh?"

What should I wear? Most of my clothes are admittedly "big night out!"

I choose a cotton skirt and a loose-fit T-shirt. And I pull on my favorite pink lace underwear set. I'm not going to pretend I don't want Travis to rip my clothes off once I get to his house—quiet night or not.

I let my hair dry naturally to make the look less formal. I add a touch of my favorite perfume and spend a few extra minutes on subtle makeup. And I'm done.

As I'm leaving the house, Hildi starts bleating louder than ever. The goat must want me to stay and play some more.

"Tomorrow," I say.

But Hildi doesn't relent.

"What's wrong with her?" Willette asks, coming to the door.

"I have no idea. It's like she doesn't want me to leave."

"Oh, she's gotten really attached, that's all..."

I pat the goat on the head. "I'll be back soon, darling, don't worry."

Hildi bumps her head on my bare calves. But as I try to leave again, the crazed bleating resumes. So much that Willette has to come down from the porch and pick the goat up to calm her.

My heart breaks a little as I hop into my truck and drive away.

When I arrive at Travis's place, the front door is unlocked—as expected, so I walk right in.

"Travis? I'm here," I call.

"You made it," Travis says as soon as I step into his house.

I take a moment to appreciate him looking so good in just a pair of gym shorts, sneakers, and a sleeveless black hoodie.

"Yeah, sorry, it took me a while to get ready."

"You look great," he assures me, and leans in for a kiss. Then his lips curl at the corners. "Maybe a little overdressed for a 'quiet night in.' But I like it."

I punch him playfully on the shoulder. "You don't have to be cheesy to make up for not texting me."

Travis back-walks toward the patio. "Who said I'm making up for anything?"

I roll my eyes and follow him outside. "Are you going to feed me or what?"

"I've put dinner back in the oven to reheat. I was expecting you a lifetime ago," he says, and leads me over to the swing. "Do you want a beer?"

"Yes, please."

He picks two out of an ice bucket on the outside table and opens them. "How was your day?"

"Rather uneventful. Shooting went smoothly and Chelsea Moreno only had one wardrobe fit." I take a sip from the beer bottle. "All in all, I call it a win. What about you? Hard day?"

Travis scratches his temple. "The whole zoning situation with the Petersons' sale on the line is turning out to be quite the headache."

"I'm sorry," I say, and soothingly rub his shoulder. "Is there any way I can help?"

The mayor shakes his head. "Nothing you can do, babe. It's a very tedious process and a hard balance to keep, but I got it under control, I promise…" Travis says, the tension in his jaw a telltale sign that he's lying.

"I know it's not my business, but…"

"You just want to help my cute face relax?" he asks, peeking at me sideways and finally cracking a smile.

"Well, yes…"

Travis leans in for a kiss. "You already have by being here."

A brush of his lips on mine, and we both get handsy alarmingly fast. Before things can roll out of control, a timer dings in the distance.

Travis pulls back at once. "Dinner is warm again."

While he's in the kitchen. I get a text from Holly and Taylor. It's a selfie of them dressed to the nines as they're about to hit a new club in the Meatpacking District. Next, they ask what I'm up to.

I take a selfie of myself on the porch with the view of the green hills behind and caption it: about to get fed and ready for dessert later.

Taylor sends me a googly-eyed face followed by two other texts:

You win!

Nothing beats sex with a hot cowboy

Travis comes back just as I'm putting the phone away, but he must catch my lingering smile because he asks, "What's so funny?"

I tell him about my friends wanting to know what I'm up to.

"And what did you tell them?"

"Only that I can't wait for dessert."

Travis drops two plates on the table.

"How about a little actual food first?"

"What's on the menu? I'm starving."

"Pulled pork, twice-baked sweet potatoes, and bread rolls with herb butter."

"Where do you find the time or energy to make all this?"

"Cooking relaxes me. I don't mind."

Kill me now. Could he be any more perfect?

After a few bites of delicious food, Travis asks, "Do you miss your friends?"

I know the question isn't as simple as it sounds. The mayor is fishing. What he really wants to know is, could you ever live in a different state from them?

I honestly don't know how to answer and I'm too tired for existential questions. I also don't want to waste the time I have with Travis agonizing about the future. I've decided I should concentrate on enjoying the present, so I give him a vague response. "Yeah, of course, I do. But not as much as I thought when I arrived here. The countryside has proven far more entertaining than I'd anticipated."

Travis takes my lead with an uncomplicated, flirtatious answer, "It's the cows, admit it—Betsy has wormed a place into your heart."

"Actually—"

"I know, I know," Travis interrupts me. "You're all about the goats."

"You stole my words."

Travis chuckles and the rest of the evening proceeds with no more hard topics looming over us. See? We can have a good time without worrying too much about what's going to happen tomorrow.

Twenty-five

Don't Rain on My Parade

I might want to ignore the future, but time keeps chasing us, relentlessly. I realize just how fast when Travis calls me at work a few days later.

"Hey," I pick up.

"Morning, sunshine, where are you? At work on a Sunday, as usual?"

"A sweltering hot Sunday, I might add. I'm presently trudging between shooting locations."

"Don't you have an army of golf carts on set?"

"Yes, but for whatever reason, I thought it'd be a good idea to exercise."

"At noon?"

"It was fine when I did it this morning." I stop in the shade of a tree because, in this heat, I can't walk and talk at the same time. And I need to preserve my fluids to make it to the community barn alive.

"Can't you ask someone for a ride?"

"They went ahead because I said I was fine walking."

"Please tell me you aren't wearing a pair of your ridiculous shoes."

I peek at my gladiator boots and sigh. "Don't make me lie to you."

"Okay, Baker, I don't want to know."

"Why not?"

"Because most of your shoes, apart from being ridiculous, have dangerous side effects."

"Such as, Mr. Mayor?"

"I'll have a presentation ready for you when you get home."

"Mmm, I'll be sure to take notes. Anyway, I should be done early. Meet at your place?"

"Yes, but that wasn't why I was calling."

"Why, then?"

"Do you want to go to the parade together tomorrow?" he asks.

I frown. What parade? Travis can't possibly mean... I check the date on my phone and, yep, today's the third of July. Independence Day is tomorrow. I've been in Emerald Creek for over a month already?

Really? Where did the time go?

It got lost, mostly between Travis's sheets.

"Sure," I say.

"Great. I have a few mayorly duties, but I should be free most of the day."

***

It turns out our definitions of a "few mayorly duties" are vastly different. Independence Day starts at sunrise with the distant boom of a cannon accompanied by chiming church bells as our wake-up call. Then Travis's schedule kicks in with his first engagement of the day: a flag-raising ceremony followed by a pancake breakfast—the food part is admittedly enjoyable except maybe for the 6 a.m. timing aspect.

The parade takes place at ten. Travis has to officially commence the event and then preside over the drum and bugle corps competition as one of the judges. Battalions of costume-period soldiers parade before the judges' dais, making me wonder how those poor fake troopers can bear to wear such heavy costumes in this heat. I don't join Travis on the dais, but keep off to the side in its shade. By the time the last corps passes, the air is filled with such noise, I can barely hear myself think. Drums beating, fake guns firing, and a few early firecracker explosions. Flags wave a salute while patriotic songs are played on trumpets, horns, or whatever other brass musical instrument people found in their basements this morning.

After the noise-filled morning, lunch takes us to the BBQ and grill festival where Travis, once again, has to be a judge for the best rack of ribs competition. Personally, if I had to choose how to spend one of the hottest lunch hours of the year, I definitely wouldn't be trudging across the fumes of at least fifty different grills.

The early afternoon is taken up by a River Raft Regatta. Bands of locals have teamed up to build the most extravagant rafts and race each other down the river. More than a few float-boats sink halfway through the race to the total delight of their crews, who enjoy the refreshing dip into the emerald waters.

A tractor ride is next, and, at 8 p.m. sharp, the fireworks show begins. The sky blazes with colors in every shade. Fireworks burst into brilliant stars above our heads and cascade toward the ground in scintillating streams. Thundering booms surround us as fireworks explode and explode, spitting colored smoke and glittering sparks into the sky. The smell of gunpowder and smoke fills the air, leaving an aftertaste of salt on my lips. The crowd claps and shouts, cheering and gasping in awe at the pyrotechnic magic.

When the fireworks show is over, I'm convinced there can't possibly be another engagement, but that's when

Travis drags me to the last ceremony of the day: a Chinese lantern launch.

What feels like the entire town gathers in an open grass field as volunteers distribute the lanterns.

I stink of smoke and sulfur and I'm exhausted—probably too tired even for sex tonight, but when Travis takes me into his arms to slow dance under the stars, I decide this is the best Independence Day I've ever had.

A volunteer arrives, and Travis grabs two lit lanterns. He hands me one, saying, "Make a wish when you let it go."

The cool night air, the sky full of twinkling stars, the rustle of the grass in the wind, all make me shiver. I let my lantern free to soar up in the air, wishing for a million more days like this one…

Twenty-six

Careful What You Wish For

The next day I receive definitive proof Chinese lanterns are very poor wish-granting instruments.

I'm sitting in the middle of my usual Monday meeting—moved to a Tuesday to accommodate yesterday's holiday—when Lionel Trumeau proudly announces, "With fast set construction here, and no more hiccups during the public space shootings, we're going to finish filming earlier than expected and get back to our original schedule. If the weather cooperates, we should be able to wrap up the production in a month or less."

The words sink in my gut like a double-edged dagger.

My face contorts in pain? Horror? Disbelief? Maybe all three and plenty more.

Lionel narrows his eyes and asks, "Are you alright?"

"I'm fine," I reply. "I mean, that's great news."

"Of course it is," Lionel Trumeau says. "That's why you look like you're about to throw up."

"No, really I'm okay," I say, forcing a smile. "I'm just overwhelmed with relief. Winthrop will be over the moon when I tell him." I gesture to the room at large. "Good job, team. If that's all from you, Lionel, we can move on to the art department."

The director still looks sideways at me but agrees with a stiff nod. Better he thinks I'm impossible to please rather than sniff out the truth.

"Margaret," I say. "You have the floor."

The key scenic artist begins to speak, and I manage to sit through the rest of the meeting, resisting the urge to projectile vomit my breakfast. Rising nausea notwithstanding.

A month? That's all I've left in Emerald Creek? I was supposed to get more! More time. More Travis.

It's not fair. The thought of leaving sickens me inside. Bitterness sucks me into a black hole of despair until my vision literally blackens around the edges. I look from face to face. Everyone's smiling and making plans. The room spins.

As soon as the meeting is over, I dash out of the barn. I make it to the line of parked golf carts, grab one, and flee to the safety of my office.

I storm inside, half hyperventilating.

I want to cry. I want to yell. I want to punch something.

But I don't. I just settle for wiping the corners of my eyes with my fingers.

I need to get control. I need to focus. I need to pull myself together. And I need to tell Travis.

When I pull up into his yard that night, I don't honk in greeting. It seems too cheerful a gesture for the bomb I'm about to drop on us.

I walk up the porch steps, and as usual, find the door unlocked.

I push my way in, calling, "Travis!"

A second later, he appears from the living room. He's wearing a blue unbuttoned shirt rolled up at the sleeves and a pair of sweatpants. The mere peek at his bare chest underneath the shirt is enough to set a zing of excitement loose in my body. But tonight I'm not here for sexy times, right?

"Hey, gorgeous," Travis greets, looking me up and down.

"Hey, yourself. Is this a bad time?" I ask, half hoping he'll say yes and tell me to leave so that we won't have to have The Talk.

"No, I was just getting changed."

"And you went for the bare chest look?"

Travis waggles his eyebrow. "You like it."

Maybe too much. I want to reply with another joke, but my lower lip treacherously trembles.

Travis is at my side in a few quick strides. "What's wrong, Baker?" he asks as he hugs me to his chest.

His warmth, his comforting presence, and the fact that I've had to keep my feelings in check all day finally become too much and I sob my heart out, ugly-crying into his shirt.

I feel the tension in his body. The need to ask what's wrong, but also the will to leave me space and time to tell him when I'm ready. He holds me tighter but says nothing.

Travis's strong arms feel so good on me that I never want to let go. But I have to. I'm not sure how long I cry, but it seems like forever. When I finally get a grip on my nerves, I pull back.

I sniff and wipe my eyes with the back of my hand, saying, "I have to go back to New York."

His forehead creases. "What?"

"I... I'm leaving early. A month, maybe less." I pause, trying to calm myself. I'm such a mess, I'm sure he can't understand me. "I just found out. I mean, this morning. I have a month left."

Travis's face crumbles like he was hit with a body blow.

"A month?" he asks, his voice pitched with surprise.

I nod.

His gaze is intense, and I know he's looking for answers. "It's not what I want," I admit.

"But you're going to leave anyway."

Going straight for the throat, I see.

I pull at the collar of my blouse. "It's too hot in here. Can we go talk outside on the porch?"

Travis gives me a stiff nod and precedes me out the door.

We sit on the swing, contemplating the view in silence for a few crushing heartbeats until I can't stand it any longer. I grab his hand and say again, "I don't want to go, obviously. But I've racked my brain all day trying to imagine my life in Emerald Creek and I've come to the conclusion—which is crazy, believe me—that I could give up New York for you..."

Travis's head snaps to me, his eyes burning with hope.

"Yes, I'd miss the city, the vibe, the energy, the buzz, the unlimited choices, and my friends. But I could live seeing them less, maybe only on the occasional girl trip. I mean, if we survived a year in lockdown with video chats, we can do it again..."

"But...?" Travis asks.

"But." I sigh. "I've spent years building my career, making a name for myself in the movie industry. And no matter how many times I try to rack my brain about it, I can't find anything that would suit me in this town... professionally, I mean."

"If I could leave my job and come to New York, I'd resign tomorrow. But I can't leave my mom."

"I know, and I would never ask you to."

Travis squeezes my hand, his voice breaking as he speaks, "So what now?"

"I don't know," I say truthfully. "I mean, this thing between us is so new I don't even know what it is." I kiss his knuckles. "But I know I don't want it to end. I want to enjoy every minute we have while I'm still here."

He stiffens at the implication, and drops my hands, his balling into fists. "And after that?"

"Just because I'm leaving doesn't mean we have to end things," I continue, rushing to get everything out. "We can still see each other. We can still talk to each other. I'm not a fan of long-distance relationships, and I know you had a terrible experience before, but I can't make a life-changing decision on the heels of a whirlwind summer romance..." I trail off.

"A summer romance? Is that what you think this is?" He flips a finger between us. "I love you."

The air in my lungs disappears.

"That's right," he growls. "I love you. I don't know how, I don't know why, but I love you, Samantha Baker. I love your brains, your kindness, your talent, and how you challenge me. I love your stupid shoes and your short skirts. I love the way your mouth pouts when you're mad and the twinkle in your eyes when we banter. I love everything about you."

I struggle to find my voice. "What?"

"I love you, and I don't want to lose you," he continues. "I don't care where you work or what your plans are, I want to be with you."

If I weren't sitting, I'd be on the floor. "You love me?" I ask, as if I'd misheard him.

"Yeah," he replies, his eyes flashing with fear and hope. "I love you. I think I have for a while, but I pushed it away because of your job. And I thought you didn't feel the same way."

My heart pushes the words out faster than my brain can process. "I love you, too," I tell him. "I really do."

I lean in and before our lips touch, I murmur again, "I'm in love with you, Travis."

We kiss like we're trying to inhale each other. Travis pulls away only to murmur against my mouth, "I love you so, so much."

"I'm glad you didn't growl it out this time."

Travis smiles against my lips, and in the most tender voice whispers, "I love you."

He runs a finger down my cheek and then kisses me again. I love the way he kisses me. I love the way the world disappears when I'm with him. I love him. I love him. I love him!

A sort of hysterical laughter bubbles out of me.

"What?" he asks.

"I might have to learn how to bake for real."

Travis raises an eyebrow. "Why?"

"If I have to change careers, what else am I going to do around here?"

"I don't know," he says. "But we'll figure it out together. We'll take as much time as you need and we'll figure it out."

Travis kisses my cheek, my forehead, my nose, my chin, my forehead again.

Sighing, I lean against him.

"I love you," I tell him again.

There's a long silence and then, "I love you, too."

Twenty-seven

The Sun for Sorrow Will Not Show His Head

On my last full day in Emerald Creek, I wake at dawn to the sound of rain pattering against the closed window. A gray weather to reflect my blue mood. Merely three weeks have passed since Travis and I declared our love for each other, but the movie is already complete. Most of the production crew left yesterday, and all I could do was steal an extra day to say goodbye.

Irony of ironies, right?

I've spent all this time obsessing over ways to find a job in Emerald Creek and always came out empty-handed. And so tomorrow I go back to New York.

"Is it time to get up?" I murmur sleepily.

"No, baby. Go back to sleep."

Travis pulls me against him, and I snuggle in, dozing off once more.

When I wake again, the rain is still pattering against the house, thunder rumbling in the distance. I'm curled into Travis's side, a leg thrown across his, my hand resting just above the steady thrum of his heartbeat while he sleeps peacefully.

His face is a work of art. That perfectly straight nose and defined jaw. The lips that give so much pleasure. Even in his sleep, his mouth is curved at the corners. That grin that, when turned on me, makes my stomach feel like I'm free-falling. Golden lashes hide his hazel-green eyes. I study the barely visible crinkle around them now that his expression is relaxed. Gosh, I love his face.

I take another look out the window. The weather hasn't improved, and neither has my mood. But Travis and I still have one day and one night together, and I'm going to make the most of it.

I pull the sheet down his body, taking my time and reveling in the view. For a lawyer turned mayor, he has more the body of a farmer or a construction worker. Powerful broad shoulders, a flat-muscled chest and stomach, and strong, athletic thighs. The mayor looks like someone who spends his days outside, working with his hands and not stuck behind a desk for most of his time. Guess Duncan knows what he's doing if he can achieve such perfection with a few training sessions a week. I must remember to send the sheriff a thank you note before I leave.

Travis opens an eyelid and catches me staring. "What are you thinking about, Baker?"

"Actually, I was thinking about Duncan," I say teasingly.

Travis rolls on top of me and pins me to the mattress. "You're in bed with me and you're thinking about another man?"

"The sheriff is also your personal trainer." I free one of my hands and trail it down his chest. "I was sending him a silent gratitude message for all this." I skim my fingertips over his ripped abs, exploring.

In response, Travis rains kisses down on me, soon followed by gentle nibbles down my neck, across my jaw. When his lips finally find mine, they ignite a fire that, in no time, builds into a scorching inferno of need.

Thunder rumbles outside the window as we make love. His eyes never leaving mine as we become one.

Later, when I come to, it feels like hours have passed. Travis's arm is still wrapped around me, pulling me tighter against him. I grab my phone from the nightstand and squint at the digits.

"It's nine o'clock!" I gasp. "We slept in."

Travis grunts in reply.

I press my face to his and whisper, "Don't you have to go to work?"

"I took the day off."

"You did?" My eyes widen.

"Yep." With his free hand, he brushes the hair away from my forehead. "I thought we should spend our last day together."

"Lucky me." I kiss his stubble-covered jaw. "Any plans in particular?"

Travis stares out the window at the plum sky. "How about breakfast to start?"

"A girl could eat."

The mayor kisses me on the forehead and rolls over to get out of bed. He's gloriously naked and I catch myself admiring the view for a moment. I can't help but smile as I watch him dress. It's almost as sexy as watching him *un*dress.

I grab the purple throw from the foot of the bed and wrap it around my naked body to search for my clothes. The underwear is pretty easy to locate, but the idea of squeezing back into the dress I was wearing last night is totally unappealing so, when I find the shirt Travis wore yesterday, I put that on instead.

We have pancakes overflowed with maple syrup and fresh orange juice on the back porch, enjoying the rainy morning.

"What time do you have to leave tomorrow?" Travis asks.

"My flight is at nine-thirty, so I'll need to pick up Celia at your mom's ranch at seven-ish to keep a comfortable buffer."

"I was thinking we could have a picnic today, but the weather isn't cooperating."

I stare at the thundering sky. "What about a porch-nic. The view is still beautiful, and the company is all that really matters."

"I like the way you think, Baker."

We finish our breakfast and he carries the dishes inside. I take a seat on the porch swing, waiting for him while I cradle a warm cup of coffee in my hands. I close my eyes, letting the rhythm of the swing lull me. Tomorrow night, I'll be alone in my apartment, 800 miles away from the ranch, from Emerald Creek, and from Travis.

The idea of returning home brings me zero joy. New York is where I've always belonged. Heaven knows I miss my friends, and I miss Manhattan. But there's no Travis Hunt in the city. And there's no movie producer job in Emerald Creek. The whole catch-22 situation keeps swirling around my head in an endless loop.

Sometime later, Travis slips a blanket around me. I snuggle into the soft material and breathe in his familiar scent trapped in the fabric.

Tomorrow will be a temporary goodbye. Travis already has tickets booked to come visit. We'll see each other again in less than ten days. Still, after two months when we've been together every night, it'll feel like forever.

Travis sits next to me, nursing his own thoughts.

"Are you already packed?" he asks after a while.

"Yeah. I took care of that yesterday. I didn't want to waste a second of today on trivial stuff."

Travis's lips curl in that familiar smirk. "That must've taken you a minute. Did all your shoes fit back into the dead-body trunks?"

I swat him, playfully. "Yes, thank you."

We eat lunch on a blanket laid on the porch, which is ridiculous considering we're three feet away from the table. But it's also very romantic. And with the rain falling incessantly around us, we don't even feel guilty about spending the entire afternoon in bed.

When the rain finally breaks at five, Travis asks, "What do you say about one last dance night? It's Wednesday after all."

Wednesday dance nights have become our thing and I couldn't think of a better way to spend my last night in Indiana. "Only if you promise to take me to Billy Bob's later for burgers."

"I can live with that." Travis's grin is wolfish.

"Hey," I mock-chide. "I'm not your appetizer."

"Are you sure? Because you look good enough to eat."

I giggle and wiggle out of bed.

"Where are you going?" Travis protests.

"If we want to get to the dance hall in time, I need to shower."

"I could help you lather up."

I lean my head on his wardrobe. "I'm going to regret this, but I have to say no."

"Are you sure?" His voice is hoarse.

"You're going to have to wait until later when we get back."

Travis laughs. "I guess I can suffer until then."

***

Three hours later, we're sliding into a booth at Billy Bob's, already making plans for Travis's first visit.

"What's the single thing you miss the most about New York?" I ask.

Travis chews his burger and thoughtfully looks away. "You can't narrow New York down to one thing."

I bite into my fries. "Come on, there must be something."

Travis rubs his chin in thought. "The problem is there are too many things. The variety of people in the city. The theater. The art showings..."

"How about fashion week?" I can't help but fish a little. I haven't asked about his ex-girlfriend once, but he also hasn't volunteered any info.

Travis shrugs. "Not particularly. And my ex is married with three kids in case you were wondering. She married an investment banker and quit her job two months later. We were never meant to be."

"I wasn't fishing," I say innocently.

Travis throws a fry at me. "You so were, Baker. Admit it."

"I'd like to assert my Fifth Amendment right."

Travis chuckles and then, shrugging, he adds, "I guess I also miss the convenience of being close to a decent Thai restaurant."

"Ah, Thai cuisine still hasn't made it to Emerald Creek. I could add 'open a Thai restaurant' to my list of potential alternative career paths," I say only half-jokingly.

He leans across the table and flashes me a dimpled grin. "No shop talk, Baker."

We agreed earlier to act as if tonight were any other night and next weekend just a romantic trip as opposed to the results of our imminent separation.

"Do you want to attend a show on Friday? I could check what's on Broadway?"

"I don't know. Sitting next to you in a dark room where I can't take your clothes off for hours at a time seems like a slow kind of torture."

I nod. "Thai take-out and plenty of naked time, got it."

Travis roars with laughter. "Sounds like a plan, Baker."

And just like that, we end up back at Travis's house.

Wordlessly, Travis slides the door shut behind us and turns to face me. I can't see his face in the dark, only make out his form in the moonlight streaming in through the window. The mayor doesn't bother to switch on the lights. Clothed in semi-darkens, he looks more handsome and feral than ever.

It isn't until I bump into the couch with the back of my legs that I realize I'm backing away.

"You look beautiful tonight," he whispers as he approaches, taking small steps to close the distance between us. He hasn't touched me yet, but my body is already humming with anticipation.

"You look pretty good yourself, Mr. Mayor," I say, running a hand down his shirt to smooth out the wrinkles. My fingers meet with soft cotton over hard muscle.

"Thank you for baking the worst cake in the world," Travis whispers.

"Thank you for... smashing it on my favorite dress?"

I feel his smile against my lips.

"My pleasure," he says.

Travis pulls my hands up to his lips and kisses my fingers, one by one.

A warm breath and then his soft lips finally touch mine. At first, it is a chaste kiss, slow and teasing. Then he takes hold of my face and pulls me closer to deepen the contact. He tastes of coffee, salted caramel, and Travis, and all of it makes my head spin. His lips feel like home and I long for more.

"You didn't get enough of me on the dance floor?" I ask breathlessly.

"Mmm, no. Not. Even. Close." He drops a kiss on my neck after each word.

Travis pulls me closer and all of a sudden, he's everywhere. His hands are in my hair, at the small of my back, on my face, his mouth is doing wicked things to the skin below my ear.

"You're driving me crazy," I say.

"That's the plan, Baker," he says, his voice husky.

Then his mouth is on mine again, and I feel myself melt into him one last time.

Twenty-eight

Night's Candles Are Burnt Out

Morning arrives too quickly. One moment I'm snuggled in Travis's arms in his bed, warm and cozy, and the next, I'm opening my truck door, saying goodbye.

"I'll call you tonight," I say.

"After ten, remember. It's council night."

I nod. Travis chivalrously swings my overnight bag across me into the passenger seat and lingers next to the open door for a parting hug. I wrap my arms around his waist and hold him for a long moment, pressing my face into his chest, never wanting to let go.

Travis's arms engulf me. "Go now if you don't want to miss your plane."

I nod and sigh. "One more kiss?"

Travis obliges and gives me a goodbye kiss I want to remember for the rest of my life.

"Talk soon, Baker," he says, kissing the tip of my nose and my forehead.

I rise on my tiptoes and give him one last peck on the lips. "I'm going to miss you, Mr. Mayor." Biting my lip, I let him go and slide behind the wheel.

Travis closes the door for me, remaining a lone figure in my rearview mirror as I pull away.

At Sagebrush Ranch, a farewell committee is waiting for me. Lined on the porch are Willette and Hildi, while Fluffy is perched on top of Celia's suitcase. My assistant, however, is nowhere in sight. From the production's black truck parked next to Willette's, it's safe to assume she's busy with her own farewells.

Saying goodbye to the animals is almost as heartbreaking as my parting from Travis.

And even Willette gets a little emotional. Travis's mom hugs me. "You're a sweet girl. Thank you for making my son so happy."

"Thank you for being so welcoming. I'm going to miss you," I say.

Willette hugs me again. "We'll be seeing you again soon. I'm sure of it."

Celia reappears, sparing me from having to answer Willette's implied question. My assistant rounds the house corner, walking hand in hand with Jerry.

They, too, kiss a long goodbye, and then Celia and I are driving to the airport.

On the plane, Celia is as quiet as I am. But her silence seems more restless than sad.

"Something on your mind?" I ask.

My assistant sighs and turns to me. "Samantha, you've been a stellar boss for me the past few years, and I couldn't've learned more from anyone else."

She's using the same tone as every man who ever broke up with me.

"But?" I prompt.

Celia wrings her fingers. "But... I wanted to let you know that as soon as we get back to the office, I'm going to put in a transfer request for the LA office."

"Are you sure?" I ask, and then I hasten to add, "I mean, I'm not asking as your boss. If you want to go to LA, I'll approve the transfer and give you a glowing recommendation. But you don't have any doubts? Why do you have to move to LA and not Jerry to New York?"

"Well, he'd get way more on-set carpenter jobs in LA than New York, while I can do the same work in both cities. And yeah, I'm sure. I love him and I have no doubts."

I squeeze her hand and smile. "I'll be sad to see you go, but if LA is what you want, we'll make it happen."

I let her hand go and stare out the window, mulling over her statement. The truth is that if I could have the same career in Emerald Creek, I'd move in a heartbeat as well.

**

I expected to feel a teensy bit of relief catching sight of the familiar Manhattan skyline from the landing plane. Instead, I'm cranky and distracted. I almost forget one of my dead-body trunks as Travis calls them at the airport and then I give the taxi driver my old address where I haven't lived in three years.

That same afternoon, I go to the office, hoping that getting back to my old routine will help me readjust. Instead, I completely space out of my first meeting, which is even weirder because usually production meetings, where new project proposals are discussed, are the best ones. And even that evening, as I go out for drinks with Holly and Taylor at our favorite cocktail bar, I find myself unexcited. I get lost alternatively staring out the window, or compulsively checking the time on my watch, making a silent countdown to 10:00 p.m. when I'll be able to call him.

"Sammy?" Holly says, waving a hand in front of my face. "Where are you?"

"Isn't it obvious?" Taylor replies. "Can't you see the little hearts with the cowboy hats in her eyes?"

I roll my eyes. "I'm not that bad."

"Honey, you're lovesick," Taylor explains. "It's okay, we understand."

"I'm not lovesick," I clarify, setting down my drink. "I just miss him."

"Well, maybe you should go home and call him," Holly says.

"Or have really hot Zoom sex," Taylor suggests.

"No, he has a town council meeting until ten."

"Well, at least your love is reciprocated," Holly says.

That distracts me. "What are you talking about?"

"Oh, yeah..." Taylor says. "You're not up to speed on the latest Holly and Justin developments."

I frown. "Justin, who? The guy at work you hate?"

Taylor winks. "She discovered the line between love and hate is a fine one."

"No! You like Justin now?"

Holly waves me off. "It's a crush at most. And it doesn't matter because he hate-hates me. It'll pass."

"Ah!" I snort. "Last time I said I had a crush that would pass landed me here."

"Here where?"

"All sad in a Manhattan bar with my boyfriend 800 miles away. But tell me more about this new office fling."

"It's not a fling because it's totally one-sided and nothing happened."

"But how did you go from hate to crush?"

"She spilled coffee on him," Taylor interjects.

"It was one of those weird ah-ha moments, you know," Holly says. "I tripped, landed in his arms, and spilled my iced latte all over his perfect Boss shirt. When he tipped me up, our faces were an inch apart for about two seconds, and then I knew I wanted to kiss him..."

"And then he took off his shirt," Taylor adds.

"We were in his office and he keeps a spare." Holly nods. "The man is too refined for his own good."

We chuckle. "What are you going to do about it?"

"Nothing. I mean, what *can* I do? I've been feuding with him for years."

Talking about someone else's love life and problems distracts me until the silent alarm on my phone goes off at 9:30. I wish the girls goodnight and head home with enough spare time to ring Travis at 10:00 on the dot. My phone rings at 9:54.

"We finished early," Travis breathes down the line.

"How was the meeting?"

Travis sighs. "Not a good one, I'm not going to lie. I wasn't able to convince the town folks to relent on the new zoning and the sale of the Petersons' downtown property fell through. Tom was distraught. But my hands are tied…"

"I'm sorry."

"Don't worry, I'll fix it. But enough sad talk about zoning and regulations. How was your trip? Did you have that famous Thai for dinner?"

"Sushi, actually, I'm saving the Thai for you."

"I'm glad because I changed my tickets. I'm flying out tomorrow night. I couldn't wait a whole week to see you."

My heart starts to race. "You're flying in tomorrow? What time?"

"I land at JFK at nine. I take it you like the idea?"

"Well, if you really couldn't resist, I mean, I don't see why not. Anything I should prepare? I mean besides a variety of take-out menus?"

"Just you."

Twenty-Nine

A Miss Is as Good as a Mile

Friday night, I go to pick up Travis at JFK airport. I wait for him at the arrivals, holding one of those silly cardboard signs, Mr. Mayor written in black marker on a white background. At least until I check the arrivals board, and a red-dotted message informs me his plane has been delayed by one hour.

I alert my driver of the delay—my company has a discount rate with a luxury airport shuttle service employees can use. Cardboard sign under one arm, I go sit on a row of plastic chairs, wondering if this is how I'll spend all my weekends from now on: in and out of airports in a never-ending struggle to see Travis whenever I can.

The minutes trickle down incredibly slow, but when his flight status finally switches to 'Landed,' all the energy and excitement flow back into my body. I stand up, sign in hand, and go wait for him at the gate.

Travis is a standout in the mismatched crowd of casual-dressed tourists: tall, overwhelmingly handsome in a black T-shirt and jeans—and mine!

When he spots me, his smile is dazzling. He meanders through the other passengers to get to me faster, and then I'm in his arms and we're kissing.

"How was your flight?" I ask when we finally let go of each other.

"Late. But I'm glad I'm here now."

Travis talks with the same resentful tone I was using in my head earlier as if the airline purposely stole sixty of our precious minutes together.

At least the limo is waiting for us outside when we finally make it out of the crowded airport.

"This for us?" Travis asks, surprised.

"Yep, you're getting the VIP treatment, Mr. Mayor."

"You shouldn't call me that in public."

I lean in to whisper in his ear. "The car has dark, tinted windows, and the passenger compartment is soundproof."

***

Our tryst in the limo takes enough off the edge that when we get to my apartment, we're sufficiently out of lust to order a late dinner.

"We just ate Thai at midnight," Travis says, arranging the white take-out cartons on the coffee table by the couch.

"It's easy to forget how it is to live in this city, huh?"

"I'm just so used to everything in Emerald Creek being closed by nine-thirty except for the White Hart."

"Yeah, I miss the pub. Amber had gotten really good at making martinis."

"Please, don't remind me of your cocktails at the White Hart," Travis says, unbuttoning my shirt.

"What, why not?"

"Because…" Travis trails off, his hands still on my shirt. "I still remember you in that dress, trying to take away my sanity."

"What dress?" I play dumb. "The green one with the white heart polka dots?"

"No," Travis says, unfastening another button. "The other dress."

"Oooooh, the naked dress, then."

"You call it the naked dress?" Travis chuckles. "Admit you wore it just to torture me."

"If I remember correctly, you were the one playing hard to get at the time."

Travis's face turns serious. "I was a fool to waste even a single night with you."

"Agreed." I lean in and kiss him. "But you've made up for it since."

"I try very hard," Travis says, the corners of his mouth quirking up as he finally succeeds in taking off my shirt.

"Yes, you do an excellent job, Mr. Mayor."

***

The next morning I'm torn between spending all day in bed, part sleeping and part doing obvious other things, and getting the most out of the day with Travis in New York.

"What do you want to do today?" I ask as we both stir awake.

His wolfish stare tells me he'd be more of the stay-in-bed-all-day school of thought, so I clarify, "I meant in the city, with clothes on."

Travis groans in mock protest. "What do you do on Saturdays?"

I check the time from the alarm clock on my nightstand. "Well, I'm about three and a half hours late for my Pilates class, for starters. But we're in time for brunch."

"Oh, there's this French bistro I used to go to."

"I was thinking of taking you to a French place, what was the name of yours?" I ask, then putting my hands forward, I add, "No, wait, we say it together on three. Ready?"

He nods.

"One, two…"

"Lafayette," we say in chorus.

I swat him. "Oh my gosh, you're such a New Yorker."

Travis brushes imaginary dirt off his shoulders, hip-hop dancer style. "Just gotta take some of the rust off."

And the day goes exactly like that. Like we've lived together in New York City forever and this is just another Saturday for us. It's amazing how perfectly we fit in Manhattan or in Emerald Creek. Country, metropolis, it doesn't matter. We're good together.

***

The high of the weekend quickly evaporates on Monday morning as I have to put Travis in a cab headed for the airport. The goodbye is just as gut-wrenching as it was when I left Emerald Creek only a few days ago. How many of these can I survive? How long before one of us gets tired?

As the weeks progress, I learn the hard way why so many long-distance relationships fail. I can see my disappointment mirrored in Travis's eyes as we video chat one night and discover the weekend he has to work at his mother's ranch for some unpostponable farming job, I have a work event in New York I can't skip. Or feel his frustration when our flights get delayed more often than not. I'm equally frustrated.

Another weekend Travis's flight gets canceled altogether and then postponed to the next day, cutting our little time together even shorter. We try to put a brave face on it. Joke about it even. But underneath the surface, I can tell the distance and traveling are taking their toll.

The next weekend is my turn to go to Emerald Creek. I book a connecting flight since there were no direct flights compatible with my schedule. But then I spend all of Friday dreading one or the other flight being delayed and me having to spend the night by myself in Washington, DC or some other random city.

Thankfully, I don't. And my stay in Emerald Creek almost goes smoothly. At least until my Outlook calendar updates around lunchtime on Sunday, informing me Winthrop has scheduled a meeting for us on Monday morning at eight.

What a dick move. Who schedules a meeting that early on a Monday? I do it only when I want to put someone off their game, show them who's boss. Oh my gosh, is that what Winthrop wants to do to me? Why?

I don't have time to wonder as I literally have to drop everything in the middle of lunch to reschedule my flights. I had planned to take an early one on Monday morning that would get me to the office at ten-ish—a totally acceptable hour for an executive. Now I have to catch a red-eye, and Travis has to drive me all the way to Indianapolis because there are no late-night flights out of Louisville.

Not exactly a happy ending to our weekend.

The ride in the truck is silent. Tense. We're both angry, not at each other, but at the circumstances that seem to keep wanting to pull us apart.

By the time Travis pulls up to the curb at the airport, I'm so rigid I'd break if I tried even the easiest of stretches. We try to keep our goodbyes loving, but it's clear how unsatisfied we both are. And I have a bad feeling about tomorrow's meeting. I'm afraid things are about to get a lot worse.

Thirty

If You Don't Have a Plan for Yourself, You'll Be Part of Someone Else's

Monday morning, I dress for a fight. A smart suit, not a hair out of place, impeccable makeup. I'm the image of a cutting-edge professional. My concealer is working miracles to hide the signs of a sleepless night. Yesterday, I arrived at home at 2 a.m. and spent the little sleep time I had tossing and turning, worrying about what Winthrop will have to say today.

But at seven fifty-nine sharp I knock on his open door, looking almost fresh-faced. Thanks, Ms. Estée Lauder.

"Ah, Samantha." Winthrop beckons me in. "I see you've survived farm life. I was worried." My boss gestures for me to take a seat before his desk.

"Worried?" I ask, sitting on the chair with my back straight and on high alert. "Why?"

The boss leans back in his leather chair, interlacing his fingers. "Usually by the time one of your movies is completed, you've already presented me with ten ideas for your next project... but this time, nothing." He whistles softly. "Total radio silence."

The boss is right, *so* right. I've taken my eyes off the prize. Between the constant back and forth with Emerald Creek, how tired I've been, the fact that Celia is gone and my new assistant, Adele, isn't properly trained yet, I haven't read a single one of the two thousand screenplays piled on my desk. Celia was a great help in screening and making summary reports of the best ones for me to choose from. But I can't trust Adele with that kind of responsibility, not yet. Of course, I can't tell Winthrop any of this.

Instead, I lie through my teeth. "No need to worry, Boss, I haven't put forward any new proposal because I'm working on something big at the moment and I wanted to make sure the pitch is up to par before I presented it to you."

Winthrop studies me for a long time as if he could see right through my *cow-manure.* "Good," he says eventually. "Wrap everything up this week and be ready to show me your proposal next week. Tamara will fit your presentation into my calendar."

I nod, ready to leave, when he adds, "I still haven't assigned anyone to the Ember Crown franchise. You'd be perfect for such a high-profile job."

I swallow—*hard.* Ember Crown is a three-part fantasy movie series shot mostly in New Zealand.

The message is pretty clear: keep your head in the game, bring me something interesting, *or else.*

'Else' translating into me becoming his ship-around-the-world plodder.

I muster a half-smile and try to keep my walk steady as I backtrack out of his office.

Tamara, his secretary, schedules our next meeting for Wednesday morning at ten.

I'm not sure if knowing the time of my professional death is more comforting or disturbing. I wobble on my stilettos until I reach the safety of my office and shut myself in. Adele has at least learned not to disturb me when my door is closed.

I lean back in my chair and turn to stare out the window at the spectacular view of New York City.

My relationship with Travis is already strained, if Winthrop assigns me to a job in New Zealand with several literal oceans dividing us, we're toast.

The alternative? Find a movie so good Winthrop won't be able to say no.

I turn back to my desk, grab the first screenplay from the slush pile, and get to work.

***

I read, and read, and read. When Friday afternoon arrives, my eyes are bloodshot and I have to buy artificial tears because I've spent all the real ones. Since Monday, I've ruffled through what feels like a million screenplays while in actuality, I skimmed maybe a third of my pile. I've been so obsessed with finding the perfect story, I forgot to leave enough time to actually put up a production plan around that mystical movie embryo that would save my love life.

Now, I'm tempted to pick one of the scripts I earmarked for potential at random and just go with it. Cancel my weekend trip to Emerald Creek and spend the next four days holed up in the office, concocting a presentation. But without the help of my team, they won't be at the office on Saturday and Sunday, the sacrifice would basically be a waste. Plus, usually, when I present something to Winthrop, I already have tentative agreements with investors, a few members of the main cast, and definitely a director in mind. But I can't call all these professionals sounding desperate. It'd be like swimming next to sharks with a flesh wound oozing blood.

This means I'm down to two possibilities: either quit my job and move to Emerald Creek, or keep my job and move to New Zealand and lose Travis in the process.

My heart is telling me to show Winthrop the finger. Yeah, that would definitely make me happier in the short term. But long term? How much time would pass before I started resenting Travis for giving up my career? How long could I stay happy in Emerald Creek doing precisely nothing?

The more I think about it, the more it seems I only have one option left.

By the time I get to the airport, my mind is set: I have to break up with Travis.

Thirty-one

It's Always Darkest before Dawn

After the security checks, I arrive at my gate only to find out my flight is delayed by forty-five minutes.

I'm equally annoyed and relieved. Now that I've resolved to break up with Travis, part of me is worried I'll lose my bearings if I have too long to sit on the decision. The other half is hanging desperately to the distant hope something will happen to allow me and Travis to be together.

To kill time while I wait for my flight's status to change to "Boarding," I go to my favorite bar. Mark, the bartender, is a friendly chap and always gives me free chips.

"Samantha," he greets me as soon as I grab a stool at the counter. "OJ, like usual?"

I nod, even if I'm tempted to ask him to add some vodka to the juice.

Mark gets to work, cutting oranges and feeding them to the juicer. Once he's done, he sets a tall glass in front of me alongside the coveted bowl of free chips.

His blue eyes linger on me. "What's with the long face?"

"That obvious, huh?"

"Well, usually when you're off to see your beau I have to put on shades to not be blinded by your smile. Or are you flying out on business this time?"

"No, I'm going to Indiana."

"Then what's wrong?"

I take a sip of juice. "I have a gun pointed at my head, and whatever choice I make, I'll end up unhappy."

Mark's reply surprises me. "You work in TV, right?"

246

Weird question. "Motion pictures, actually. Why?"

"Well, to quote a famous TV show to you, what do you do when a person has a gun to your head?"

I blink, waiting for the punch line.

"You take the gun, or you pull out a bigger one. Or, you do any of 146 other things."

Despite myself, I smile. "A *Suits* fan, huh?"

"Who isn't?"

I chuckle. "Maybe the royal family? Anyway, I'm pretty sure I already tried 145 possible solutions." At least I've read as many scripts in the past five days. "And no matter how hard I rack my brain, I can't seem to come up with a way to fix things."

"Then you've still got another try." Mark winks. "If you don't like your odds, change them. Go find your unicorn." He points a finger to the sky. "And that's your flight they're calling."

Mark is right. I quickly pay my bill and stroll to the gate area.

Change my odds... mmm, where do I find a bigger gun?

***

On the plane, I pass out the second we take off because... lack of sleep and everything. But my brain stays active even while I'm unconscious. In fact, when a hostess shakes me awake upon landing, I'm on the cusp of having a life-changing idea. I stretch my mind's fingers as if I could still touch that idea, but the big revelation remains elusively just out of my grasp.

Still, unformed ideas keep spinning in my head. The solution is out there somewhere, I only need to find it.

At the arrivals, I greet Travis with a quick kiss and get into his truck, still concentrated on searching for the missing piece of the puzzle.

I'm so absorbed in my own thoughts, I don't even notice Travis stewing next to me. At least until he breaks and asks, "You seem a little preoccupied?"

"Well, of course, I'd come here to break up with you—"

Travis hits the brakes with such force the truck lurches to an abrupt stop, skewing to the side of the road dangerously close to a ditch. The engine rattles and then dies of its own accord. Good thing we're on a dirt road skirting the borders of his mother's property—a shortcut to his neighborhood—and no other vehicle is around or we might've caused an accident.

"Are you out of your mind?" I say, heart still pounding in my chest for the surprise.

"Gosh, Samantha, you said you want to break up with me. Forgive me for not being super Zen about it."

The mayor must be really serious if he's calling me Samantha. "I said my intention *had been* to break up with you, *past* tense."

"I take it you've changed your mind?"

"Yes."

"Care to elaborate?"

"You know the meeting I had with my boss on Monday?"

"The one you kept insisting wasn't important and after which you started dodging all my calls?"

I nod guiltily.

"Yes, I know."

"Well, Winthrop said that I either present him with a grand project by next Wednesday or he's going to assign me to a three-part movie series in New Zealand."

Terror takes hold of Travis's features and he rakes a hand through his hair. "And?"

"I don't have a project to present."

"So, you're moving to New Zealand."

"That's what I thought when I left home."

"And now?"

"Now I think we need a bigger gun."

Travis shakes his head. "You're not making any sense."

"We need to change the variables, only I haven't figured out how yet."

Travis ponders for a moment and then says, "Well, I've had this idea… but I didn't want to share it with you until I had a better look at the numbers, but, since we're in a hurry…"

I make a give-it-to-me gesture.

"Lake View Acres has officially gone on the market after your lease expired, and you've always told me how convenient it was to have a whole ranch as your set, how much money you saved compared to booking studio time in LA… so I was wondering, what if we bought the ranch together? You could leave your job in New York and we could rent it out to other movie productions. I mean, you've so many connections in the industry… and I know it wouldn't be exactly the same job you do now, but it'd still be movie related—"

I raise a hand to make him quiet, cogs whirring furiously in my brain. Until the last piece of the puzzle slips into place and the idea that was eluding me finally takes full form. It's like I've been hit by lightning. "Theodore Abraham Hunt, you're a genius!"

"So you don't think it's a stupid idea?"

"No, it's absolutely brilliant!" I beam at him.

"Does that smile mean you're quitting your job and we're buying the property together?"

"Oh, no, I'm keeping my job."

"How?"

"Because you just handed me a bazooka."

Thirty-two

Diplomacy Is the Art of Letting Someone Else Have Your Way

Anticipation fills me as I wait for Winthrop's reaction to my presentation. The head of Denouement Studios is once again holding my future happiness in his palm, only this time I also have him by the short hairs.

My boss leans back in his chair. "Why do I have a feeling you're going to do this whether I say yes or no?"

Travis asked me the same thing. The business plan is solid. Travis and I spent the last four days working endlessly on the proposal. We both called in every favor we were owed to put together a bulletproof financial plan with an unquestionable upside. So why cut Winthrop in on it? Why not go at it alone?

I told Travis it's always better to have friends in the movie business rather than enemies. And now I tell Winthrop the same thing, making it perfectly clear at the same time that he's correct in assuming I'm doing this whether he's in or not.

"But I'd rather do it with you," I conclude.

Winthrop leans his elbows on the desk. "Walk me through the numbers again…"

"This is how much the property costs," I say. "And that's how much we'd save in studio rental fees over ten years, assuming we filmed just one movie per year in Emerald Creek. This figure shows the tax subsidy the state of Indiana is offering over five years for new companies operating within the state. Creating our own filming studio in Emerald Creek would save us millions of dollars. The property, with the hills, the lake, the river, and the flat pastures, is really versatile. We could shoot a million different things on it."

Winthrop sighs. "So you want to make Emerald Creek the new Atlanta?"

"Emerald is the new black," I say.

"And we'd be partners."

"Yeah, fifty-fifty."

"What I don't get is why you also want to open a movie theater in town?"

"Because there's a property on the market downtown that'd be just perfect," I say, referring to the Petersons' building on Ironwood. The zoning issue wouldn't be a problem if we turned it into a movie theater. "And any respectable studio needs a movie theater. We could host premieres there, private showings for investors, pre-screenings. It'd be truly complementary to the studios. Plus the owners are in a hurry to sell, so we'd get it for a good price. But, of course, the movie theater isn't essential."

"No, I like it." Winthrop chuckles. "I like all of it. All right, Sam, I thought you'd gone soft, but I'm happy to see your teeth are still sharp. And you really wouldn't mind moving to Indiana permanently?"

The truth is I'm practically dying to go, but I need to play it cool with my boss. "The opportunity is too good to pass up, and I'd still be keeping an office here and travel for work. I wouldn't exactly be stuck there all the time."

Winthrop knocks twice on his wooden desk. "Okay, Samantha, I'm in."

***

Four hours later I'm on a plane headed to Emerald Creek to surprise Travis with the news that Denouement Studios Emerald Creek is happening. My head is buzzing with everything I have to do, start a company, build a movie studio, pack my apartment... I'll be swamped in work for the next million years and I've never been happier.

My surprise-the-mayor-with-the-good-news plan goes smoothly until my rental car blows a tire on the dirt road shortcut from his mother's house to his place.

I get out of the car, searching the horizon for any sign of other human life. There isn't any. No one except Travis and his mom, and now me, uses this road.

I see only three options.

One. I try to change the tire myself. Not really an option.

Two. I call the tow company. But Joe, the owner knows me and knows that I'm dating Travis so, with my luck, the gossip that the mayor's girlfriend is stranded on a dirt road somewhere would spread across town with the speed of fire and reach City Hall before I do, thus ruining my surprise.

So, three, I might just call the man himself and ask him to come save me.

Travis picks up on the third ring. "I've been trying to call you all day," he skips hello.

"I know, my phone was off." I toy with him a little.

"Didn't the meeting go as planned?"

I could give the mayor another mysterious answer, but I don't have it in me to torture him. "My phone was off because I was on a plane."

Travis's voice takes a hopeful tone as he asks, "A plane headed where?"

"Oh, this little town in the middle of nowhere that's about to become the new Hollywood of the Midwest."

"Your boss went for it?"

"Yep, I'm officially the new head of Denouement Studios Emerald Creek."

"Wow!" he whoops. "Why didn't you call me to tell me right away?"

"I wanted to surprise you."

"So why are you calling me now?"

"I blew a tire."

"Mmm, we have to up your survival skills, Baker, if you want to fit in the country lifestyle. Where are you?"

"Five miles off the dirt road down to your mother's ranch."

"I'll be right there."

Travis hangs up.

Ten minutes later, I'm searching the sky for the telling puff of dust of an incoming vehicle but find none.

Instead, I hear the thunder of hooves coming from my right. I turn toward the field and spot Travis atop a massive black horse, galloping my way. Horse and rider leap over the fence in a tournament-worthy jump and come to a spectacular halt just a few inches shy of my nose.

I look up at him. "Show off."

Travis flashes me his signature good-boy-misbehaving grin.

"What are you doing off riding in the middle of the afternoon, Mr. Mayor?"

"It's past office hours by a long shot," he says. "And I was too worried to sit still in an office. I needed some fresh air, so I took Smokey for a ride." He pats the beast's neck.

"Are you going to get off that horse and kiss me or what?" I ask.

"I'd rather you got *on* it."

"You're not changing my tire?"

"I could think of a lot of better ways to spend the evening. We can come back for the car tomorrow."

"So, we're just going to leave the car here by the road?"

"Yep."

I shrug. A while ago, I might've protested about leaving my suitcase in an unattended car for an entire night, but now I know no one in Emerald Creek would ever steal anything from it.

Travis extends a hand toward me and I take it.

He pulls me up onto the horse and turns to me as I sit in the saddle behind him. "Welcome home, Baker. Should I start the papers to make you an honorary citizen of Emerald Creek?"

"I'd like that very much, Mr. Mayor," I say with a grin so wide it threatens to split my cheeks.

We kiss until Smokey neighs beneath us. Guess the horse doesn't like to sit still either.

"Hold on tight," Travis says as he turns the beast around and, with a toe-curling, "Yee-haw," sets the stallion to a gallop.

The wind blows into my hair, and I wrap my arms around Travis's waist. I squint my eyes against the low glare of the sun, and a freeing chuckle bubbles out of me as I realize we're *literally* riding into the sunset.

Epilog

Today Is the First Day of the Rest of Your Life

I thought this would be another typical Friday night in Emerald Creek. Get home from the office, if you can call over 200 acres of green hills and flat pastures an office. Kiss my boyfriend a good evening as I arrive home, perhaps coax him into giving me a foot rub before he feeds me. And then a movie before bed, totally skippable if the bed part becomes too urgent.

Instead, things become unorthodox the moment I turn onto Travis's road—my road, too, now—and face a swarm of people walking in the opposite direction toward the town's center. It's like the entire neighborhood is on exodus. What's even more peculiar is how everyone in the crowd is wearing the same colors: blue and green. Over baseball caps, painted warrior-style on their cheeks, or draped around their shoulders as silky flags.

Did I somehow miss the memo that today is Emerald Creek Day or something?

At home, I find Travis waiting for me on the porch with an impatient pout.

He checks his clock and scolds me. "You're late."

I slam the door of my brand-new red pickup. "Late for what? Did we have a commitment I forgot about?"

As the unofficial First Lady of Emerald Creek, I get to show my love and support for the mayor at all his formal gatherings.

"No," Travis says, hopping down the porch steps to scoop me up into his arms. He kisses me and, late or not, the mayor takes his time. When he drops me back to the ground again, he adds, "I wanted it to be a surprise."

"Oh?"

"You were here only during the summer, but you should know fall in Emerald Creek is all about high school football."

"Oh."

Travis's face falls. "You don't like football."

"I don't know, I've never been into sports. I only watch the Super Bowl because I find the commercials funny."

Travis groans as if in actual physical pain.

"But until a few months ago I wasn't into small towns either, so…" I shrug.

"We don't have to go if you don't want to."

"No, really, I'm curious. Is the home team any good?"

Travis answers with a series of stats I can't make heads nor tails of, but that should mean that, yeah, the team is okay.

"What should I wear?"

"Just a pair of jeans and your high-wedge sneakers."

The mayor's footwear vocabulary has greatly improved since I've moved in with him.

I go upstairs where he turned one of the bedrooms into my personal closet. He had it built in record time and ready as a surprise for me on the day I officially moved into his house. I sigh, true love and all, and run my fingers along the orderly shelves of shoes until I find the ones he referred to. To complete the outfit, I put on a pair of Capri jeans and a T-shirt. I don't own anything in blue and green, but maybe there'll be a concession stand at the stadium where I can accessorize.

I needn't have worried. When I get downstairs, Travis is waiting for me, holding a blue and green football jacket.

"How would you feel about wearing my old jacket to the game?" he asks.

"You played football?" I take the jacket from him and drape it over my shoulders, marveling at how many things we still have to discover about each other and also smiling, thinking we now have the rest of our lives to do so.

"Star of my team, two times state champions, go Panthers, who-hoo…"

"Wow, you're really into this, aren't you?"

"I loved playing in high school and even better in college. I went to Notre Dame on a full athletic scholarship."

"Isn't Notre Dame one of the best college teams in the country?" Even I know that.

Travis winks. "Sure is."

"So you must've been good."

"Could've gone professional."

"Why didn't you?"

Travis gapes at me. "I guess I have to thank Hollywood for that."

"Hollywood?"

"Yeah, a movie I watched, actually. **Concussion**, with Will Smith."

"Yeah, great movie." I shiver, remembering the worst scenes of the movie describing the long-term effects of repeated head traumas. "I'm glad you didn't go professional. Was it hard to turn that world down?"

"Oh, yeah, when you're a football player at Notre Dame it's like being a god walking among mortals. The feeling wasn't an easy one to give up, and I can only imagine what playing in the NFL could've felt like. But professional football is a cruel world, too. You get injured and you're out. I didn't want my life to be tethered to the good health of my kneecaps."

"Very sensible, Mr. Mayor."

He pokes the tip of my nose with a finger. "Plus, if I'd gone professional, I would've never met you."

"Oh, who knows? You could've developed a second career in Hollywood, and I would've been your producer, and maybe we would've fallen in love after a passionate on-set romance."

Travis frowns. "That happens often with all the good-looking actors you associate with? Should I worry?"

"Nope, it actually never happened. But if you'd walked on one of my sets…"

"You would've worn the naked dress to work on the second day?"

"Probably."

"And I would've fallen for you just as hard and fast." Travis swings an arm over my shoulders and kisses the top of my head. "Should we go now? Before it gets too late?"

"Sure."

We join a few other latecomers hurrying toward St. Mary's High. I've never been on a date to a football stadium, not even when I was a student myself. My high school was all about basketball, so the games were played in the gym, and they never attracted a crowd as big as this one.

Emerald Creek's is a legit yearbook-style football stadium, with cheerleaders, a pep band, giant screens, and basically the whole town looking on from the bleachers.

"Wow," I say. "You're really serious about football in this town."

Travis raises his eyebrows. "Yep! Want to grab something to eat before we sit?"

"Sure."

We buy two deliciously unhealthy, bacon-wrapped, deep-fried danger dogs and French fries and eat them on the bleachers while the players are introduced. I'm amazed at how they each get their video presentation. Particularly because the photography looks very professional.

"So you lied when you said there were no producer jobs in Emerald Creek."

Travis wipes a drop of ketchup from his mouth with a napkin and frowns. "What do you mean?"

"A professional made these videos."

Travis smirks. "Actually, the school's media department produced them."

"Well, I want to know who filmed that and recruit them."

"Easy, Tiger. Let them at least graduate first."

"Or we could start a summer internship program at the studios."

"That would be amazing, Baker."

I smile, thinking how Emerald Creek feels more like my home with every day I spend here.

We polish off our food just as the game kicks off. The stadium lights beam bright in the night sky, and the players get into action.

"Take a seat, ladies and gentlemen, you're gonna need it for tonight's most anticipated first game of the season," the announcer's voice booms through the speakers. "It's a beautiful night for football and our Panthers are ready to roar. Wilkins makes the kick at the five. Adams on the blocking. Gets outside. He's at the twenty. He's at the thirty.

Out of bounds at the thirty-five-yard line and, ladies and gentlemen, this game is on!"

The game is fast and furious, so I don't have time to think as I'm dragged along with the excitement of the crowd, cheering, yelling, and jumping on the spot every time the home team scores points.

Half the time, I'm not really understanding what's happening on the field, but I'm loving the atmosphere, the tension in the air, the screaming.

The score goes back and forth, and the Panthers seem to have it. But we're down six points going into the last quarter and I'm getting worried… The other team has the ball and the quarterback passes it downfield, but Bryson Wilkins intercepts the ball and starts running it back toward the goalposts.

The stadium roars as the Panthers tackle and block one opponent after the other protecting Wilkins with the ball until…

"Touchdown!" Travis screams next to me, and I jump around like a manic pixie.

I throw my arms around Travis's neck and kiss him full on the mouth.

"This is the best date ever," I yell over the booming cheers of the crowd, then glue my eyes back to the field.

There are only a few minutes left on the clock, but anything could happen. I watch every second of the game with my heart in my throat, knowing that Emerald Creek is so close to winning.

Then the Panthers have the ball again.

"The home team is gonna score!" the announcer screams through the loudspeakers. "The ball is on the fifteen-yard line. Wilkins takes the ball, and he's one of the more experienced players, so let's keep our fingers crossed he'll get this done for us. It's Wilkins on the left, toward the center…"

The whole stadium holds its collective breath and then… "He scores!" Travis and I are screaming along with the rest of the crowd, "We won! We won!"

Watching a game in person is really different from seeing it on TV. Wow, who knew? It also helps to have a team to cheer for.

As the players return to the locker rooms, Travis and I begin the slow process of leaving the stadium, stepping in line with all the other spectators heading for the exits.

As we get outside and lose the protection of the crowd surrounding us, I'm super glad to have Travis's jacket to wear. At the beginning of September, the days are still hot, but the nights can get chilly.

"Did you have fun?" Travis asks as we walk home.

"Are you kidding? It was amazing!"

"Well, football season is only starting. We should go to more games."

"I'd love to."

"Unfortunately, the next one is going to be an away game, so we'll have to watch it on TV."

And the plan was to watch the live broadcast, but then I pulled a little surprise for the mayor and dressed for the game in a Panthers cheerleader outfit, complete with hair ribbon and pompoms.

The mayor got turned on all right, but the TV never did.

The next afternoon we're watching the replay, cuddling in the living room when a loud, repeated honking in the backyard distracts us.

We pause the game and go out on the patio to see what's happening.

Travis's mom has parked her light-blue pickup next to mine and is getting out in a frenzy.

"Mom," Travis calls out. "What's up?"

"I've had it with that goat," Willette says. She opens the passenger door and Hildi hops off the seat to the ground. "Bleating all the time like a lovesick cat. She's clearly your goat now."

Hildi bounds toward us. I squat down to welcome her and almost get knocked over. She bumps her head under my chin frantically, truly acting more like a cat than a goat.

That's when I notice a perky silver-tabby tail heading our way, too. Two seconds later, Fluffy joins Hildi in smothering me in cuddles.

Travis smirks and raises an eyebrow, asking his mom, "And the cat?"

Willette throws her hands up in the air. "Same traitorous breed as the goat. Well, enjoy them. They're all yours now."

Willette starts to get back into her truck.

"Mom," Travis calls after her. "Don't you want a cup of tea or something?"

"No, I'm off to the shelter to adopt a couple of kittens."

"Aww," I say.

"Nu-uh." Willette shakes a finger at me. "I love you to bits, dear, as if you were my own daughter, but from now on you're staying away from my cats before they all want to move here like these two traitors."

She leaves, and Travis squats next to me and the animals. "Guess now I'll have to fight to get your attention."

"Oh, please, there's no competition," I tease. "The animals will always win."

Travis starts to grab me, but I'm faster. I wiggle free of our new pets and run off the porch toward the yard. Unfortunately, the mayor's stamina is superior to mine. He tackles me halfway through my escape and gently lowers me to the ground. The kindness is short-lived, however, because next, he proceeds to relentlessly tickle my sides until I'm screaming for mercy.

That's when Hildi comes to my rescue. She's small but determined and butts her little horns into Travis's side.

"Ouch," the mayor flops down beside me, yelling, "I'm outnumbered, it isn't fair."

Hildi hops onto his chest and studies him as if assessing if he's still a threat or not.

Travis raises his hands in surrender. "I promise never to tickle again."

Hildi gives him a tentative sniff and then licks his cheek.

From the porch, Fluffy observes the scene with a look of disgusted detachment. "Thank you for helping," I yell.

Travis pulls up on his elbows and, turning his head toward me, says, "I bet he's here only because he wants to sleep in your bed."

I raise an eyebrow. "Same as you, then?"

"You're getting a little impertinent, Baker."

"Oh, is that so, Mr. Mayor?"

Despite his promise of a few minutes ago, Travis is back tickling me. Not even Hildi can stop him this time.

And if I had to capture happiness in a moment in time, it'd be like this one. Me laughing my head off in the grass with my man, my goat, and my cat.

Note from the Author

Dear Reader,

I hope you enjoyed reading *Sweet Love and Country Roads,* thanks again for your immense patience in waiting for this book. I apologize again for getting distracted by other projects along the way, but I'm glad we finally got here. I hope you enjoyed this book as much as the others in the *First Comes Love* series. If you picked up this book as a standalone and this is the first time you heard about the series, you can check out the other books on the series page on my website: https://camillaisley.com/novels/first-comes-love-series/. (Or scan the code in the next page.)

Book 4, To the Stars and Back, is where we first meet Samantha and also the story of how Lana and Christian got together. And while I'd suggest reading the books in order, they're all standalones so you can start where you want. Oh, yes, and book 1, Opposites Attract, is free in eBook. This is another enemies to lovers rom-com.

In case you were wondering what derailed the completion of this book for so long, it was the writing of three standalone Christmas novels: Home for Christmas, Fool Me Twice at Christmas, and A Christmas Caroline. You can also find out more information about these three novels on my website.

Now, I have to ask you a favor. If you loved my story, please leave a review on Amazon, on Goodreads, your favorite retailer's website, or wherever you like to post reviews (your blog, your Facebook wall, your bedroom wall, in a text to your best friend… a TikTok video!).

Reviews are the best gift you can give to an author, and word of mouth is the most powerful means of book discovery.

Thank you for your constant support!

Camilla, x

Scan these codes to:

Visit the First Comes Love Series page

Join my newsletter

Acknowledgments

Thank you, readers, for all your heartwarming messages and cool pictures and reviews. You are my tribe. Without your constant support, I wouldn't keep pushing through the blank pages.

Thank you to Rachel Gilbey for organizing the blog tour for this book and to all the book bloggers who participated. I love being part of your community.

Thank you to my street team, and to all of you who leave book reviews. They're so appreciated.

Thank you to my editors and proofreaders, Arnetta, Helen Baggott, and BBB Publishing for making my writing the best it could be.

And lastly, thank you to my family and friends for your constant encouragement.

Cover Image Credit: Created by Freepik

Printed in Great Britain
by Amazon

17732229R00157